MY KINDA
Song

Summer Sisters - Book 3

LACEY BLACK

♡ *Lacey*
Black

My Kinda Song

Summer Sisters Book 3

Index

Also by Lacey Black

Rivers Edge series
Trust Me, Rivers Edge book 1 (Maddox and Avery) – FREE at all retailers
> ~ *#1 Bestseller in Contemporary Romance & #3 in overall free e-books*
> ~ *#2 Bestseller in overall free e-books on another retailer*

Fight Me, Rivers Edge book 2 (Jake and Erin)
Expect Me, Rivers Edge book 3 (Travis and Josselyn)
Promise Me: A Novella, Rivers Edge book 3.5 (Jase and Holly)
Protect Me, Rivers Edge book 4 (Nate and Lia)
Boss Me, Rivers Edge book 5 (Will and Carmen)
Trust Us: A Rivers Edge Christmas Novella (Maddox and Avery)
> ~ *This novella was originally part of the Christmas Miracles Anthology*

Bound Together series
Submerged, Bound Together book 1 (Blake and Carly)
> ~ *An International Bestseller*

Profited, Bound Together book 2 (Reid and Dani)
> ~*A Bestseller, reaching Top 100 on 2 e-retailers*

Entwined, Bound Together book 3 (Luke and Sidney)

Summer Sisters series
My Kinda Kisses, Summer Sisters book 1 (Jaime and Ryan)
> ~*A Bestseller, reaching Top 100 on 2 e-retailers*

My Kinda Night, Summer Sisters book 2 (Payton and Dean)
My Kinda Song, Summer Sisters book 3

Standalone
Music Notes, a sexy contemporary romance standalone

*Coming Soon from Lacey Black
Book 4 in the Summer Sisters series, My Kinda Mess (Lexi and Linkin)
A Holiday Anthology Novella, still untitled

Dedication

To everyone who has ever fallen for their best friend.

Lacey Black

Chapter One

Abby

It's a Summer sister tradition that on the first Saturday of each month, the six of us get together. We take turns picking the location or activity, anything from margaritas and a movie to wine and painting classes at the small gallery uptown. One thing, though, is as certain as the sun rising over the Chesapeake Bay every morning; there will be alcohol involved.

Always.

The pleasant July night is perfect for a beachside round of disc golf; or at least that's what AJ said. It was her month to choose our activity, and since she's enjoying the heck out of her summer away from the teenage kids she teaches at the junior high, she opted to live it up along the Bay. We're one of several groups playing tonight, which is higher than normal. Of course, the main reason for the extra bodies on the beach isn't just because of the gorgeous evening. It's because the band Crush is playing.

Levi's band.

As much as I try to tune them out, his deep vocals can be heard all the way over here, on the opposite end of the public beach. He's been the lead guitar player and backup vocalist since they started the band when we were nineteen. I can still recall the day he called me at school and told me his news. We celebrated together on my next trip home from college the one way we always did: a movie and strawberry ice cream.

I push the memory out of my mind and focus on now. My next throw is coming, and I'm trying to figure out how to get out of it. I hate sports. Okay, I don't hate them, I'm just not good at them. Bowling, mini golf, Frisbee golf, you name it, I stink at it. The whole sports gene was just used up by the rest of the Summer sisters by the time I came along.

Let's roll back around to disc golf, or Frisbee golf as some like to call it. The object is to take your plastic disc (think Frisbee) and throw it into a basket on a pole. There are chains and a technique to it, but I don't really care about all of that. I'm basically here for the margaritas. Oh, back to the game. It's like golf, except without the club. You throw your disc and try to get it in the basket. The person with the least amount of throws wins. I never win.

Our beach is considered a nine-hole course. It's not sanctioned by the powers that be, the Professional Disc Golf Association. (Yes, that's a real organization. Look it up.) It serves its purpose to those who enjoy the game in Jupiter Bay. Six holes are positioned along the beach, whereas the remaining three can be found just off the sand in areas of dunes and tall grass.

I suck not only at sports, but well, anything that doesn't involve words. I like to read, always have, which is why my job as an editor for Stonewell Publishing is heaven-sent. I get to work from home, editing and correcting manuscripts for romance authors all over the world. The best of the best write under the Stonewell name, and I'm lucky to be attached.

"Abby, your turn," Payton hollers as she stands by and waits for me to throw.

"Are you all set to move at the end of the month?" I ask, taking aim at the big chain-made basket.

"All set. Everyone's available to help, right?" she asks, opening another can of beer.

"Did you really leave us a choice?" AJ quips, a smile on her face.

"Nope. You'll all be there. I'll make lunch," Payton adds.

"You'll make lunch?" Lexi asks, her eyebrow posed high into her hairline, an ornery smirk on her face.

"Well, Dean will make lunch. Whatever. Same thing. Don't be a brat, just be at my house at eight a.m."

"We only get lunch? You're making us move everything out of your place and into either storage, take it to Goodwill, or to Dean's. That calls for dinner too, I believe," Jaime says, glancing over her shoulder towards the crowd on the beach.

"Stop it. He's out there somewhere watching you. His lips are probably going to fall off because he hasn't kissed you in like," AJ says, checking her watch, "fifty-five minutes. Poor baby."

"What did I do to you? Is tonight pick on Jaime night?"

"Nope, that was last night," Payton adds.

I can't help but laugh. "Anyway, I'll be there," I tell Payton.

"Good. Bring Levi. We need more muscle."

Ah yes, Levi. The man we're not discussing right now.

I don't acknowledge the statement, but instead, turn towards the basket. I let the disc fly, but it doesn't go anywhere near the intended target. Instead, it flies to the right by a good ten feet. At this rate, I'll never get that stupid round thing inside the stupid hole.

Huh. Much like my sex life.

"Grandpa stopped by the shop yesterday and grabbed flowers for Grandma," Payton says.

"That's sweet," I chime in.

"It was, until he asked me to make an arrangement with pussy willows and poppies," she mumbles.

"Gross. Why is there a flower called pussy willow?" Meghan asks.

"It's not even a flower. It's a plant. It's actually called the Salix Discolor, and they grow wild along ditches and places where water gathers."

"But why pussy willow? They look more like cocks than pussies." Lexi looks deep in thought as she contemplates the answer to her question.

"Why are we talking about this?" I ask.

"Because our grandparents always talk about the sex, and they're rubbing off on us," Jaime says. We all giggle at her reference of *the sex*. It's how Grandma always refers to it.

"Poppies are fairly popular though, right?" AJ asks, taking her shot at the basket.

"Yeah, if you like hairy ball sacks. Grandma always says they look like balls."

"Or vaginas! Don't forget that everything looks like a vagina," Meghan adds through her laughter. It's so nice to see her smile.

Our grandparents helped raise us, and are the most inappropriate couple on the face of the planet. Their constant groping, mixed with language that would make a sailor blush, makes them over the top in the PDA and embarrassment departments. But we love them, even with the constant mortification that follows in their wake.

Our dad, Brian, is amazing. When my mom died sixteen years ago from ovarian cancer, it took a toll on everyone, especially him. He was left alone to raise six girls ranging from nine to seventeen. But he did it. Sure, he had the help of our grandparents, our mother's parents, but he made sure to stay an active part in our lives. He took a job flying private planes that didn't take him away as much as the commercial jets, he did everything he could to attend ballgames, dance recitals, and award assemblies. He rarely missed a milestone and has remained very much a part of all of our lives.

My sisters all talk over each other, laughing at stories and teasing each other mercilessly. We're brutal in a pack, competitive by nature, and loyal to a fault. I'm second to youngest of six girls. Yes, all girls. I'm also a twin. I can see you now, panicking at the thought of trying to keep all of us straight, so I'll try to help you out and keep it simple.

First, there's Payton. She's the oldest and owns Blossoms and Blooms, the small floral shop in downtown Jupiter Bay. She's also getting ready to move in with her boyfriend, Dean, and his daughter, Brielle. I adore that little girl. She's the first child in the Summer family, even though she's technically not flesh and blood. But that doesn't matter to us. She's already as much a part of the family as if she were actually born into it.

Up next comes Jaime. She works for Addy's Place, a program where kids who come from hard situations can go after school for help with homework, a healthy snack, or just to hang out socially. She's dating Ryan, though my sisters and I all expect a proposal soon. They live together with their deranged cat, Boots.

Third is Alison, or AJ. Teacher. Coach. Smartass. She's one of the remaining single ones, and I don't foresee that changing anytime soon.

Meghan. Oh, sweet, heartbroken Meghan. It's hard to talk about Meg. She's fourth in line, and recently lost her fiancé in a car accident. Josh was…everything to her, and our family. She's learning to navigate a new normal right now, and all we can do is be there for her when she needs us.

As I mentioned, I'm a twin, so that leaves Lexi. Alexis is my mirror image, even though we are nothing alike. She's fierce and feisty, and loves to stir the pot with her big wooden spoon. She's married to her high school sweetheart, Chris, but there are rocky waters there.

She's also my other half. When I need to talk, to cry, to laugh, she's my first call. Lexi and I share a special bond that most don't quite understand. I mean, we shared womb space for nine months; that's something pretty gargantuan.

Then there's Levi, but we don't need to get into him right now. I'm here tonight to have a good time with my sisters and don't need the distraction of letting my mind wander in his direction. Just know that he's my friend.

My best friend.

And I might be a little bit in love with him.

Chapter Two

Levi

I scan the faces in the crowd, but don't see the one I'm looking for. Dozens of half-drunk girls are swaying along to the music we play, singing every note. There was a time when seeing their lustful eyes, watching me play, was the biggest high ever. And it is, don't get me wrong, it's just that things might have changed.

Playing with Crush is fun, but it's not what I live for anymore. It's a way to unwind after a long-ass workweek. If I'm not on the rig, working as an EMT for Jupiter Bay Hospital, then I'm at the station as a volunteer firefighter. Both are an adrenaline rush that I crave. Just like playing in the band has been.

But now things are different. I'm getting older, and hopefully wiser. Yes, I know I'm only twenty-five, but back when we started six years ago, it was all about the music, booze, and girls. And there were plenty to go around, believe me. Now, it's still the music, but it doesn't own my heart the way it used to. There's still plenty of the other two. Most places we play give us free drinks, and most women we meet are ready for a little one-on-one time with someone in the band. Oh, and I used to take full advantage of it, all that I could. Girls were practically handing it out like cocktail napkins at a party. But lately, I'm just not looking for a quick hookup. Does that make sense?

I guess I'm just getting tired of all this bullshit.

My band mates say I should be having the time of my life, living up the fame that comes with being a small town, local musician. Oh, and I do, believe me. I get passed more phone numbers than a phonebook everywhere I go. Blonds, brunettes, redheads of all shapes and sizes. Thongs, double D's, black mascara, and stilettos. I have my pick of the party everywhere we play, but lately, they're just not doing it for me.

We're getting closer to a break, and damn, could I use one. I need some water to rehydrate, and I wouldn't mind finding Abby. I haven't seen her since the sun set and we started to play. She was out on the poorly lit Frisbee golf course with her sisters, enjoying another night with the girls. It kinda makes me jealous that they're so close, especially because my only sibling is a brother who doesn't live around here anymore. He's super smart, went off to college, and now lives in New York, raking in the dough for a finance firm.

Much smarter than me, that's for sure. He's all straight-laced and proper, and I'm all tattoos, piercings, and rock music. Sure, I went to the community college and worked hard to be an EMT. Those classes were fucking brutal for someone who hated school, especially when you mix in volunteering for the local fire department AND playing in a band. But I made it through.

Some nights, I wasn't sure how. I'd call Abs who was away at State. Sometimes when my mind gets going in fourteen different fucking directions, I need to hear her voice. It grounds me, soothes the turmoil brewing in my head. That's why, after almost fifteen years of friendship, she remains the only constant in my life. Well, besides my job and my parents. Abby is the one person who knows me, inside and out, and doesn't give a shit that I sometimes transpose letters when reading or that I can't balance my checkbook to save my life. She doesn't care about my status in the band or how great my ass looks in my uniform pants. (Don't judge–I hear it all the time.) She's one of the only girls to know I cook and bake better than Martha fucking Stewart and that I make my own laundry soap.

I know you're wondering, so I'll tell you. The whole laundry soap thing happened after Abby talked about having sensitive skin and how difficult it was to find a laundry soap that didn't make her break out. Do you know the kinda shit they have on Pinterest? Well, I found this recipe for this do-it-yourself laundry soap. Long story short, it worked so well for her–and smelled so fucking clean–that I use it myself to this day.

She's my rock, my constant, my best friend, if it's okay for dudes to say they have one. But she is, dammit, and I can't imagine my life without her.

And she's out there somewhere in the night, I can feel it.

When we finish our set, I put down my guitar and jump off the hay wagon we're using as our beachside stage. We've played many shows atop this wooden beast over the years, that's for sure. As soon as I head towards the cooler and start digging for a bottle of water, I feel long, slender fingers slide up my back and wrap around my shoulder. I don't know who it is, but I can tell you who it isn't. Abby would never touch me like this, even though part of me wouldn't mind that one fuckin' bit. Just the thought of her fingers –

No. I will *not* go there.

"Hey, handsome," the owner of the hand purrs in my ear. Her body is now pressed against my back, ample tits smashed against me. I can feel nipples through the material of my shirt, which doesn't bother me much, since I am a red-blooded, heterosexual male.

Turning around, I come face to face with the owner of the hand. Ahh, yes. I've had those hands on me before. "Crystal," I croon in a deep voice. "Lovely to see you this evening."

Her hand slides from my shoulder, down my chest, and lands on my abs. Apparently, she doesn't care that I'm a bit sweaty from playing. Instead, it seems to only wind her clock that much more. "I'd let you see a lot more of me later tonight," she replies with a coy smile.

I bet she would.

"Ahh, thanks for the offer, darlin'. I'll see how my night goes and get back to ya," I answer without committing. She keeps her hand on me, running a single finger down towards the button of my pants.

"We had such a great time before," she coos while biting her lower lip.

"That we did," I respond, even though nothing really stood out from our night together. Unfortunately, those kinda nights were more frequent than not. Booze and music would take hold and leave me a little on the wasted side by the end of the gig. Those were the nights where the girls all blended together into one big wild, drunken night. Well, probably about two years' worth of nights. Fine, call it three.

"We could have some fun again," she says, her finger dipping into the top of my pants.

A year ago, my dick would have already been hard and ready to play. Tonight? I just want to grab some water and head over to find my friend. How pathetic am I?

"Ahhh, maybe later, sweetheart. I gotta run and catch a friend," I tell her with a wink. She practically orgasms from that one little action. I've learned to perfect the wink since I was a horny teenager. My band mates call it The Panty Dropper. Yeah, we're dicks. What can I say?

"Levi," she whines, pouting to the extreme. Crystal actually sticks out her bottom lip, silently pleading for me to take her behind the hay wagon and give it to her right now. Ain't happenin', sweetheart.

"Yeah, maybe later," I say, taking a step back and dislodging her finger from my pants. I take one, then two steps backwards before turning towards the beach. "See ya later," I throw over my shoulder as I step into the crowd and start looking for my girl.

No.

Not my girl.

My *friend.*

My Abby.

Abby. Just Abby.

Even after I stop and say hey to a few guys I know and get chest-crushing hugs from the chicks, I make my way towards the edge of the beach. It doesn't take me long to find her sisters there, laughing and carrying on like a bunch of banshees. Ryan and Dean are right there, watching over the girls with a hawk's eye. It still feels weird not to see Josh there, Meghan's fiancé. I also realize real quickly that I don't see Abby.

"Hey, guys. Having a good night?" I ask my friend's sisters; women I've known for fifteen years.

"Levi!" Lexi hollers, barely taking her beer bottle away from her lips.

"You guys sound great tonight," Ryan says as he throws a protective arm around Jaime's shoulder.

"Thanks." I take a long gulp of water, practically finishing off the bottle. "Who won?" Oh, if that ain't a loaded question, I don't know what is!

"AJ, the cheater," Payton grumbles, swaying into Dean's arms.

"Whatever, harlot! I won fair and square," AJ defends.

"If you call shaving strokes off the holes as fair and square, duckface, then I guess you did."

"Did you just call her duckface, Payton?" Meghan asks with a smile and glassy eyes.

"I'm working on my cursing around little ears. I got upset and called someone fuckface once and Bri was there to hear. She repeated it like a friggin' parrot for a week," Payton explains.

"Oops!" Meghan giggles.

"Yeah, it was all fun and games until I got a call at work from her sitter," Dean adds.

"I made that up to you," Payton coos, not-so-subtly moving in front of him and rubbing her ass on his crotch.

"Yes, you did," Dean concedes with a laugh.

"Hey, where's Abby?" I ask casually. Or at least I hope it's casual.

"Oh, she went for a walk," AJ tells me.

"She's been funky lately, Levi. Did you piss her off?" Leave it to Lexi to not sugar coat something.

"Not that I'm aware of," I say with a smile. "I'll go look for her."

Throwing goodbyes over my shoulder with a quick wave, I head off toward the darkened beach, away from the lights and the people and the noise. I walk about a hundred yards, scanning the tall grass around the golf course for any sign of her. There's a few couples every now and then making out and a group of guys bullshitting, but I don't see my–

Abby.

Another fifty yards or so and the beach is vacant. The crowd is a distant hum, drowned out by the waves crashing on the sandy shores of the beach. The salty air tickles my nose, the almost-full moon casting a glow off the Bay.

That's when I spot her.

She's standing along the water, small waves crashing over her bare feet. Plain black sandals dangle from her fingers. Her arms are wrapped around her chest in a protective manner or to help keep herself warm. Moonlight bleeds from her hair, shiny and sleek, as she gazes out at the vast mass of water.

She looks beautiful.

Abby's always been gorgeous in that simple, girl next door kinda way. She wears minimal makeup and no-thrills, non-revealing clothes. She's modest and shy and sweet in a way that most women could only dream about. Her heart is worn squarely on her sleeve, and she'd do just about anything for anyone. She's honestly the best person I know, and I've always wondered how I got so lucky.

That's why I can't fuck this up.

"Hey," I say, joining her along the water's edge.

Abby jumps a bit, so lost in her thoughts that she didn't hear me approach. "Oh, hey."

"Watcha doing down here by yourself?" I ask, not caring that water is soaking my boots.

Instead of answering, she returns her gaze to the water and shrugs her shoulders. I look out at the rolling waves, wondering what's got her so forlorn. She hasn't even said anything, but I can feel it. Years of gauging and learning her moods, her smiles, her tears, has me pretty much an Abby expert. Other women? Fuck no. But this woman? I'd like to think I know her as well as she knows me.

"Everything okay?" I ask, taking a step closer to her without moving my eyes from the Bay.

"Yeah," she responds, a little too chipper. "Meghan came tonight, and it was so great to see her smiling real smiles again."

"It's gonna take some time," I tell her. No, I don't have a clue firsthand what I'm talking about, but I've seen enough death in my line of work to know that it takes time until you're feeling a bit more human again.

"I know. She's doing well, though, I think."

"She is. She's strong and she has the support of you guys," I remind her. Abby's answer is a small smile.

Finally, after three long minutes, she glances over at me. Her green eyes are so bright, even in the dark. The moonlight is reflecting off them so vividly, it's like the moon casts shadows in her eyes every night. The breeze catches her hair and flings long, dark strands into her face. Without even thinking, I react. Grabbing hold of a cluster, I gently move it away from her eyes. In doing so, my pinky finger grazes across the apple of her cheek.

I hear her gasp upon impact. My finger tingles where it touched her smooth, pale skin, a sensation that is new to me. Don't get me wrong, I've touched Abby a lot in the fifteen years we've been friends, but never in a sexual way. Never. She's my friend.

But that slightest touch? Like a few others over recent months, it causes my heart to actually palpitate and crazy lightning bolts of lust to shoot through my body, making it hyperaware of her proximity. The scent of something fruity (probably that lotion she likes from the bath store uptown) wraps around me, choking me with a mixture of familiarity and newness. Her hair, blowing in the breeze, tickles my arm, making me want to wrap it around her body and pull her into my embrace and push her and these unwanted feelings away, all at the same time.

Friends.

Clearing my throat, I take a step sideways, out of the line of fire for her hair and her scent. "Are you gonna come listen to us play? Your sisters are all up there," I ask, glancing down at my watch and noticing our fifteen-minute break is almost up.

She hesitates, and it doesn't go unnoticed. Something's going on with her, and I hate that she won't talk to me about it. "Listen, Abs, you know you can talk to me about anything, right? I can tell something's going on. Whatever it is, I'm here for you." My heart practically jumps out of my chest, my hands twitch to touch her hair again, so I shove them in my pants pockets instead and roll back on the heels of my boots.

Glancing at me, her emerald eyes speak of confliction and hope. What the hell is going on with her?

"Yeah," she finally whispers. "I know."

"Good." Taking one hand out of a pocket, I extend it towards her. "Come on. I've gotta get back on stage, and your favorite song is in this set."

Her smile is warm and genuine, and I can't help my own that spreads across my face in that moment. Abby reaches for my hand, hers feeling warm and acquainted as I wrap my fingers around hers, and we step out of the surf. The water is gone as we reach drier land and continue to head towards the beach party, but I don't let go.

And neither does she.

"You catchin' a ride from someone tonight?" I ask.

"Ryan or Dean will give us all rides home. I rode with Jaime so my car wouldn't be stuck here all night," she says, her warm voice matching the warmth of her hand.

"You could stay 'til the end and ride home with me," I offer casually, though my heart is beating anything but a casual pace.

"Oh, thanks for the offer. I'm not sure I'm going to stay." I glance over at my friend and see storm clouds still in her eyes. I can't let go of the feeling that something is bothering her, but she won't tell me. Fuck knows I can't force her to talk to me if she doesn't want to. I can only assume she'll come to me when she's ready. All I can do is be ready to listen.

Several couples litter the beach the closer we get, upbeat rock music pumping through the massive speakers we use. I can see her sisters and their significant others on the outskirts of the party, but my legs suddenly feel heavier, leaded. I'm so preoccupied at trying to figure out a way to stall our arrival to her little group that I don't even see the flash of yellow or the half-dressed woman before she's squealing my name and throwing herself into my chest.

The impact of her sends me back a few steps, my hand dislodging from Abby's. "I've been looking for you," she coos loudly.

Crystal wraps her long legs around my waist and plants her lips squarely on mine. The shock of the moment leaves me completely motionless. I stand there like an idiot, unsure how in the hell I went from walking with Abby along the beach to having Crystal plastered against my chest and kissing me.

"Get a room," someone yells, pulling my attention away from being kissed by someone I'm not really interested in making out with.

I pull back, Crystal's smile wide and mischievous. That's when I glance around and see Abby standing there, wide, stunned eyes trained directly on me. Her sisters are standing right behind her, their own faces showing displeasure and disgust. *Shit!* How did this happen?

Wiggling my body, I try to dislodge the woman attached to my chest like some sort of spider monkey, but when I do, she takes the move as more sexual, and purrs. Yeah, she actually fucking purrs like a cat and wiggles her barely-covered ass in my hands. Apparently I grabbed onto her when she launched herself at me.

Dropping my hands and grabbing her waist, I help remove Crystal from my body. She doesn't go far, though, and practically plasters herself to my side. A lump rises in my throat and lodges firmly in my esophagus, blocking my airway. Guilt creeps up my back and smacks me upside the head. I shouldn't feel guilty, but I do. I'm not dating anyone, and if I wanted to bang Crystal fourteen ways to Sunday, that's my business. But the fact that I don't want to, and this little scene is happening in front of Abby and her family makes me feel guilty.

I open my mouth to speak, but nothing comes out. Great, I have a half-dressed woman plastered to my side, my best friend is across from me looking like I ran over her puppy, and I'm suddenly mute. Just fucking great.

"Can't wait for later, Levi." Crystal draws out my name like it's sixteen syllables. The sound of her sexpot voice doesn't turn me on the way it used to. Instead, I hear the whiny undertone, which is equivalent to nails on a chalkboard.

"Looks like you don't need me to hang around," Abby says to my left. When I glance at her, she's wearing a big, bright smile— almost too bright. It's plastered on her face perfectly, but it's not real. I know Abby's real smiles and that shit ain't one of them. She glances over her shoulder and sees Dean. "Dean, you don't mind dropping me off at home tonight, do you?" Her voice is soft and sweet like always, but it lacks authenticity.

"No problem, Abs," he says while Payton kills me with eye daggers. Seriously, what the fuck did I do to her?

"All set. You can go home and *entertain* Crystal. Don't worry about me. I'm fine. I'm good. I'm all taken care of." Quickly, before I can get a word in edgewise, she turns and grabs one of the drinks in Jaime's hands and takes a long gulping pull. I'm not even sure she realizes what she's drinking, but by the looks of it, she doesn't care.

"Yay! You don't have to babysit the little friend tonight," Crystal says behind me.

My gut tightens and my body tenses. Abby stands statue-still. Shit, the air doesn't even move. I'm pretty sure even the noise evaporates around us. Abby doesn't even turn fully to face us; I can see the hurt on her beautiful face.

Without even thinking, I grab Crystal by the arm and pull her towards the stage. She's shuffling beside me, teetering unsteadily on platform sandals. Who the fuck wears those kinda shoes to the beach? The guys are already on the stage, preparing for our final set of the night, when I move her just out of earshot.

"What the fuck was that?" I ask quietly.

"What?" she giggles, her blond hair flying in her face. I make no move to adjust the strands.

"That back there. Why would you treat Abby the way you did? I don't babysit her," I direct, my voice growing louder with agitation.

"Oh, come on, it was a little joke. Besides, everyone knows she has a crush on you. She follows you around like a lost puppy." She giggles again, which just pisses me off that much more.

"Are you kidding? Follows me around? She's my friend, dammit, and not that I owe you or anyone else in this town an explanation, but last time I checked, friends are allowed to do things together."

"Okay," Crystal says. She runs her hand up my chest once more, causing me to take a big step back.

"I gotta go. We're supposed to be on," I say, turning towards the stage.

I only get a few steps away when she adds, "I'll wait for you after the show."

I don't even stop walking. "No thanks. I've got plans with Abby tonight."

"But…" she starts, but I tune out the rest of her whining.

Back on stage, Gage instantly starts heckling me about where I was with Crystal. I don't bother telling him I wasn't with her because he sure as shit won't believe me. He's one of those guys who latches onto something and won't let go. Like a dog with a bone, he'll keep needling me until I give him the juicy details. Only this time, there are no details to give, but that doesn't matter. He'll just accuse me of keeping my dirty little secrets to myself. We've been down this road before.

Grabbing my guitar, I give it a quick tune, making sure everything is just right. Dexter starts tapping out the beat on his drums, and Andy and I join in on guitar. Gage belts out the opening notes of "Ring of Fire" by Johnny Cash and the crowd goes nuts. It's not the typical rock music we usually play, but when we find a good song that the fans love and we enjoy playing, then we go with it.

After another two songs, it's time to slow it down. Gage heads off stage to take a quick break, and I step up to the mic. I usually sing backup, but for three songs during our show, I take the reins and sing lead vocals. This song is one of them. It's my favorite song to sing because it's Abby's song.

Way back when we were in grade school, I caught her humming it as we walked home from school. She was going to help me work on our Constitution assignment at her place, which happened every week or so. That particular day, she was quiet, lost in thought, so I let her be. Suddenly, she started humming, and it didn't take me long to catch on to the tune. She had the voice of an angel, I remember thinking, and wanted to beg her to sing something for me. I had already discovered my love for music, but knowing that Abby shared this passion with me was like kismet. When I asked her about it, she just shied away and hid behind her books. I went home and started working on that song on my guitar. It took a while, but eventually, I got it down, and have been playing it ever since.

I start strumming the opening notes of Jeff Healey's "Angel Eyes." Continuing to play the song I know by heart, I scan the crowd until I see her, standing in the back, a soft smile on her face as she sings along to the song. Everything and everyone around us just fades away. It's as if we're the only two people on the beach. The way she watches me kicks my heart into overdrive, because I know, when it comes to this song, she only has eyes for me. Not that I want her eyes on me or anything. I mean, we are just friends. But *if* it were something more than friendship, then I'd be the luckiest son of a bitch to have her there with me.

Closing my eyes, I sing the words I've known by heart for fifteen years to my best friend. I can picture her out there saying the exact same words at the exact same time. We've sung this song together for years. Not publicly, of course, because she'd rather strip naked and do the chicken dance in the rain in the middle of Main Street than to get on stage and sing. In the privacy of her apartment or mine, we've belted out the words on several occasions. Abby actually has a beautiful voice. She just refuses to let anyone but me hear it.

When I reach the end of the second verse, I open my eyes and scan the crowd. She's still there, standing in the same spot, watching me and singing along. I give her a knowing grin as I finish off the song strong, singing it for her. For her because she loves it, not because it means anything more than that. She's my friend, remember? We've covered this.

Why does it feel like I'm completely full of shit?

Chapter Three

Abby

First time I heard that song, Jeff Healey stole my heart. Then I heard ten-year-old Levi Morgan belt out the words, and I was a goner. My best friend can sing, even though he prefers to play guitar and provide backup vocals, but he always sings that song for me.

When he finishes, I hold my breath and wait until…there. He does it. He points to me from the stage, a huge smile spread across his handsome face. The ladies go wild as if he's pointing to them, but I don't pay them any attention. My eyes are locked on his, my smile as wide as the one he throws at me from the stage.

"You two are so stinkin' cute. Why don't you just screw and get it over with?" AJ slurs beside me.

"Screw! I wanna screw! Not Levi because that'd be like doing the sex with my brother, but I wouldn't mind a little bit of the sex," Lexi chimes in, her words just as slurry as AJ's.

"Stop calling it *the sex,* Grandma! You sound just like her!" Jaime exclaims. She's right. Grandma always calls it *the sex,* and apparently Lexi has picked up on the habit.

"She's right," I tell my twin. "And I'm not having the, you know, sex or anything with Levi. We're friends."

"Friends who should screw," AJ retorts with a snort, finishing off her drink. "I'm done. I'm drunk. I'm ready to go," she says, swaying a little too much towards Ryan. Fortunately, he doesn't mind that she's practically using him as a place to rest.

"Me too. I'm just drunk enough for road-head," Jaime yells over the music. Ryan's face lights up like he just signed with the Yankees.

"I like road-head," Ryan adds to the conversation, a hopeful gleam in his eyes.

"Please wait until you've safely dropped us all off," Meghan begs.

"Or until you're safely at home," I add.

"You don't understand the concept of road-head, Abs," Jaime says with a laugh.

This may be true, but I'd rather them be on the safe side. I wouldn't want to risk my life and that of those around me to give a little BJ on the way home. Suddenly, completely unwarranted, but Levi's face pops up in my semi-drunken mind. For some reason, I doubt any BJ I'd give him would be little. In fact, I might have caught a glimpse of a very large, very hard penis when he was getting out of the shower in my dorm room, at college one weekend. I'm pretty sure he took care of the problem with my roommate.

Picturing the scene all over again makes me giggle. Back then, I remembered being completely shocked (and maybe a little excited). Like ninety percent shocked and ten percent excited. Fine, seventy/thirty. Maybe fifty/fifty. I had only seen one peen in person and it *wasn't* anywhere close to the size of Levi's.

"What are you laughing about?" Payton asks, glancing through me and looking straight into my guilty conscience.

"Nothing." Yeah, might as well just tattoo the phrase *thinking about penis* across my forehead.

"I don't believe you, but I'm too drunk to try to get it out of you right now. Let's head out," she says, leading our group towards the parking lot. "Get it? *Head* out," she adds with a laugh. Dean rode here with Ryan so he can take Payton's car, which only leaves AJ's behind in the lot. We'll get her back here tomorrow to pick it up.

As I climb into the back of Ryan's truck, I glance back over to the stage where Levi is performing. He probably doesn't realize I've left yet, but I'm sure he won't care. He'll have company later tonight and doesn't need to worry about trying to get me home. Even if my home is directly across the hall from his own. At least I'm not right next door and have to listen to loud *stuff* coming through the walls.

Thank goodness for small favors.

* * *

It's not even eight and I'm ready to head out. Most Sundays are spent completely opposite of the rest of my days: leaving the house. As an editor for a large publishing company, I spend most of my days behind my computer screen. But on Sundays, I do everything I can to get out and enjoy a little fresh air.

Today, I'm meeting Lexi at her salon for a color and cut. To me, hair is hair, and it doesn't matter to me what mine looks like, but Lexi is a perfectionist beautician and would rather die from paper cuts than let me walk around without highlights and a regular trim.

Whatever.

My hair appointments are almost always on Sundays, when the shop is closed and we can talk about anything and everything.

It's one of our bonding times as twins, and I look forward to it like clockwork every eight weeks. The best part is I don't have to do my hair or makeup to go out. She'll fix my hair, and often plays around with new eye colors or smudge-proof lipsticks.

I gather up my purse and tablet, hoping to get a little reading in while I'm under the dryer. And not work-related reading, I'm talking about something I want to read for enjoyment. Something that's already edited and corrected. Today's selection is somewhat of a regency novel. I normally stick to straight rom-com romance, but since I'm working on stepping outside of my box, I figured it wouldn't hurt to give other genres a try too. And this is still romance; it's just set in another time period.

Grabbing my keys from my purse, I step through my door and into the hallway. I pull it closed behind me, turning the lock to confirm it's secure, when I hear the door behind me open. Levi has always been an early bird, using the sun rising as his excuse to go for a run, so I prepare to greet my friend.

Only this isn't Levi.

She's wearing a dark purple dress with tall black sandals. Her jet black hair is pulled back in one of those messy buns that some women have the natural born ability to create, and her pretty face is makeup free. She doesn't notice me standing there, staring, but turns to face the inside of Levi's apartment.

"Thanks for last night, Levi! I had a great time," she says, throwing a wave over her shoulder before shutting the door. The woman notices me for the first time and gives me a shy grin. "Oh, hi," she says, looking down at her clothes that are clearly from last night.

I don't respond; I can't. My heart pounds with the force of a thousand drums in my chest, my throat tightening up and making it impossible to breathe. I didn't realize it was possible, but I think I just felt my heart break a little in my chest. The onslaught of pain is almost deafening as blood swooshes in my ears.

The woman walks to the end of the hallway and waits for the elevator. Apparently, Levi didn't give her the same lecture about not taking the elevator in buildings where there are just a few floors. That's because she's not a friend; not like I am. I'm safely tucked away in the friends-only zone, where you worry about the other's safety, but don't ever picture them or think about them in any situation that doesn't fall within the strict friends-only parameters.

And that's where I am.

Friends. Only.

I slowly make my way to the elevator and push the button. It takes it a few moments to make the ascent back up to the third floor, so I use those moments to consider my options. One, I continue to pretend I don't have the hots for my best friend and pine away for him, hoping that over time he'll realize that he's secretly in love with me too. Two, I move on. I accept that Levi and I are friends and nothing more will ever come. The thought makes me hurt.

No one said life was ever easy.

As I get into the elevator car, I smile a little knowing that I'm going against something he's always said. I'm getting into an elevator and only using it for three floors. It could break down or the city could suddenly be overtaken by severe weather and I'd be trapped. But today? I just don't give a crap.

In my car, I crank up the radio, blasting Joan Jett, as I make my way towards Hair Haven. A new plan starts to take shape, one that already has me nervous. This next stage will force me to not only step outside my comfort zone, but to jump over it and keep going. This is the start of something bigger than dull old Abby. The sister who works from home and sometimes doesn't even get dressed that day. The one without the trail of single men following behind her (that's AJ) or the one who can flirt as if it were as natural as breathing (that's Lexi). I'm the one who cries at beer commercials and could never get a pet because she can't bear the thought of losing it one day.

I'm just Abby, plain and boring.

But not anymore.

It's time to get up and move on. Time to show myself that I can date and have fun and be carefree. It's time I become someone different than the ordinary girl I've always been. Move over simple Abby because outgoing Abigail is coming.

I can do this, right?

Right!

The street is practically empty at eight a.m. on a Sunday morning, so I'm able to park directly behind Lexi's vehicle. The front door is unlocked for me, but I throw the latch after I step through it. One time, we had a man stop by and ask for a cut. He saw the lights on and thought she was open. Since then, we've always locked ourselves in. And if any of the other sisters show up–which has happened on many occasions–she just runs over and lets them in.

Easy peasy.

The lights are on and there's plenty of natural sunlight filtering in through the large front window. There are four workstations in the little shop Lexi works at. The owner gave her a shot right out of beauty school and served as her mentor as she navigated her first few years of being in the business.

"You look like you didn't get much sleep last night," I say to my twin as I walk over to her station.

"I'm dog tired. I couldn't fall asleep last night to save my life. And for once, it didn't have anything to do with Chris snoring."

"He snores?"

"Like a freight train."

"Is there something you can do?" I ask as I slide into the chair.

"Besides a pillow over his face?" she quips. I glance up at her face and see the slightest grin play on the corner of her lips. She's joking. At least, I hope she is.

"I wouldn't recommend that," I say as she wraps the cape around my neck.

"No, you're right. I would never do that."

"Good."

"Orange isn't really my color," she says before grabbing the box of foil squares and the pan of color that she already mixed up for my highlights. "I think we should add this reddish highlight in with the blond." She makes it sound like a suggestion, but it's not. It's already happening. That point is perfectly clear by the red highlights already made up, brush sitting in the pan.

We make small talk about our other sisters, about work, and about the weather, but I know the hard stuff is coming. Both Lexi and I use these two-hour hair sessions as a way to dig in and talk about the good stuff. And by that, I mean Lexi will nag me until I finally spill whatever's on my mind, and she'll overshare everything I really don't want to know about. Namely, her sex life–or lack thereof.

Instead of waiting for her to start grilling me, I decide to be bold. "I'm going to try Internet dating," I say after a few moments of silence. She almost has my head completely foiled, and the brush stalls against the strands of hair she's coloring.

"Really?" she asks, concern etched on her face.

"Yep. I've already made up my mind." I leave out the reason why.

"Okay."

Again, we're silent for a few moments while she finishes and helps move me towards the dryer. Before she can put the lid down over my head and turn on the heat, I stop her hand with my own. "Will you help me?" I whisper. Fidgeting with my tablet on my lap, "I don't really know how to talk to guys and so I might need a little coaching, Lex."

The woman who mirrors my appearance squats down before me. "Of course I'll help you. I'll help with anything you want. I'll come over and we'll make you a kick-ass profile. I heard of this new site, PerfectDate.com, that's supposed to be good at pairing profiles based on their compatibility. It advertises itself as finding the perfect date will lead towards your perfect forever. Or some shit like that."

"I like it. Let's do it."

"Okay. What about this afternoon? I'm not doing anything and Chris is probably working on something and won't even notice I'm missing," Lexi mumbles, getting the dryer ready.

"Everything okay with that?"

She shrugs and gives me a sad smile. "We can talk about that later." Then, she flips on the dryer, essentially ending the conversation.

My mind races to the prospect of setting up a dating profile. A picture, talking about myself, verbalizing what I'm looking for in a potential future spouse. It'll all be there in black and white. Can I really do this? Well, we're about to find out.

Ready or not, here I come.

Chapter Four

Levi

I wake up cranky. My neck has a crick in it from falling asleep wrong on my pillow, my mouth is dry from drinking too much, and the headache got progressively worse after Jessa left my apartment with the slam of the door.

Jessa. Not exactly the woman 1 had planned on bringing home last night. Of course, by home I mean the building. Abby has her own place across the hall. After I finished her song, we jumped right into the next one. I was anxious to get done and tear down so I could grab my friend and head back to our building. Unfortunately, she slipped out with her family before the set was over. Without saying goodbye, I might add. Not a wave, a smile, not even a kiss my ass.

Afterwards, that's when things got real. Crystal was looking to hook up again, but I just wasn't feeling it. Apparently, she forgot about me quickly and moved on to the next man in line, which happened to be Dexter, our drummer. He barely helped pack up our shit before he had his tongue down Crystal's throat, his hand down the waist of her tiny little shorts.

The problem with this was that his sister, Jessa, was in town for the weekend. She was at the show, supposed to stay with her big brother, but the dumb fuck opted to invite his new *friend* home with them. It was either force Jessa to listen to her brother bumping uglies with a town tramp or invite her to crash at my place in my guest room.

She made her decision, which was why I didn't sleep for shit last night. I'm not used to having company in my space, so every time she moved in bed, every time she got up to get a drink or piss, every time she coughed, I heard it. Eventually, I got up and slammed back a bottle of Jack. The burn in my stomach and the rush of sweet intoxication helped rock me to sleep. Slept like a damned baby, too.

Sundays are my day off from my workout routine, which consists of running, some free weights, and taking out a little aggression on the heavy bag. After popping a few Tylenol and taking a hot shower, I finally feel human enough to head out in public. I'm in desperate need of some groceries, and I was hoping to have Abby over for dinner tonight. I'm on the rig again Monday, so I might as well take advantage of having an entire weekend off and spend it with my best girl.

My phone dings with a text. Swiping the screen, I find a message from my buddy, Tucker. We both work for the hospital and have many shifts together, since neither of us minds working overnights. He's also a volunteer firefighter. Tuck and I get along well and like to grab a drink after a long shift. I guess you could say he's the male version of Abby, but without the wandering eye. No way in hell do I check out Tuck's ass or tits the way I might steal glances of Abby's.

But that's not something to talk about right now.

Tuck: *I'm dehydrated. Need fuel. Lunch at café at noon. Be there, fucker.*

Realizing I'm starving, I shoot off a quick reply with an equally derogatory insult confirming the lunch plans, and grab my wallet and keys. I don't bother knocking on Abby's door to invite her along since she's at her sister's shop this morning. They'll spend all morning there doing all that girly shit that isn't necessary. She's

41

gorgeous in that simple, girl next door kinda way that guys always acknowledge. Fortunately for me, those that notice Abby just take a second look. Abby's kinda awkward when it comes to guys so it rarely makes it past the second date.

Not that she's dated much, to my pleasure. Not sure why that makes me smile, but it does. Mostly because I don't want her with some douchebag who only wants one thing. You know, a guy like me. Or at least how I used to be. I'm no saint, by any means, but I'm not the manwhore I prided myself on in my late teens and early twenties. She dated that weirdo, Colton, for a while. Damn, I hated that guy. He was…well, he just… I don't know what it was, but he grated on my nerves. When she dumped him, I was the first one there to celebrate.

Good riddance, jackwad!

I jump in my truck and head towards the fire station. I have about an hour left until I meet Tuck, so it's as good a time as any to stop by and grab my gym clothes and bring them home to wash. Plus, there's always something there to keep you busy for a little while. Since we're all volunteers, paid a small wage for calls, we congregate once a week for a meeting and do what we can to clean, organize, and maintain our gear and equipment. Most of us use the gym in back to workout, but there's only a handful of guys that actually will do a bit of cleaning up after the gross fuckers that sweat all over everything and make the locker room smell like a cross between nasty ass and swampy feet.

Before I know it, it's a few minutes before noon. My bag packed with dirty clothes is thrown in the bed of my truck as I head off to the café to meet Tuck. He's already in a booth when I get there, chugging a glass of ice water. By the way he carries the suitcases under his eyes and he gulps water like he may never get it again, I think it's safe to say that ol' Tuck went out and tied one on last night.

"Long night?"

"Fuck. My head is throbbing."

"Where'd ya go? I didn't see ya at the beach," I ask, taking a drink of the water the young waitress slides in front of me. She gives me a coy grin, which is rewarded with a wink that makes her giggle, before heading off to her next table.

"I don't know how you do it. You've got more pussy lined up than anyone I know," he says, shaking his head and watching the waitress walk off.

"Anyway, last night?" I redirect, not wanting to discuss the tail I get or could get.

"Headed up to Lucky's before I was gonna show at the beach. Brenna was there in that fucking skirt the same size as an Ace bandage, which told me one thing: she was on the prowl. Heard that dick she was seeing left again, so I bought her a drink. One turned to five, which turned into a BJ in the bathroom before I took her home and rocked her world half the night. There was tequila and body shots somewhere along the way, and damn if I'm not hurtin' this morning."

The giggly waitress comes back a few moments later to take our order. I'm ready to order my standard when I think about that chicken wrap that Abby always gets. "Grilled chicken, bacon, and ranch wrap with onion rings, please." Tuck notices my odd choice and raises his eyebrow my way.

When the waitress is done lingering at the table, she heads back to put in our order. "Abby's rubbing off on you," he says, his look pointed and direct.

"It looked good last time we were here so I thought I'd give it a try."

"Mmmmhmmm," he says, taking another drink of water.

"What does that mean?"

"Nothing. Just that you and Abby seem to spend a lot of time together."

"We're friends," I remind him.

"You and I are friends. Guys and girls can't be friends, at least not for very long."

"I've been friends with her for fifteen fucking years, dude."

"Yeah, well, you're a freak of nature. Anyone else in your shoes would have bagged her by now."

"Don't fucking say that. I'm not bagging Abby, nor will I."

"But you want to," he says, causing me to choke on air. "Oh, come on, Levi. I've seen the way you look at her when you don't think anyone is watching. You'd make a shitty spy, brother."

"I don't look at Abby like that," I retort, but know it'll fall on deaf ears. Plus, I'm not really sure I can argue his point. These weird images of Abby and me together have popped up in my head a lot lately, and they're seriously fucking with me.

"You do. Why don't you just take her out for real?"

Closing my eyes, I let them drop down to the tabletop. "I can't. She's seriously the best thing in my life. I need her to be a part of it, man, and if I take it to the next level, I'll fuck it all up. Then where would I be? Without her in my life at all, that's where."

"So just mess around with her. Like a friends with benefits deal," he suggests, and I instantly want to punch him.

"Does she look like the friends with benefits type? Besides, Abby's too good for that shit. I don't want to play games with her or hurt her, and that's what I'd end up doing. I'd hurt her, and I won't do that." I'll just keep her tucked away in the friends category until this pesky crush thing I've developed is over.

Easy peasy.

God, I sound like her.

"Well, if you're not gonna screw her, mind if I do? Her ass is fucking fantastic."

And just like that, I see red. I actually lunge across the table at my friend, ready to throw five years of friendship down the drain, and all because he talked about Abby's ass like it was his next meal and he was starved.

His laughter permeates my muddled thoughts. "That's what I thought. Dude, just take her out. Quit fighting the feelings that I know you have, or you'll end up losing her to some douche who treats her like a fucking princess. Then where will you be? You think she'll need you in her life as much when she's got a man who worships the ground she walks on?"

The thought causes the stone in my stomach to drop to my toes. It's almost painful to think about her with someone else, but I refuse to put myself in the place of that man. Because, in the end, I'll only hurt her like I do everyone. I'm no good for her, but she has no idea how much I need her in my life. She's the sun, the moon, and the fucking stars. She's beauty and goodness.

She's mine.

But she's not.

"Whatever," I mumble as my wrap is placed in front of me.

"Just think about it, man. I'm not saying you have to propose to the girl or anything, but I really do think you're making a mistake by not trying to see if there's anything between you guys."

I nod in consensus and dive into my food, the entire time thinking about my beautiful best friend who'd be eating this exact meal right now if she were here. Thinking of her makes my heart beat faster and the food I'm consuming turn sour in my stomach. I wish there were an easy answer to this dilemma I find myself in, but there's not. I won't risk my friendship with her, even if that means she finds someone else who treats her like the amazing woman she is.

But that image just makes me angry.

See my predicament? It's like a double-edged sword. On one end, I have a woman I'd be lucky enough to call my own. But if things went south with the relationship, then I'd be without my friend. On the other end, I maintain my friendship and risk losing her to another man. At least with that option I'd still have her in my life.

Basically, either way, I'm fucked.

* * *

I pull the taco dip out of the fridge and get ready to head over to Abby's place. I texted her earlier and told her I had chicken wings in the cooker and whipped up taco dip with fresh guacamole. To finish off the meal, I threw some cookie dough in the oven and baked her fresh chocolate chip cookies.

Her text reply was instantaneous and said that I could come over anytime. I almost dropped everything and went over right then and there, but decided to wait until I got laundry finished. I'm on the schedule Monday night, so tomorrow will involve me catching as much sleep as I can during the day to get ready for the night shift.

There's a baseball game on my TV, but it's mostly just background noise. I glance at the score every now and again, but I haven't been able to sit down and watch more than a few batters at a time.

As I switch my last load from the washer to the dryer, I find myself humming along to the song that reminds me of a certain brunette. She sang along with me last night while I was on stage, and smiled widely when I gave her the acknowledgement that always comes at the end of the song.

Abby actually has the voice of an angel. I'll never forget the first time I actually heard her sing. She blew me away at the age of ten. I've tried to get her to sing with me on stage, but she won't. Hell no, not my shy, sweet little Abby. She'll belt it out when it's just the two of us messing around, but the thought of singing in front of people, on stage, terrifies her.

That's another thing that's just hers and mine. I'll play guitar and she'll sing with me. I actually recorded her one time with my phone. I got about two minutes worth of video before she caught me. Her face at the end, a mixture of horror and excitement, has kept me company on nights that I'm working late and missing her. I could probably call her and she wouldn't mind, but I refuse to do that in the middle of the night, even if she works from home and sets her own hours. Instead, I pull out that video and watch her sing, eyes closed and swaying to the silent music that isn't there because I stopped playing to grab my phone.

That's between the two of us, though. Don't you fucking say a word, okay? No one besides her knows I took that video, and I told her I deleted it. But I didn't.

I couldn't.

It's almost four when I gather up my bags and get ready to head across the hall. Locking my door, I balance a grocery bag of food, a platter of dip, plate of cookies, and the small cooker with honey barbeque glazed chicken wings. I look like your typical twenty-five year old Betty Crocker.

I don't even knock, just let myself in like always. "Hey!" I holler as I kick the door closed and head into the kitchen. "Why was your door unlocked?" I don't get an answer, but instead hear giggling. If I had to wager a guess, I'd say the laughter is coming from either Lexi or AJ.

Walking from the kitchen, I head towards the hallway. The layout is the exact same as mine, except the mirror opposite. The first door on the left is the bathroom, which is empty. The door across the hall is the master bedroom. I stop and glance inside, and even though I've seen it before – hell, I've slept in it before – it makes my dick take notice of the big bed.

Embarrassment courses through me as I realize I'm getting a full-on chubby staring at my best friend's bed. The pillows that cradle her head, the blankets that slide along her porcelain skin, shit it's all there, flashing before me like the start of a porno.

Quickly, I clear my throat and head to the last door, the one for the second bedroom. In my apartment, it houses my small weights and a twin sized bed for a spare. It's the same bed that Jessa slept in last night. Abby's other room serves as her office. Since she works from home for a big publishing company, she transformed that space into her home away from home during the day.

Inside, I find my girl–no, my friend–sitting at her desk with two brunette heads bent down and looking at something over her shoulder.

"Oh my God, Abs, look at that one! I think that's a bong he's holding in his profile pic," AJ says, causing Lexi to laugh and Abby to groan.

"Gross," Abby says. "Wait look at this one."

"Oh, he screams bad boy. Click him," Lexi exclaims.

"His ears are pierced. A lot," Abby says.

"I bet he has other things pierced too," AJ chimes in.

"Hey, don't knock piercings. Some of them are really...effective," Lexi quips with a smirk, making me do a double take at my girl's twin. Shit, there I go again. My *friend's* twin.

"There's a story there, I can tell. Spill," AJ directs.

"Motorcycle boy in high school had a piercing," she whispers conspiratorially before giggling.

"Really?" Abby asks curiously, turning towards her sister with a cute little blush. Her hair is different. Even through profile view, I can see it's lighter, with a caramel colored highlight blended through.

"Oh, yeah. They're...nice," Lexi adds with a wink.

Choking on air, I do everything I can to hold in my own laughter. Unfortunately, I'm unsuccessful and three sets of eyes glance over at my position in the doorway. "What are you ladies doing?" I ask, stepping into the room.

Abby looks guilty, while her sisters look amused.

"Internet dating!" AJ exclaims, gleefully.

"You're gonna try that crap? I would have thought you wouldn't waste your time and energy on that bullshit, AJ," I say, stepping up behind Abby. My nose instantly catches a whiff of her shampoo. It takes everything I have not to bend down and run my nose along her scalp.

"Not me, big guy," AJ teases with a knowing smile. "Abby."

Abby's trying Internet dating? My Abby? The earth stops moving on its axis at this startling revelation. Air is sucked from the room by some invisible vacuum. I might even be stroking out right now; my heart is beating so fast and furiously in my chest. My Abby? Internet dating?

What. The. Fuck?

Chapter Five

Abby

Lexi called AJ before we were even finished at the salon and invited her to join us at my place. Apparently, if I was gonna give this whole Internet dating thing a try, I was gonna do it with the help from two of my sisters.

"First things first. We need to settle on which site. Here's a list of some of the popular ones," AJ says as she keys in sites into my Internet browser.

The first thing I notice is the sheer quantity of sites she's pulling up. There's general dating ones, ones particularly for the wealthy, even sites for finding country boys and cowboys. It's almost overwhelming right off the bat, and I haven't even started the process of setting up my profile.

"I've already told her we'd use PerfectDate.com," Lexi tells our older sister.

"That's a really good one, and from what I've found there's quite a few singles on the site from our area. Not just Jupiter Bay but also Ridgewood and other towns that are within a short drive," AJ says, inputting that site into the browser next.

"What about this one?" I ask, pointing to one with a catchy name.

"No, you don't want that site, Abs. That one's nothing but a bunch of people looking for hookups and sending dick pics," she says, waving her hand.

Lacey Black

"Maybe I want that," I say shyly, unable to stop the blush.

"Not those kind. The men on there whipping out their dicks aren't the good ones you actually want to see. Trust me," she says.

"Why did you bring it up if you aren't going to let her use it," Lexi asks, chastising our sister.

"I had a profile on there once, but I was getting hookup requests from just as many women as I was men, so I deactivated my profile."

"That's what all of these are? These are ones you've tried?" I ask, shocked because, my goodness, there's a lot of them.

"Not all of them, but some. I kept a list though and would try a new one if I wasn't getting many results on one of the others."

"Wow, there's a lot to this, huh?" Worry suddenly creeps up my spine. Maybe Dad's right and I shouldn't do this. There are a lot of crazies out there.

"Don't get all nervous now, Abs. I won't let you get into trouble. Dating sites can be perfectly safe and effective at finding your true match," she says with a smile.

"And how'd that work out for you?" Lexi asks, a mischievous gleam in her eyes.

"Still a work in progress," AJ mumbles before bringing up the site we agreed to use.

She gets up from my office chair and points. "Sit. First thing we need to do is create your profile. Then, we'll help you sort through the frogs until you find a prince."

Turning to face the monitor, I move the cursor until it's hovering over the words *Sign Up*. Do I really want to do this?

Images of Crystal's arms and legs wrapped around Levi last night flash through my mind, unwanted and unedited. I'll never get the picture of the other woman exiting his apartment in the early morning out of my head either. They both keep repeating over and over again, reminding me that I'll never be what he's looking for.

I'll never be who he wants.

So this is the best way for me to squash this little crush I've developed on my best friend once and for all. I'll find someone who enjoys watching cheesy 80's rom-com movies and eat caramel corn with me, and finally be able to spend time with Levi without the butterflies fluttering in my belly.

Except that Levi likes watching those cheesy movies and the popcorn is always his idea. So maybe I start watching something else. No biggy. I can do this. For my own sanity, I have to try.

I. Can. Do. This.

I create my profile with all of my personal information, as well as my credit card details. Now comes the fun part. Glancing at both of my sisters, they're anxiously chomping at the bit to jump in and help me write the perfect profile that'll attract men aged twenty-five to thirty-five in the Jupiter Bay area.

"Profile name," I say aloud.

"Don't use your name. Everyone uses nicknames or sexual innuendos like Super69 or BigDaddyDic," AJ states.

"BigDaddyDic? Why would you want to date someone named that?" I ask.

"Why wouldn't you?" Lexi retorts with a snort.

I type in the first thing that comes to mind. AngelEyes. I keep my eyes on the monitor and to the next category so that I can't see the judgment on my sisters' faces. Occupation? Editor.

"No one uses their real occupation, Abs," Lexi says.

"You just have to embellish it a bit more. Like a fast food worker might call themselves a culinary expert or a chef extraordinaire."

"Really? People really lie about their careers?" I ask, flabbergasted at the idea.

"Of course they do! People lie about everything on these things. I mean, I bet sixty percent of the profile pics aren't even of themselves," AJ adds.

"Then what's the point?" I ask. "Why do all of this if the person you're talking to isn't even the person you think they are?"

"Listen, Abs, this is great practice for you," Lexi says. "You want experience at dating and this will get you that."

"Yes. Your first goal is to set up a profile. Next, we'll take the quiz, which will help narrow down guys who have the same interests as you. Then, we'll scan through the guys and see if anyone draws your interest. From there, you strike up conversations," AJ instructs.

"No talking about romance novels, though," Lexi adds.

"Right. And Levi. You can't talk about your male best friend when you're trying to attract a new male into your life," AJ says.

So begins the process of setting myself up on a dating site. I answer the questions in the quiz as truthful as possible, even though Tweedledee and Tweedledum are chirping in my ear, trying to make me sound better than I am. The thing they may not realize is that I really am that boring and lame.

After the quiz, PerfectDate.com has matched me up with fourteen potential date candidates. Together, we set out to find out if my future someone is in the mix.

The first two are nixed right away. The first, someone with hair longer than my own. Not that there's anything wrong with it, but it's just not for me. The second had a culinary expert listed as his occupation, and I just couldn't stop thinking about him flipping burgers at the local Burger King. Not that it's not a reputable job, but I keep picturing a thirty-five-year-old man, living at home with his parents, playing video games all day long, and going off to work at the BK every night.

The third guy has potential. Shaggy blond hair that reminds me of the surfer type, with striking blue eyes. His hobbies are completely outdoorsy, and even though that's not my thing, I can't get over the fact that I need to start somewhere, right? So, I click the thumbs up beside his profile, which categorizes him for me to make contact with later.

"Oh my God, Abs, look at that one! I think that's a bong he's holding in his profile pic," AJ says, causing Lexi to laugh, while I groan. Drugs definitely are a deal breaker for me.

"Gross," I grumble, sliding past him. "Wait look at this one."

"Oh, he screams bad boy. Click him," Lexi exclaims.

"His ears are pierced. A lot," I notice.

"It bet he has other things pierced too," AJ chimes in, her green eyes lighting up with something dirty.

"Hey, don't knock piercings. Some of them are really...effective," Lexi adds, her own smirk plastered across her face.

"There's a story there, I can tell. Spill," AJ directs.

"Motorcycle boy in high school had a piercing," Lexi whispers before breaking out into a giggle fit.

"Really?" I ask, completely curious now about the whole piercing thing. I mean, is his, you know, pierced? A nipple? Why am I blushing? Why do I find that thought completely hot?

"Oh, yeah. They're...nice," Lexi adds with a wink.

A gasp mixed with a laugh is muffled from somewhere off to the side. I glance up and see Levi standing in the doorway. "What are you ladies doing?" he asks, walking into the room. I forgot he was coming over for dinner tonight, but mostly I feel slightly guilty for looking at guys right now. And that's just plain silly, right? I have nothing to feel guilty for.

"Internet dating!" AJ exclaims, happily.

"You're gonna try that crap? I would have thought you wouldn't waste your time and energy on that bullshit, AJ," he says, stepping up behind me. I can practically feel the heat radiating from his muscular body.

"Not me, big guy," AJ teases with a knowing smile. "Abby."

I swear he chokes on the very air he breathes.

"Abby?" he asks, glancing down at me with hard eyes. "You can't do that," he says automatically.

"Why not?" I ask, defensively.

"Because...well, you're...it's not safe."

"I'm not meeting up with all of these guys, Levi. There's no reason for you to freak out and go all big brother protective," I tell him.

"Besides, when the time comes for her to meet up with these guys, we'll make sure she's in a public place and that one of us always knows where she is," AJ reasons.

"Guys? As in more than one?" he asks, glancing down at me again. There's something strange in his features today. He looks scared or worried, twisted with hurt and rage. But he's doing his best to camouflage it with curiosity.

"Of course, more than one. You always start with many and weed them out until you find that one perfect date," Lexi adds.

"That's the name of the site. PerfectDate.com," I tell him. "It'll be good for me to meet new people. Lord knows I don't meet anyone working from home every day."

"Why do you need to meet new people? You have your sisters. And me," he says, seeming completely at a loss, which just makes me feel weird and uncomfortable. I didn't expect him to turn into my dad at the thought of me trying Internet dating.

"Exactly, Levi. I have my sisters and you. I can't date any of you," I remind him.

"Or have sex with any of us," Lexi mumbles to AJ.

"And Abs needs to have the sex, Levi," AJ adds loudly, causing a whole new level of mortification to set in.

"Let's not talk about that," I beg before turning my attention back to the monitor.

Ignoring all conversation around me, because really, who needs to listen to her sisters and male friend talk about her sex life, or lack thereof, I finish flipping through the matches the website gave me. At the end, I have five prospective matches to work with.

I'm already exhausted by the time I return to my own profile, that I really want to just shut down the computer and dig into the greasy, messy chicken wings that I can smell in the kitchen.

"Oh, look, Abs! You have your first message," AJ notices, pointing to the little envelope icon that shows the number one over the top, indicating that I have a message.

"I can look at it later," I suggest, ready to power down.

"No way. I want to see who it is," Lexi says, and I swear I hear Levi grumble behind me. When I glance his way, though, he's as cool and calm as ever.

"Fine." Clicking on the icon, the message pops up. It's from GraveDigger413, one of the cuter guys I saved. His message pops up on the screen, and I can feel my sisters leaning in on both sides of me to read over my shoulder.

> *Hey, AngelEyes. Noticed your profile pic first but then my attention was pulled to the fact that you love to binge watch 80's rom-coms. Me too. Would love to chat more with you.*

Levi snorts over my head, clearly reading along with everyone else in the room. "What the fuck ever. He's only saying that shit to get in your pants."

"Excuse me?" I ask, turning to face him. My agitation with him is reaching an all-new record high. "So, what's he bullshitting me about? The fact that he noticed my profile pic, or the fact that he likes the same movies as I do? Because I'm pretty sure *you* like watching those kinda movies with me too. So if he's lying, then are you?" I ask, standing up and crossing my arms.

"Burn!" Lexi yells, causing AJ to bust up laughing.

"I'm not lying, I do enjoy them."

"So it must be the fact that he thought I was attractive? What, because I'm not a model, then I'm not attractive?" I can't stop talking. Why can't I stop?

"That's not what I meant. You're putting words in my mouth," he defends, but it falls on deaf ears.

"You know what? I'm putting myself out there for the first time in my entire life, and I could really use your support right now. If you can't handle that, then you should just go."

"You want me to go?" Hurt reflects in his hazel eyes, which look greener today than ever before.

"If that's what you want." Crossing my arms again, we stare at each other in a silent standoff.

"This is like foreplay," AJ whispers to Lexi.

"I wish I had popcorn," she replies quietly, but of course, I hear both statements.

Levi turns towards the door. "I'll be back."

"You're leaving?" I panic, my words rushed. Did I really piss him off that much with this whole dating site thing?

He stops at the doorway and turns back to face me. Ignoring my sisters, he keeps his eyes trained only on me. "I forgot something at my place. I'll be right back, I promise." He throws me a quick grin before walking out of the room. I hear the sound of my door closing a few moments later and finally exhale the breath I didn't realize I was holding.

"That was kinda hot," AJ mumbles.

"Stop it. We're friends. We still fight and argue, just like we all do."

"That was like sexual tension at its finest," Lexi smirks.

"Agreed."

I glare at AJ.

"Whatever. Anyway, it's time for you both to go. I'm gonna get ready for dinner and then it's a big night of watching television and eating chocolate chip cookies," I say, leaving my office and hoping they both follow.

When I reach the living room, both sisters hot on my heels, I turn and face them.

"Promise me you'll communicate with some of those guys. You don't have to meet up with them right away, but just talk. You know, get to know them," Lexi says.

"Fine. I'll check my profile for contacts again before I go to bed."

"Good," AJ says before leaning in and giving me a tight hug. As soon as she pulls back, I'm engulfed in another equally big embrace from my twin.

"Call me tomorrow and let me know how it's going," she instructs.

"Yes, we'll expect daily updates," AJ adds.

"Daily? Can't I just text when something actually happens?" I ask.

"That too, but for now, I want to know how it's going every day," AJ replies.

Conceding, I finally say, "Fine."

A few minutes later, my sisters are gone and I'm left alone in my apartment. All around me I see traces of Levi, from the slow cooker of yummy chicken wings on the counter to the fresh tray of my favorite cookies on the table. Since he's being a butt, I go ahead and help myself to a cookie. Taking a big bite, I groan out load, the warm gooey chocolate melting over my tongue. This man is deadly in the kitchen.

Walking over to my television, I find the movie I've been thinking about watching tonight. It might not be an 80's movie, but it's still one of my favorites. Levi's not a fan, but since he's on my shit list today, he no longer gets a say. Tonight, after we eat, we'll devour cookies and watch *10 Things I Hate About You.*

Oh, Heath Ledger. I miss you.

I pop the movie in the DVD player and cue it up, ready to go. Then I make my way back into the kitchen and get ready for dinner. I can't help but wonder if this whole dating thing is really a good idea or not. I guess it's worth a try, right? I mean, if it doesn't go well, I could close my profile and walk away. I'm not out anything but a fifteen-dollar per month service fee. I want to try it, but don't want it to cause problems between us. He'll either learn to deal with it or he won't.

Right?

Right. My decision made, my resolve set, I make sure the wings and taco dip are on the table with plates and napkins. There's no need for silverware because one of the joys of wings is eating them with your fingers and then licking them clean afterwards. I grab two beers from my fridge and place them on the table with the food. Glancing down, I realize I'm all set.

Now, where the heck is Levi?

Chapter Six

Levi

I must pace the entire length of my apartment fourteen times before I find myself in front of my own computer. Grabbing the laptop, I head into the living room. First thing I notice when I glance at the mirror above the couch is that my hair is all crazy and standing on end from grabbing it and running my hands through it while I practically walked grooves in the carpeting. Next thing I notice? The flush of annoyance and possible rage coursing through me. You can practically see it radiating from my body.

Why would she want to date? She doesn't need to date. At all. She's perfectly fine sitting in her apartment all day, working her ass off, and then hanging out with me at night. What's so wrong with that?

Then my mind flashes back to the things Tuck said. How would I feel if she met someone who treated her the way she deserved to be treated? Fuck. Me. She's going to meet someone who'll treat her the way she's always deserved to be treated, isn't she? *Isn't she?!* My head pounds and my heart gallops. This can't happen.

She's my friend and it's my civic duty as part of the friend code to watch out for her. So much can go wrong on those stupid dating sites. What if she chats with a guy who seems perfect, then he turns out to be a serial killer who wears women's skin as clothes? No, not likely, but the danger is still very much alive and out there.

And my danger? I'm at risk of losing my best friend.

Fuck that.

Powering up my laptop, I know exactly what I have to do. There's only one way to keep her safe from becoming some psycho's skin suit and that's to monitor the situation and keep a close eye on her. It's the most logical thing any good friend would do, right?

Fuck no, I'm not going to tell her. Would you?

She'll get all pissy and claim I don't trust her enough to do this on her own. She'll accuse me of being overprotective and slightly stalkerish. But it's what I have to do. Keep watch on my girl – my friend, excuse me – and make sure she doesn't fall victim to the woos of Internet dating.

First thing's first: set up my own profile.

I type in PerfectDate.com into my browser and wait for it to pop up. My leg is bouncing so much, my computer practically jumps off my lap. Running my hand through my hair once more, I click the button to sign up. It only takes me a few minutes, but I'm in, in no time.

Profile name? Has to be something she won't recognize. Can't be my name, right? I mean, I'm not that big of a dumbass. Got it! She used her favorite song, so I'll use mine. SimpleMan. Everyone knows Skynyrd, right?

Up next, profile pic. Well, again, can't use my pic, even though she used a really great picture from last Christmas. It was actually one I took, believe it or not. We had just finished up our gift exchange and were getting ready to head to her dad's place for lunch. I'm always invited to every family function, and try to go to every one when I'm not working. My own family isn't nearly as close as hers, and my parents had planned on a late Christmas dinner. Therefore, it was completely logical that I go with Abby.

Anyway, back to my point, I took that damn picture with my new camera. She bought me an expensive Nikon since I was always complaining about the quality of pics on my phone. She helped me set it up and then let me snap a few pics of her while we were messing around. No – not that kinda messing around. I don't take pics during those times. Well, not anymore. Always comes back to bite you in the ass. Know what I mean?

Yes, I'm off track here. Back to my point. I took that damn pic. I own the rights to it and I didn't give her permission to use it as a profile picture on some fucking dating website. She looks stunning and radiant in the picture, which is why I sent it to her. Now she's using it against me.

Traitor.

Well, I can't use my own picture or she'll know it's me, so I grab a folder on my desktop and strum through some of the band photos. There I find a close-up shot of my favorite guitar. It's not one I use on stage, but one that sits in my spare room on a stand, and only brought out for special occasions.

Like when I'm playing for Abby.

I quickly upload the photo to my profile, and fill out the rest of the garbage they require to set up shop on their stupid site. I don't need to lie to make sure I'm compatible with Abs; I already know I am. I just have to be vague enough that she won't realize who she's dealing with.

Once I get myself all squared away, I wait while it pairs me up with other singles in the area. Sixty-five matches. What the fuck? Okay, so I might have left some of the categories a little too vague.

I'm not interested in sixty-four of them, but I have to click through them until I find my girl. My friend.

Not bad face, click past. Huge knockers, click. Bird-beak nose, click. I run through them all, taking in their profile pic, but not reading anything about them. I'm not here to date, I'm here for my friend.

After what feels like ten thousand clicks, I finally find her. Her gorgeous face smiles at me from the screen and my heart flops around in my chest like a fish on the sand. Her hair is down, hanging loosely around her shoulders, just the way I like it best on her. Her green eyes radiate excitement and happiness. You can't tell it from the picture, but she's holding the hardback book with her name folded in the pages. It's a specialty shop I found online that does all kinds of book projects. She loved it.

Again…moving on.

I click the like button on her profile and pull up a message. It takes me only a few moments to think of what I want to say before I hit send. There. Sent.

Feeling much better and lighter about the whole situation, I shut down my laptop and get ready to head back to Abby's. Before I can open my door, I remember that I was supposed to have come back over here for a reason. Checking my place, I find a bottle of bourbon on top of the fridge that I pull out for special occasions. No, this doesn't constitute as one of those times, exactly, but if I go back over there empty-handed, then I basically just look like one of those douchebags she's going to be talking to on the Internet.

Bottle in hand, I head back over to her place.

Letting myself in her front door, I walk into the kitchen like I don't have a care in the world. She's standing there, wringing her hands together, and wearing a look of concern on her face. "Everything okay?" she asks, worrying that lush bottom lip of hers between her teeth. I almost groan.

And my cock turns to stone.

"Yep, great," I say, a little too chipper for my own liking, turning slightly to cover my hard-on.

"Are you sure? You were gone quite a while for only grabbing a bottle of alcohol," she says, causing me to glance down at the bottle in my hand. Of course she'd notice that I was gone for roughly twenty minutes and only returned with booze.

God, I'm a dumbass sometimes.

"Oh, yeah. Sorry. I had to use...the bathroom." Really?! What. The. Fuck.

"Oh. Well, you could have used mine," she says meekly.

The only response I have to the statement is that I needed the privacy of my own bathroom, but I really don't want to focus on my shitting habits right now. "Anyway, I brought this. To celebrate."

"Celebrate?"

"You know, the whole...dating thing. That's a big step. Good news. Really great news. Fantastic, actually."

She just looks over at me with concern and disbelief in her eyes. "If you say so. It's no big deal, really," she says casually, walking over to the kitchen table. She has it all set and ready to go. Setting the bourbon down on the counter, I join her.

Walking her way, I stop directly in front of her. Unable to stop from touching, I grab a hold of her recently cut hair. It's a small change, only a couple of inches of length, but I noticed right away.

It's the extra colors that have me all beside myself. They somehow bring out her green eyes even more. "You changed your hair," I say, not letting go of that strand.

"Yeah," she says, her voice gravelly and deep.

"It looks…great."

"Thank you," she whispers.

Eventually, when the touch borders on creepy, I drop her hair and take my seat. "I had lunch with Tuck today," I say as a way to steer the conversation to anything other than the elephant in the room: dating.

"Yeah? What's he been up to?"

"Same ol' Tuck."

"Sleeping with everything with a vagina?" she asks with a laugh, but I also know she means just that. Tuck's a bit of a manwhore. He's definitely working his way through all of the single ladies in town, and some that aren't so single.

"You know him well."

As we finish dinner, we talk about the book she's working on for an up-and-coming author from California. Her technique needs a bit of work, according to Abs, but her stories are unique and keep you flipping the pages.

"Does she write girl-porn too?"

"No, she's not an erotic writer," she chastises me with a shy grin.

"But you've edited some, haven't you? You've had your hands on some of those dirty office romance novels or the ones where the girls are supposed to call the Dom Daddy, right?"

The blush is fast and furious, and I know I've hit the nail on the head. My mind wanders rapidly to all of the different storyline scenarios that she could have read, working her tail off on making the book as polished as ever. But then my wayward dick creeps into the equation, and suddenly, I'm wondering about a different kinda polish. Guys have to either find a willing female to take care of the problem, or they take care of it themselves. Lately, my problems have all been solved on solo runs.

But what about Abby? Does she get turned on reading about Doms and subs and find herself with her own little problem that needs solved? Does she take matters into her own hands, which frankly, is fucking hot. There's nothing sexier than watching a woman making herself come with her own fingers. Suddenly, the very idea of Abby doing just that, late at night when no one is around, could quite possibly be the sexiest thing I've ever pictured.

And cue the massive hard-on, folks. My cock is unexpectedly so hard I could pound nails through concrete.

"Did you hear me?" she asks across the table.

"I'm sorry, what?" I mumble, mortified, trying to picture everything under the sun that could kill this boner. Emma and Orval using their playroom is usually a surefire way to ease the tension in my pants, but for some reason, now I just picture what it would be like to have Abby in one of those pleasure rooms.

Fuck.

"I offered to get the movie ready to go while you grabbed the cookies," she says again, standing up and collecting the paper plates from dinner.

My eyes are riveted to the sexiest pair of tight grey yoga pants that I've ever seen. Are those new? Does she always wear slick body-hugging material that makes her ass look good enough to eat off of? I watch as she walks into the kitchen, her hips swaying gently with each step, and I realize that nothing short of a good ol' fashioned spanking is going to get this boner to go away.

My mind replays dirty images of my best friend over and over again, and all I want to do is act them out in real life. Especially the one where I watch her finger herself. *That* fantasy is all-star spank bank material.

"I went ahead and grabbed the cookies. I know how much you want it," she teases, holding the plate out for me to see. But my eyes aren't on the plate extended in front of her. Oh, no. My eyes are captivated by the lush mounds of creamy tits, barely concealed behind a black tank top.

Kill. Me. Now.

Where in the hell did that thing come from? Has she always worn something so revealing, so provocative?

"Are you okay? You're looking all flush," she says as she heads towards the living room. I have yet to stand up, because if I did, she'd have a front row view of my soldier standing at attention.

"I'm fine," I choke out.

I watch as she walks to the TV and turns on the DVD player. She bends over and places the cookies on the coffee table, my dick practically crawling through my jeans. I should look away, and really, I try, but it's futile. My eyes betray me and watch every move she makes as she heads to the couch and plops down on her end.

"You coming?"

Not yet, but hopefully soon.

"Yep!" I chirp in a high-pitched voice that sounds like the one I had at thirteen. Clearing my throat, I carefully stand up and adjust my body so that she can't see my front. "I'm just gonna use the head first," I tell her as I head towards the hallway.

Inside the bathroom, the walls start to close in on me. Glancing at the tub, I picture her naked body with water cascading down her smooth skin. I actually have to bite my lip to keep the moan from slipping out.

I'm trapped inside my best friend's bathroom with a boner that won't quit, and there's only one thing to do. I should be embarrassed about what's about to transpire in her private space, but I'm not. I can't be. I'm too wired, too horny, to even give a flying fuck right now.

I practically push down my pants like they're on fire. My cock is throbbing, pushing against the cotton boxer briefs trying to conceal it. Oh, but there's no concealing this baby. I'm more excited than a John on two-dollar BJ day. There's a huge wet spot on the front of my skivvies from pre-cum seeping from my dick. When my underwear are somewhere down around my ankles, I take my cock in my hand and give it a squeeze.

And I groan.

Clamping my mouth shut, I listen for Abby. Did she hear me? Will she realize that I'm in here cleaning the pipes just so I can sit out on the couch with her without her knowing there's a third person in the room with us: namely, my dick.

Hearing no movement, I start to stroke. Oh, this is going to be embarrassingly quick, but I don't care. My balls are already aching and probably bluer than Papa Smurf. I start to move my hand in long, quick strokes, pleasure coursing down my spine. I close my eyes and try to picture anything but the one person I shouldn't. But there she is, in bright Technicolor.

Abby.

I picture her hand in place of mine, her mouth and tongue licking the wetness off the tip. God, I'm such a fucker and shitty friend, but I can't stop. I want her to be on her knees in front of me, her eyes looking up at me, vulnerable and trusting. I want her hand to slide up and down my rock-hard erection. I want her soft fingers to stroke my balls. And above all, I want her tongue on me when she discovers just how fucking amazing a dick piercing can be.

Before I can stop it, my orgasm barrels down on me. My balls tighten as lust tickles the base of my spine. I fire off more cum than would probably be considered normal, but I don't care. My legs practically give out, my body sagging against the sink. Wave after wave of pleasure rips through me until I'm left spent and content.

Finally opening my eyes, I realize that in my rush to come, I didn't exactly have a plan for the mess. And since I'm pretty much considering this to be the most embarrassing day of my entire life, I blink my eyes to find white beads of jizz all over her soft pink robe hanging from the hook on the wall in front of me.

Just fucking great.

I rush to pull up my pants, balling up my boxer briefs in the meantime, which makes it pretty much the most uncomfortable thing going on in my pants right now. Grabbing a handful of Kleenex, I try to clean up the mess as much as possible. Have you ever gotten cum on your clothes? Yeah, it pretty much leaves a white, hardened residue behind which basically just screams spoodge.

Before I can toss the Kleenex in the wastepaper basket, a soft knock sounds on the door. "Levi, are you okay?"

Fuck a duck. No! No, I am definitely not okay!

"Yep, fine. I'll be out in just a sec," I tell her. She doesn't say anymore, to which I am most eternally grateful for, and heads back into the living room.

I try to right my boxers and my jeans, clean up the result of my jack session, and head back out into the living room to face the firing squad.

"Are you sure you're feeling all right? You're all flushed and your ears are bright red." Her concern would be welcome and comforting if I didn't feel so guilty about jacking all over her robe.

"It must have been something I ate," I tell her, gingerly sitting down on the couch. I'd rather her think I've been shitting my brains out than what I was actually doing in the bathroom.

"Come here," she says softly, setting a pillow in her lap. Of course, my dick takes note of her innocent little phrase.

I should definitely head home and end this mass of embarrassment right now, but I'm too weak. When it comes to Abby, I'm all puppies and roses and sunshine. So instead of running for the door, claiming I have food poisoning, I opt for door number two and lie my head down on the pillow in her lap.

Welcome to my own brand of heaven and hell.

Chapter Seven

Abby

Something's not right with Levi. He's acting all weird, and if it weren't for the dilated eyes and the flushed cheeks, I would think something was slightly wrong with him. He's been acting strange since he arrived the first time earlier this afternoon, but I'm sure he just has a little bug or something.

Right now, he's laying his head on my lap, and it takes everything I have not to sigh with contentment, and maybe even groan a little with excitement. No, not the reaction I should be having right now considering my best friend isn't feeling so well.

He lies on his back, his hazel eyes staring up at me, and I swear somewhere in my stomach I feel the flutter of a thousand butterflies. My heart beats a fast chorus of hope and yearning in my chest. God, why did I have to develop a crush now?

His eyes search my face, and I swear he can see into my soul. Which isn't a good thing since what I'm thinking about is probably considered crossing that imaginary friendship line in the sand.

"Are you feeling better?" I ask, worried that he'll figure me out too easily.

"Yeah," he says, clearing his throat. "Much."

I grab the remote and start the movie. Levi turns on his side and moves his hand beneath the pillow. Directly. Over. My. Youknowwhat! He doesn't seem to notice, or if he does, doesn't care. I swear I'm going to come out of my skin at the closeness of his hand to a place his hand has never been before.

Tingles of awareness start between my legs, making me want to wiggle in my seat. But with his head in my lap, that's probably not a good idea. So instead, I sit perfectly still, barely breathing, and praying that I can hold it together long enough to make it through the movie.

"Really?" he says, glancing at me over his shoulder as the flick gets underway.

"It's a classic."

"You just want to see Heath Ledger."

"True. His hair is shaggy and long and makes me want to run my fingers through it." Levi's gasp makes me look down from the television to see I have my hands in his hair. It's longer on top, while short in back and around the sides. His hair is silky soft, and though it lacks the curls of Heath's hair, it's still almost orgasmic in itself. I tense, which causes me to tug the strands wound through my fingers. The slight pull causes him to groan. G-R-O-A-N. He groans almost sexually from pulling his hair. It makes me hyperaware of the fact that his hand is still so very close to the junction of my legs and that it has been a very long time since I've had anything in that general vicinity that isn't a vibrator.

"Sorry," I practically shout, pulling my hand from his hair.

"S'okay," he whispers. "I liked it."

And for some foreign reason that I have yet to figure out, I actually put my hand back on his head. I make sure to keep it simple, easy movements; more like brushing his longer hair away from his forehead. Surprisingly, I find myself relaxing into the couch more, even though I can't move my legs.

Levi senses this and sits up quickly. I start to think I went too far with the whole hand-in-his-hair thing, so I'm surprised when he tells me to sit more in the corner of the couch. He takes my legs and spreads them. Heat creeps up my neck and lands on my face, but he doesn't seem to notice. One of my legs is extended the length of the couch, so he lies next to it, positioning the pillow between my legs. Yep, right there between them. The place where I'm all achy and wet.

My God, I hope he doesn't notice! Or worse yet...smell it.

I want to jump up off the couch and hide until he leaves, but that's not going to happen. Before I can put my great game plan into motion, he moves my other leg up on the couch, essentially wrapping it around him. He's lying between my legs. Levi. My best friend. He's lying between my legs, people. Do you hear me?

This is so not going to help the crush. In fact, it might have just thrust it straight into Lustville.

"Comfy?" he asks, adjusting his bigger body to snuggle in real close to the place friends aren't supposed to be.

"Yes." My voice sounds high-pitched and chipmunky.

And just like that, we watch the movie. I laugh when it's appropriate and cry when Heath breaks Julia's heart, but all the while, I'm still very much aware of Levi's very close proximity to my special lady place. By the time it gets to the end of the movie, and we've each consumed no less than four cookies each (fine, I've had six), my eyes begin to droop. Levi hasn't stirred much in the last thirty minutes, which makes me wonder if my friend is still awake or not. I could shift slightly and look, but I don't want to move a single muscle and risk breaking this crazy nice bubble we're in.

So I don't.

Instead, I fall sleep.

* * *

Why in the heck is my apartment so warm? I've cocooned myself into my blanket so tightly, that it feels like a second skin, restricting and stifling. I can't even move. It's a weird mix of softness and hardness all over. Cracking open my eyes, I focus on the television in the living room, but can't figure out why I'm still on the couch.

Then it hits me.

Well, a hand does, anyway.

Levi moves his hand, whacking me in the chest. But don't worry, he soothes the sting with his large, calloused palm by running it up my side and palming one of my breasts. His face, which is cushioned against the other breast, burrows in deeper and he rubs his nose against my nipple.

Hello!

I gasp as need sweeps through my body, my nipples erect with desire. Our legs are completely entwined, his erection–oh my God, his very large erection–is against my thigh. One of my hands is resting against his back, while the other is back in his hair. My word, the man has the hair of a god. We're basically hugging, lying next to each other on a very small couch.

I don't know what to do. We're locked in a completely inappropriate embrace that is so far over the friend line that I can't even see it anymore. I've jumped over the line, and the worst part is I'm actually enjoying it. Oh, I'm enjoying it so very much. I should get up, go to my room and hide until he leaves (or until I die, whichever comes first), but I find myself snuggling in a little deeper into his warmth.

Traitorous body.

"You smell so good," Levi mumbles, again running his nose against the outline of my breast.

I try to figure out what to say, what to do, when he finally starts to come to. His hands flex, gripping my breast tightly, and his lower half starts to grind against me. Then suddenly, he stills against me, his body going rigid–and I'm not talking about the *other* body part that's quite…hard.

"Abby?"

Swallowing hard, I squeak, "Mmmhmmm?"

He doesn't move. "Why are your boobs pressed against my face?"

"Technically, I think your face is pressed against my boobs," I quip, unable to breathe.

"You could be right." He moves quickly, pulling his body apart from my own, and sits up on the opposite end of the couch. His hair is unruly and wild, and makes my fingers twitch to feel those silky strands once more. "I take it we fell asleep watching the movie?" he asks through a yawn.

"Yeah." My words are more choked.

"You probably have to get to work," he says, standing up and turning away from me.

Of course, since I work at home, I don't have to go far. "Yeah." Again with the one-word answer.

"Is your coffee pot ready to go? I can start it for you before I go," he suggests like any good friend. And here I am, the complete opposite of a good friend. I'm trying to figure out how to get him back on the couch and back asleep so we can see how far his wandering hand would have gone.

Bad friend.

Levi can't even look at me, which tells me just how uncomfortable he was to wake up with me in his arms. It's mortifying that I was all excited and ready to jump his bones, and he's just trying to figure out the easiest and quickest way out of here. I pull myself into a sitting position and tuck my legs against my chest, holding on tightly and pleading for this moment to end, for our friendship to still be intact when he goes.

There are certain lines that can't be crossed, and I pray this wasn't one of them. I'll just pretend it didn't happen, to never ever talk about it again. Then, when he goes about his carefree life as if he didn't have his morning wood pressed against his best friend's thigh, well, then I can too. Easy peasy.

Only, that's something I don't think I'll ever forget.

Chapter Eight

Levi

Nothing has ever felt better than waking up with Abby in my arms. Nothing. And I've woken up with plenty of females. She's the chocolate cake of females, my friend.

I'm off the couch so damn quick you'd think my ass was on fire. No, I'm just trying my damnedest to conceal the biggest hard-on I've had since my days as a horny teenager. Turning towards the kitchen, I head over and start the pot that she already prepared last night. It's one of her nightly habits.

Hiding behind the counter, I turn and look at her. She's holding her legs tightly against her chest, a chest that I'm now very familiar with thanks to my wandering hand and face. She looks humiliated and uncomfortable and won't make eye contact, which was never my intention. Hell, I don't even know what my intention was, but I need to get out of here before I make the situation worse by dragging her into her bedroom and using the baseball bat I'm trying to suppress in my pants to make her scream. (That's a good thing.)

"I'm on tonight, so I'll catch up with you later," I holler over my shoulder, heading towards the door.

For some reason, my hand stalls on the knob. When I spin around to say something, *anything*, I find those mesmerizing green eyes on me. Well, on my ass, to be exact. Excitement races through me, different than a few moments ago. This thrill comes from knowing that she might be fighting a similar attraction. Maybe not as severe as my case of lust for my best friend, but if she's stealing glancing at my ass–and it really is a nice one–then, that counts for something.

At least it does to me.

I don't bother waiting for her eyes to return to mine. I walk out the door with a smile on my face and a boner, still very present, in my pants.

Chapter Nine

Abby

As soon as he's out the door, I want to combust into flames. Why do the most embarrassing things happen to me? Well, I guess, technically, Jaime might have that title after all the crazy things that happened to her when she was first dating Ryan, but I'm definitely coming in a close second.

He couldn't get out of the apartment fast enough.

Away from me.

Jumping up, I run to my room to get ready for the day. I can shower at any point, but I'll at least log on and check email and my schedule for this week. My assignment will take my full attention, which is typical. When I get a manuscript from my boss, I always give it everything. Cutbacks over the last few years affected our publishing company, as well as many others. With all of the e-retailers allowing anyone to publish, they call them Indie Authors, well, it's taken its toll on the publishers–big and small.

It was my attention to detail and my ability to turn around an assignment quickly and efficiently that ultimately secured my job. There were other editors who had been with Stonewell longer than I had, but took too long to turn around the product.

As I boot up my computer, I find notifications on my brand new app. It stares back at me from my desktop, taunting and assuring. I hover over the email icon, but find myself moving the mouse to the PerfectDate app. Without thinking, I click.

The sign-in page appears. I input my username and password. Sign In.

While the page loads, my bladder reminds me that I haven't emptied it yet this morning. In the bathroom, I go ahead and brush my hair and teeth before heading into the kitchen and grabbing a cup of coffee. Of course, pouring the cup only reminds me of the man who started the pot for me this morning. He's always right there, never far from my thoughts.

Cup in hand, I head back into my office and get cozy in my chair. There'll be time for a shower and change of clothes later. Right now, my curiosity is piqued and I need to see if this stupid site has matched me with my perfect date. Pun intended. Hardy, Har, Har...

Three new messages and two thumbs up. Well, that's encouraging.

The first message is from a guy named DanTheMan. I choke on my hot coffee when I read his opening line. *Beauty is a rare gift and I can't wait to treasure the shit out of you.* Is he just stating that I'm beautiful and he'll spend the rest of his life treasuring me? Or is that some sort of sexual innuendo and his idea of treasuring me is with his peen?

Help me, Lord, I don't think I can navigate this landmine that is Internet dating.

The next message is a little more cut and dry. Hammer&Nails is a carpenter by trade and enjoys quiet dinners at home or along the Bay. Okay, I'm intrigued. His message to me is that he thinks I'm pretty and would love to chat a bit more with me. He's from Ridgewood, which isn't too far of a drive, so if it ever came to the point where we decide to meet, it's within a short drive. So I send him back a casual reply, and wait.

The third message grabs my attention as soon as I see his user name: SimpleMan. My mind instantly goes to Levi. Dammit! Why do I have to think about him right now? Pushing him out of my mind, I click on the message. It's a warm greeting and doesn't hint at any sort of sexual reference. Before I can even think about it, I'm already replying.

AngelEyes: *Hi. It's nice to meet you, SimpleMan. Your name jumped out at me right away. It reminds me of a friend whose favorite song is "Simple Man" by Lynryd Skynyrd. Does the name have special meaning?*

Send.

Yeah, so much for not thinking about the pesky best friend.

A few moments later, the little bubbles appear, letting me know he's replying.

SimpleMan: *Hey. Actually, your friend must have good taste in music. It's one of my favorites too. I'm a huge fan of all kinds of music, especially Skynyrd. You?*

AngelEyes: *Me too. I listen to country mostly, but enjoy rock music, thanks to a friend who's in a band.*

SimpleMan: *Excellent choices. What about your user name? Is that just a reference to your amazing green eyes or does it mean something else?*

AngelEyes: *Thank you for the compliment. It's an ode to my favorite song.*

SimpleMan: **types out a few lines from the song**

AngelEyes: *Did you sing it while you typed it? *Smiley**

SimpleMan: *Of course! That's the only way.*

I smile at the screen, surprised at how easy this whole Internet dating thing is. Settling into my chair, I continue to type.

AngelEyes: *Can I ask what you do?*

There's a significant pause, and that makes me nervous. I go from thinking that talking to SimpleMan is super easy to wondering if I've crossed some invisible Internet dating line and you're not supposed to ask about the profession. Is that a thing? Like asking women their weight? My God, I've already messed this up, haven't I?

Then the bubbles appear.

SimpleMan: *I'm in public service. You?*

Vague, but he doesn't know me well yet, so I won't press for more information. Instead, I type out my response.

AngelEyes: *I'm an editor for a publishing company in New York. I get to work from home.*

SimpleMan: *Cool. Does that mean you get to hang out in your pj's all day long? *winky face**

I should lie, shouldn't I? I mean, no man wants to know that the woman he just started talking to on a dating site is still in yesterday's comfy clothes, hasn't showered, and might still smell like her best friend that she copped a feel of this morning. Especially if it's a male best friend. Though, I'm not sure it would be much better with a female best friend, right?

AngelEyes: *Something like that *smiley**

We end up chatting for the next thirty minutes, and before I know it, it's way after my starting work time. I should have logged in ten minutes ago, and if I'm not careful, I'll find an email from my boss in my inbox, concerned that something is wrong.

AngelEyes: *It has been great getting to know you, SimpleMan. I've got to get to work.*

SimpleMan: *Sorry to keep you! Hope you're not late. It's been great chatting with you. Any chance you'll be on again later?*

Do I want to be on later? Before I can reply, he shoots me another message.

SimpleMan: *I have to work later, but I'll try to pop on and say hi at some point. Have a great day, AngelEyes.*

AngelEyes: *You too. Talk to you later.*

I'm breathing hard, like I just ran a mile. My heart races with excitement and nervousness at the prospect of getting to know SimpleMan on a more personal basis. It's weird because I haven't thought about Levi for the last forty minutes or so, but the first thing I want to do when I log off the computer is call him and tell him all about SimpleMan.

Oh, the muddy waters in which I swim.

Chapter Ten

Levi

I'm smiling the biggest fucking cheesy grin as I log off from my laptop. That's also when the guilt starts to settle in. I just talked to my best friend for forty minutes and she has no idea it was me. This whole guise started as a way to watch over her and protect her from the potential predators that troll social media and dating sites.

But now? Now it feels different.

It was the most natural thing in the world to talk to her, even if it was under unusual circumstances. And by that, I mean lies. It's not my intention to keep the truth from her, but I'm doing it to protect her. I'll tell her soon, though. Hell, I tell her everything, which may be why this is so difficult and fun, all at the same time.

It's fun talking to her unfiltered. Yeah, I know I could just pick up the phone or walk across the hall and talk to her anytime I want. I get it. You don't have to remind me. But this is more fun, even if slightly wrong.

What do I expect at the end of the day? I still have no clue, but I'm more aware of things that I didn't notice before. Like the way she smiles when she's enjoying her first cup of coffee after her shower. Or how about the way her touch makes my skin tingle. What about how her green eyes sparkled in the moonlight while she looked out over the Bay. Or my personal favorite, how she felt in my arms when we woke up together on the couch.

Yeah, I liked that one. The proof is in my pants.

I'm not about to start dissecting whatever is happening between Abby and me. No matter how I think I feel, nothing can come of it. She's my best friend, and I won't do anything to jeopardize that. Hell, she's more than my friend. She's my family.

I probably need to get laid, but that kinda sours my stomach. The thought of getting busy between the sheets with some random woman doesn't sit well at all. In fact, the hard-on I've been sporting since I woke with my head pressed against Abby's tits dies a very quick death. The thought of screwing someone else makes me feel…guilty.

Which is why I need to figure my shit out, move past this weird little crush thing I've developed, and proceed with my life, friendship intact.

Easy peasy, right?

Right.

I'll tell her I'm SimpleMan soon, we'll have a good laugh, and we'll continue on with our friendship. But right now, I'm not thinking very friendly. What I'm thinking about is the complete opposite of *just friends.* These thoughts are dirty and make my jeans rub uncomfortably against my cock.

Waking up with Abby in my arms was heaven. That's the only way to describe it. She was warm and soft and curvy, just the way a woman should be. Her long, lean fingers were gripping my hair, and just the thought of how it felt when she tugged makes my dick hard again.

Lying there, I knew where I was the moment I woke. Yeah, I knew who I was with too. Her scent surrounded me. Her touch encompassed me. She moved against my leg, grinding her body and working me into a complete frenzy. As soon as I realized what was going on, I tensed. Stupidest fucking mistake ever because then she tensed and things got weird.

I should have keep my hands to myself, but I was weak–and a man–and her sweet body just felt so damn right in my arms and hands. Dammit, did she feel so fucking amazing. My mouth waters to know what it would have been like if she hadn't been wearing a shirt, my face pressed against her glorious tits. My mouth inches away from those perky nipples. Oh, you bet your ass I noticed that part too. I groan just at the thought.

Do you know what I need to do? Stop thinking about my best friend's nipples. But now that the thought seed is planted, it's growing like a fucking vine, working its way up and wrapping around my brain. I want to know – no, I *need* to know what they look like. Are they small and dark or a dusty rose color? Either way wouldn't matter to me, but it'll be interesting to see how I'm able to have a conversation with her without wondering.

My cock still throbs in my pants. I'm a damn perv and a shitty friend, but for the second time in less than twenty-four hours, I rip my pants off and grab my cock. I haven't jacked off this much in the last few years combined, but here I am, dick in my hand and thinking about the one person's nipples I shouldn't be.

God, I bet they're magnificent. Just like the rest of her will be. Closing my eyes, I call upon the mental image I created of her naked. Even as a figment of my dirty imagination, I'm sure it doesn't do the real thing justice. She's gorgeous fully clothed; could you imagine what my Abby will look like naked?

I don't even chastise myself for referring to her as mine. Nor do I bother arguing the fact that I said *will* look like naked, not would. Because right now, my sole purpose in life is to see every inch of her naked body. I want to see it, touch it, taste it, and fucking own it. I want her beneath me, on top of me, wrapped around me, bent over.

I want it all.

With her.

I shoot my load all over my shirt, groaning and moaning through my release, all while picturing the way she'd look riding me.

What the hell am I going to do? I can't stop thinking about sleeping with my friend, which can't happen. It's practically a law.

But what if it did? What if it was every bit as spectacular as it was in my daydream? You know, the one I just had while whacking off?

I'm going to hell.

* * *

It's a long week, even though I'm not on the rig as often. It'll be my weekend to work, which means less hours during the week. But that hasn't stopped the fire calls from coming in. Two bonfires that got out of control and a couple of minor accidents. Throw in our regular weekly meeting on Tuesday, and it's been fairly constantly busy.

The band wanted to practice a bit on Saturday to perfect a new song we hope to add to the show, which means I had to figure out how to sleep between getting off early Saturday morning and going back late Saturday night. That was fun. A couple hours here, another one there. The guys have been awesome at only scheduling gigs on the weekends I'm off, though we've had requests. I hate turning down a chance to play and make a little extra dough, but my job with the hospital has to come first.

Sunday brings a cookout at Jaime and Ryan's place. It's two when my alarm wakes me up from a dead sleep, giving me six hours of slumber. Good enough for me. Crawling out of bed, I jump in the shower so I don't smell like ass and gather up the mini fruit crepes I made last night before heading in to work. I won't be there as early as the girls, but will still make it in plenty of time to eat with the gang. If I had to guess, they're probably engaging in some sort of rivalry game of horseshoes or beanbags.

They're crazy competitive, even though my Abby is probably the least aggressive of all of them. Payton and Lexi take the crown on that title, for sure. Meghan's just as laid back as Abby, but without the shyness. AJ's full of the Summer spirit and has plenty of fire. Jaime too.

Abby's spirited, but it's not as well known. She keeps a lid on it, only pulling it out when dealing with her sister or when we're together. There was a time in high school when I dared her to run around my house in her bikini. Any other girl would have stripped down in a heartbeat. Hell, maybe even had left the bikini in my room with her clothes.

But not Abby. That's why I made the bet, because I didn't think she'd do it. After losing (and frankly, I don't have a clue why we even bet anymore), she showed up at my place, donning a bright pink bikini beneath her clothes. I was completely aroused when she came out of my room, her entire body flushed, and headed towards the front door. I've never wanted to slow time as much as I did the day I watched my best friend run around my house in a borrowed bikini.

91

Oh, did I mention it was January? Chilly enough to catch a cold, but not enough to kill the boner in my pants. That was just one of many of the Abby-inspired hard-ons I've had. I realized that day that my best friend was fucking gorgeous. She hid behind big shirts and long pants. Her shorts were–and are–always sensible and modest, never too short – and her boobs always tastefully covered.

But I'll never forget that day. The day Abby showed me her sassy side.

Pulling into the driveway leading to Ryan and Jaime's place, I find the entire family already there. Brian's car is even there, which makes me smile. He's been working a lot less lately and spending more time with Meghan. After Josh's death, her dad stepped in and is doing everything he can to help her out, including just being there when she needs her dad.

I grab the container of fluffy desserts and head around the house towards the backyard where I know the family is gathered. The first person I run into is Ryan. He's turning off the hose, kicking water out of his shoes.

"Hey, man. What the hell happened to you?" I ask, nodding towards the remnants of mud all down his leg.

"My girlfriend and her sisters happened. There I was, minding my own business, when they decided they wanted to play mud volleyball."

"It hasn't rained in the last two weeks," I remind him with a smile on my face.

"You would be correct. So Jaime got out the hose and turned the old garden area behind the garage into a mud pit."

"Sounds kinky," I laugh.

"You'd think, except when it's six girls, and they're all related and so competitive that they'd sooner tear your eyes out than let you win anything, it kinda kills the fantasy," he says while shaking water from his shoes. "Anyway, Jaime hollered at me to come see and the next thing I knew, I was ankle deep in mud and it was being flung at me."

I can't help it, I laugh. "So where are they now?"

"Behind the garage, acting like children."

"And Brielle?"

"In the middle of the mud pit in a pink dress, refusing to get out."

Laughter comes from all around. I hear it filtering from behind the garage, it comes from Brian who just walked up to shake my hand, and it bellows from Dean, who's videotaping the muddy antics on his phone.

"I have to see this," I say, setting my dessert down on the table.

When I walk around the corner, I'm completely stricken in place by the sight. The small volleyball net is set in the middle of the square, which isn't big enough to really play the game on. Something tells me they just don't care. Payton, Abby, and Jaime are on one side of the net, while the other three man the opposite side. Brielle sits directly where Ryan said she'd be: in the middle of the court, right below the net. She's playing with a Barbie doll, giving her a mud dress.

Everyone is completely wet and covered in mud. They're all in t-shirts and shorts, but it's the way Abby's shirt molds to her body that has my full attention. Her long hair is pulled up in a ponytail, high on her head, and her face is streaked with mud. Those long legs that were entwined with my own only a week ago are covered in drying mud, her feet bare and caked with brown.

I'm hard. Like harder than the oak tree in the middle of the yard kinda hard.

"Better put that hard-on away, boy, before it falls out and beats someone on the top of the head," Orval snaps as he walks up and stands beside me.

"What?" I ask, flabbergasted and unable to hide my smile.

"Oh, you heard me. I know a chubby when I see one. Hell, I've got one now thinking about my Emmie coming over and playing in the mud with me."

My bark of laughter draws Abby's attention. The smile she gives me is as warm as the sun, yet hesitant. We haven't seen each other very much since I woke nestled against her amazing chest with my morning wood begging to be played with. For me, it's a combination of busy with work and trying to squash the lust I've developed for her before I see her.

Gauging by the way my dick is crawling out of my pants to get to her, I'd say it didn't work.

I have talked to her via texts, but also through the dating app. Of course, she doesn't know that's me, but whatever.

"Thank God Jaime has a brown thumb and wasn't using the garden, otherwise her vegetables would definitely not be fit for consumption," I quip, watching as the girls try to keep the ball from hitting the ground.

"True, son. She's never been able to grow dandelions, not like Payton. That girl could take a dying plant and nurse it back to health. Emmie's that way too."

We watch them play for a few minutes. Dean walks over and joins us, a wide smile across his face. "Hey, man." He sticks out his hand and I shake it readily. I've come to really like and respect Payton's boyfriend. "Don't get too close or you'll find yourself with mud flung at you."

"Like monkeys flinging shit," Ryan grumbles as he walks up and stands beside us. He's wearing a new shirt and flip-flops, but still has residue of mud on his arms and legs. Even though he's trying to act all tough and upset, I can still see the hint of a smile on his lips and the way his eyes light up when he watches his girl. "So much for growing a garden," he says, shaking his head.

"Unless you were going to grow it, I don't think Jaime had any intentions of planting zucchini, tomatoes, or cucumbers," Orval says. "Besides, a woman only needs one zucchini in her life, and as long as you're packing a good one, which I know ol' Ryan is, based on the moans coming from that bed and breakfast last summer, well, that's all that matters." That's when Ryan chokes on his beer, spraying it from his mouth. Thank God no one was standing in front of him.

"What are you guys over here talking about?" Abby asks, walking up and standing in front of me. I get a good look at my girl–shit, no my friend. The sun bounces off the mud streaks in her hair, and there's a big clump on her chest. Mud, not hair. My fingers twitch to remove it for her, maybe copping a bit of a feel while I'm at it. But then everyone around us would see and that'll just turn the relationship spotlight on Abby and me. No thank you.

"Zucchini," I tell her with a bright smile.

"Zucchini?" she asks, crinkling up her adorable little nose. "You boys are weird."

"Payton loves zucchini," Dean mumbles, making me crack up.

"Yeah, anyway, Meghan had to go to the bathroom so we need you to come over and fill in for her." Then the little vixen bats her eyelashes at me.

"Not gonna happen, sweetheart. I'm wearing good shoes," I say, pointing down at my crappy pair of old Nikes.

"Get your rear out there before Lexi comes over here and makes you," she retorts, that sweet and innocent smile spreading across her face. "You know she doesn't play fair."

"Fine. You want me? You got me," I quip with fire, stripping my shoes and socks off and throwing them on the ground. Abby smiles sweetly before rejoining her sisters.

"You're going in there? You realize this is a trap, right?" Dean asks, glancing from me to where the girls all smile warmly and innocently.

"Oh, I know," I say as I strip my phone and wallet from my shorts. Then, as if I didn't have a care in the world, I reach behind my neck and pull off my t-shirt. A gasp comes from my left, and if I had to wager a bet, I'd say it came from Abby. "Here," I say to Dean, tossing my shirt in his direction. "It's my favorite. I don't want it to get muddy."

Taking a quick drink of my beer, I walk towards the makeshift volleyball court with a smile on my face.

"Wait, did she say Meghan went to use the bathroom? In the house?" Ryan asks. "Jaime!"

"It'll be fine, babe. Mud washes," she replies sweetly, throwing in a wink for good measure.

The mud is cold between my toes as I walk out on the opposite side of the net from my friend. I keep my shades over my eyes for the sun, but they also hide the fact that they're zeroed in on one woman. She wouldn't know that though because her eyes are planted firmly on my chest. Martians could touch down and steal her sisters, and unless they landed directly on my abs, she wouldn't have a clue.

"Abby! Pay attention," I holler over the net. "This one's coming at ya." Throwing a cocky smile her way, I grab the nasty, wet ball and throw it in the air. I hit it hard and to the right, aiming for the corner of the court where she'd have a hard time getting it. She moves, but not quick enough and basically face-plants in the muck.

"Point!" AJ exclaims from our side of the court, giving me a high-five.

"Ready for another?" I ask, glancing her way. She's getting up off the ground, flicking mud and clumps of grass off her body. Lucky fucking mud.

When she's in position, I do it again, except this time I hit it a bit short so she has to move forward. Jaime tries to go for it too, but neither of them is quick enough and the ball lands between them in the mud.

"That's two," I bellow, as the ball is whipped back at me.

"You wanna play hardball, Mr. Morgan? Fine. Bring me your best shot. I bet you won't get a third point," she throws at me with venom. And I'll be damned if my cock doesn't respond again.

Or maybe it's the fact that her mud-caked shirt has ridden up and a strip of her stomach is showing.

Grinning a wide smile, I toss the ball in the air and let it rip. This time, it aims straight at her. I put a little too much heat behind the ball and my heart actually stops when I realize it's heading straight for her. *For her head.* She tries to duck, but it's no use. The gross as shit, muddy ball slams into the side of her head and my girl goes down.

Hard.

I'm already on the move before her sisters even have time to yell. Diving under the net, I drop to my knees in the mud beside her unmoving body. She's on her side, her face slack, the left side of her forehead turning a nasty shade of red. "Abs!" I holler, trying not to move her. If she has a neck or head injury, I could do more harm than good by trying to move her.

Shadows surround me as everyone gathers around. "Abs, can you hear me?" I say, bending down to get closer. I can tell she's breathing, which is a good sign. "Abs?" I whisper by the side of her face as close to her ear as I can get. I'm so consumed with guilt and fear that I don't even know it's happening until I'm falling.

No, not falling.

I was pulled.

My face plants firmly into the nasty, cold mud, as cheers echo around me. Shocked, I pull myself back up, wipe the shit from my face, and glance over at my friend. She's laughing so hard, tears are running down her cheek, mixing with the dirt and creating streaks of filth down her glowing face.

"Gotcha!" she exclaims, trying to cover her mouth with her hand.

"Oh, you're going down," I say, just before I pounce on her. The force of my body weight knocks her off balance and flat on her back. Her hands grab heaps of mud and she flings it at my bare chest. My body covers hers as I latch on to her hands and hold them above her head. Suddenly, this fun little game in the mud is something completely different, something completely dirty. And no, I'm not talking about the mud.

My body is nestled between her legs, lining my hard cock against her pussy. Heat flares to life in her eyes, replacing the playful look that was there just a moment ago. My body is on fire for her, and there's nothing I can do to cool it.

And honestly, I don't know that I want to.

"That wasn't very nice," I whisper, both of us holding completely still. The sounds of laughter are all around me, but I don't pay anyone else any attention. Instead, I hold her arms with one hand and take a handful of mud with the other. Our eyes are locked together as I bring my hand up and set it directly on her chest, right above her magnificent tits. The oozing slime runs down her neck.

Her gasp can be heard for miles, I'm sure. "You are so gonna pay for that," she says with force, but it's lacking heat.

"Oh, I don't think so, angel. You're kinda in a predicament here. You can't move."

"Maybe not now, but I'm keeping score Levi Morgan. I will get payback for this."

Bending down until we're a mere breath apart, I whisper, "I look forward to it."

And then I almost kiss her. Her lips are swollen and so fucking sexy that I almost throw caution to the wind and kiss my best friend. She must sense where my mind is because I watch, helplessly, as that little tongue of hers slips out and wets her lips. I groan. Yeah, fucking groan.

"Come on, guys, we're gonna hose off before running through the shower," Jaime says beside us, breaking the magical bubble we were just in.

And just like that, the moment is gone. Realizing exactly where I am and who is around me, I jump up and discreetly adjust my pants. Abby gazes up at me, a heady cocktail of embarrassment, laughter, and lust swirled together in those green eyes. Extending my hand down to her, she reaches for it. It's warm against mine as I help pull her up from the mud pit.

Turning around, I find most everyone is already over by the hose, cleaning themselves off. Well, everyone but Grandma who stands alongside the net with a huge knowing smile on her face. I can practically see the mischief and the calculating going on in her head.

"What?" Abby asks, straightening up and letting go of my hand.

"Nothing, Abs," Emma says, shaking her head politely.

"I'm gonna go over and hose off," she mumbles before turning and all but running to where her sisters stand beside the water spigot.

"Having a good time?" Emma says, stopping me before I head over to the hose.

"Uh, yeah." She continues to smile at me, making the hairs on the back of my neck stand up. "Okay, I'm gonna go over and wash off."

"Sure, sure. It must have been a really good time, Levi," she says behind me. "Otherwise, I'd be worried about the baseball bat you're hiding in your shorts right now." I drop my head and refuse to turn around. "Nothing to be embarrassed about, boy. By the looks of the bat, I'd say you're more than capable of playing a full nine innings, and then some. Just make sure it's my Abs who is playing with you when you start swinging for the fences."

"Ugh," I groan before turning around.

"You can try to deny it all you want, child, but I see it in your eyes. And I feel it when you're together. When the time is right, it'll happen, I know it. And it'll be wonderful and everlasting. Until then, go wash off and shower." I turn and head towards the girls, my mind reeling from her statement. "Oh, and Levi?"

"Yeah?" I ask, turning to face Abby's petite little grandma.

"No need to put a shirt back on. The view is marvelous this time of year," she quips with a smile and a wink.

Shaking my head and unable to stop my laughter, I head towards the hose with a crazy beat in my heart and a wide smile on my face.

Chapter Eleven

Abby

Levi runs his hands up and down his bare chest, washing off most of the remaining mud. My heart is pounding, my mouth watering, and my eyes glued to every ab gloriously defined in his tanned skin. There's like eight of them. Did you know guys could have more than six? Seriously. It's magnificent, the freezing cold water cascading down his stomach, wetting his shorts.

"Abby, reel your tongue back in your mouth, honey," Grandma remarks with a straight face.

"What? I'm not...no...it's not hanging out." Smooth, Abby. Real smooth.

I don't look up, but can feel Levi's eyes on me. Instead I take the time to finish wetting my hair. We're the last two to get the shower, and I'm pretty sure all of the hot water will be long gone by the time it's our turn. Not *our* turn, our turn. We're not, like, showering together or anything.

And now I'm thinking about showering with Levi. My best friend. That would mean we'd be naked together, his impressive erection that I've felt against me twice in the last week, very prominent in the shower with us. All week long I've thought about how it felt to wake up in his arms with that erection between us. Now that I've gotten a little taste of it between my legs–albeit with clothes on–I'll never get the image out of my head.

Stupid, pesky, unwanted crush!

When he's fairly clean, he turns off the water and steps forward. Gently, he takes my chin and side of my head in his hands, and turns my head to get a better look at the lump near my forehead. I'm not gonna lie. Getting nailed in the head with a volleyball wasn't a Sunday afternoon picnic. Oh, it hurt. It just didn't make me faint the way I portrayed. That little part of my plan just kinda happened, and it worked out perfectly.

"You'll have a knot on your head for a few days," he says, his breath fanning across my face making me shiver.

"I'll be okay," I croak.

"Of course you will. You're badass." His eyes remain locked on mine, his hands unmoving from my face.

"Shower's yours," Lexi hollers as she comes out of the house, breaking the moment again.

I take a step back, putting a little distance and breathing room between us. Glancing over at my friend, we both pull out our hands and form a fist. "One, two, three," Levi counts as we both pound our fists in beat with the counting before throwing out our hand.

"Paper wraps rock! I win!" I exclaim, reaching over and wrapping my hand around his, demonstrating how my paper beats his rock in a game of Rock, Paper, Scissors.

"You cheat," he says with a smile before nodding towards the back door. "Go. Save me a little hot water."

I turn to head to the house when I realize my hand is still wrapped around his. "Sorry," I grumble, dropping his hand as if it were something that slithered. Turning around, I make my way to the house as quickly as possible.

"There are some shirts and shorts sitting on my bed," Jaime says. "Throw your dirty stuff in the washer. I'll start it before we eat."

The hot water feels amazing as I wash the slime and grime from my body. I use my sister's shampoo and rinse the rest of the mud from my hair. As I wash my body, I can't help but notice how tingly and sensitive it is. My nipples harden as I run my soapy hand along my body, picturing someone else's hand as I go.

I should feel guilty thinking about my friend while I shower, but I can't seem to find the gumption to stop. Instead, I picture how those hazel eyes blazed into my soul when we were lying in the mud. I recall exactly how his body felt against me, his large erection pressed against my center. There was something else to that, but I can't put my finger on it.

Instead, I go ahead and put my finger on something else. Me. My body is humming with need and wet with want. Between the water and my own juices, my fingers slide easily over my swollen clit. I almost groan with pleasure as lust slams through me. With my eyes closed, my fingers start to move quicker, my breath labored and choppy. It's his face I see, his touch I feel. It's the image of my best friend with his hands between my legs, and maybe his mouth too, that causes me to fly over the edge.

Yep, I just had an orgasm in my sister's shower, with my entire family outside in the backyard. Shame slams into me as I try to control my breathing. I can't believe I just did that. Not only in someone else's house, but with images of my friend to carry me over the orgasm threshold. I'm such a loser. No wonder I'm single.

Getting out, I notice the flush to my cheeks. I grab one of the last fluffy towels from the closet and quickly dry off. I didn't pay attention to what I grabbed from Jaime's clothes on her bed, and I'm starting to regret that decision now. Glancing in the mirror, the neckline of the tank top hangs down, showing off several inches of cleavage. The shorts are comfy, but much shorter than I normally choose. I should probably switch them out when I leave the bathroom.

Throwing a brush through my hair, I pull my long locks up into another high ponytail. My makeup is all but scrubbed clean, but instead of stealing my sister's makeup, I opt to just go all-natural. Even though I think my skin's blotchy, it's just going to have to be fine for the rest of this evening.

Grabbing the towel and throwing it in the full hamper, I open the door and slam into a wall. No, not a wall because this unmovable object has arms and legs. Levi wraps his arms around me to keep me from falling. "Woah, angel," his deep voice croons.

"Sorry," I mumble, pulling back and getting a look at him.

His eyes bore into me with an intensity I've never experienced before. My cheeks start to heat up again as I think about what I just did in the shower. His smile starts small and slowly widens into something almost predatory. I swear he knows what just went down in there. It's like it's written on my forehead with black magic marker. *Diddled to thoughts of you.*

"Shower's yours," I say, slipping around him and practically sprinting for the doorway. His soft laughter follows me down the hall and all the way down to the kitchen. I'm outside like the hounds were nipping at my heels, and maybe that's a good analogy for Levi. A hound.

The guy has been sleeping around since he was old enough to figure out what that thing was used for. He lost his virginity as a freshman at fifteen to a girl three years his senior. I know because he bragged about it. Not to anyone, just me. I'm lucky like that. I got to hear about all of his conquests over the years.

Except for recently. He hasn't mentioned them in a while. Thinking about it, I can't remember the last one he brought up. Susie, maybe? God, she was last summer. I know he still gets around. The proof is in the pudding; or in the way that gorgeous woman snuck out of his apartment not too long ago. But he didn't brag about it; didn't even mention it.

That makes me glad that I don't have to hear about all of the women he's sleeping with. Until this pesky little crush thing goes away, I'm not sure my heart can stand the details. But should I also be worried that he's *not* bringing it up to me? I mean we tell each other everything. Does this mean something has shifted, potentially changing our friendship?

Now *that* hurts my heart to think about.

That's why I need to keep my distance. No more mud wrestling or flirty banter. He can't help it, but he also doesn't know the effect it has on me. The best thing I could do is not engage in teasing and not touch him. Touching him is bad. It leads to dirty thoughts and self-induced orgasms in your sister's shower.

By the time dessert rolls around, everyone is relaxed and having a great time. Well, most everyone is relaxed. I'm tense and fidgety. There's a pair of hazel eyes that have been glued to me since dinner. Levi sat beside me on the picnic table, which isn't a big surprise, but I couldn't help but focus on the way the hair on his leg tickled mine. As soon as I was finished eating, I got up and went to sit under the tree by Brielle. He watched me as I moved and has been observing me ever since. It's like he noticed my nerves and could sense that I was hiding.

I can feel those eyes on me. He's sitting in a lawn chair across our makeshift circle, which gives him the perfect line of sight to gawk. I do my best to ignore him, and the crazy way my heart beats in my chest, but it's difficult. Brielle and I are playing with dolls and it takes everything I have not to glance up and look at him.

"Who wants dessert?" Grandma hollers from the back door.

Jaime jumps up to help her carry out two containers of homemade ice cream that she and Ryan made the night before with Brielle. Bri had spent the night so Dean and Payton could go have dinner with some of his friends who were in town. Since it's July, they spent the night making several batches of flavored homemade ice cream in a churn that he picked up at the hardware store. Bri loved it, I'm told; especially taste-testing every flavor.

The dolls and I are left behind as Bri jumps up and heads towards the table. I know Levi brought a dessert, one I didn't get a chance to try ahead of time since I haven't really seen him much lately. Not since we woke up on the couch last weekend. Yeah, Bri isn't the only one who is used to taste-testing all of someone's creations.

"Levi, what are these?" I hear my sister Meghan ask from the table.

"They're mini crepes. The ones on the left are blueberry, the middle ones strawberry, and the ones on the right are raspberry with a yogurt glaze." My ears perk up instantly.

"Raspberry?" I ask as I stand up, my tongue surely hanging on my chin.

I don't even hear him approach. I'm too busy watching which ones everyone else takes, hoping that there'll be lots of raspberry ones left for me to steal. I mean take home. "Of course I made raspberry ones," he says quietly behind me. His voice is low and husky as he leans in and adds, "I know you love them."

A shiver sweeps through my body as goosebumps pepper my skin. Wrapping my arms around my midsection, I wonder if the temperature dropped suddenly. You know, maybe with the sun getting ready to set has made it about twenty degrees cooler than it was a few moments ago?

Or maybe the temperature rose a good twenty degrees.

I can feel his breath against the nape of my neck, and another tremor races through me. My breathing is shallow and my body very much aware of his close proximity. In fact, I can practically feel the material of the shorts he borrowed from Ryan graze against the back of my thigh. God, he's so very close.

"Come on, angel. Let's get some ice cream before it melts and fill you up on the raspberry crepes before they're gone," he says. Levi places his hand on my lower back and applies a little pressure, which causes me to move. As we approach the table, I notice the warmth still firmly planted against my lower back. Again, cue the shudder.

He doesn't let me get far after our bowls are full of dessert. I try to sneak away and sit over in a chair by my dad, but it doesn't work. Apparently, Levi doesn't understand my need for space or the fact that he's causing me sexual anxiety. Well that, or he doesn't care. Every time I glance his way, I find his eyes on me. They're...different. They're darker and laced with something I'm not used to being directed towards me. They look almost lustful.

Again, this is all new to me. Sure, I've had boyfriends, but none of them looked at me the way Levi is right now. Like he wants to forget his ice cream and gobble me up instead. It's making my brain go haywire. I know I'm reading more into it than what is actually going on. I'm crushing on him, therefore seeing things that aren't there. Namely, his desire for me.

Suddenly, Grandma comes out of the kitchen with a large butcher knife. It's so out of place that it draws just about everyone's attention. I watch as she walks over to the ice cream and starts to scoop some into a bowl. Then she adds two crepes on top of her sweet treat, grabs the knife and walks over to the picnic table to sit beside Grandpa.

"Uh, Grandma? Why do you have that knife? You know you don't need it to cut ice cream, right?" AJ asks nervously from across the table.

"Of course I do, sweet girl. This knife isn't for dessert," she says, setting it down in front of her. "This knife is to cut the sexual tension floating around Abs and Levi. It's so thick, I'm afraid it might choke someone."

Speaking of choking, the ice cream I'm eating goes down the wrong pipe and I all but sputter and spit chocolate ice cream all over myself. I'm probably even drooling it down my chin right now as I gasp for air. Levi reaches over and pats me on the back as all eyes focus on me.

Kill. Me. Now.

When I finally find words, I glance at my grandma. "There's no tension, sexual or otherwise. We're friends," I say lamely.

"Keep telling yourself that, dear." And with that, she turns back to her dessert and eats like she didn't just embarrass the crap out of me in front of my entire family. Including Levi. Everyone snickers around us.

I'm divorcing my family.

Later that night, as everyone is cleaning up the backyard before we leave, I find myself alone with my twin. Something has definitely been off with her lately, but I can't quite peg what it is. Stress, I'm sure. She's been evasive for a while now when it comes to Chris and their struggles to conceive. I feel horrible for her, especially in light of Payton's confession a few months back. What if Lexi has the same thing – that PCOS – and even though all of the tests she's had done lately don't lead in that direction. In fact, all of the tests came back clear.

Is it Chris? Is there a problem with him? Not that I want to think about my brother-in-law's sperm count, but maybe it's low and his little swimmers just aren't getting to where they need to be? I'm no doctor, but I do know he hasn't yet been to see any one of the physicians she has been recommending. That's one thing she *has* told me.

"Where's Chris?" I ask as I pick up any cans or bottles still lying around from the gathering.

"I don't know. Probably at home."

Glancing over, I give her a look. "You don't know?"

"Nope," she says in a huff as she picks up a doll dress from the ground. "I don't know because I left without inviting him."

"You didn't invite him? Today?"

"Nope. He barely shows interest in going anywhere with me anymore, so I just decided to avoid the entire discussion. I would have just gotten some stupid excuse that he has a policy to write, or a client to take to lunch. I'm over it, Abs. Like really, *really* over it." She finally stands up and looks at me. Her eyes are filled with tears and my heart breaks a little more for her. My twin sister has had her share of ups and downs with her husband, but lately, there seem to be a lot more downs.

"What are you saying?" I whisper, making sure no one is around to overhear.

"I don't know," she grumbles, throwing the doll dress down on the table. "I just…I don't know how much more of this I can handle. He won't talk to me, and when he does, he just keeps assuring me that everything is fine. It's not fine, Abby. Not by a long shot."

"You know I'm here for you if you need me, right?"

"Of course, I do," she says, wrapping her arms around my neck. After a brief hug, we both pull away. "How's the Internet dating going?"

Glancing around again, I turn my attention back to her. "It's going. I've talked to a few guys who seem nice. There's potential there for a date. One is really pushing for it. But there's this other guy, SimpleMan, and I don't know, I just really feel a connection with him."

"Yeah?" she asks, her green eyes brightening for the first time since we started our conversation.

"Yeah. We haven't talked about meeting up or anything, but I can see it leading there. We talk every day. Like multiple times every day." I can't fight the smile on my face.

"What about Levi?" my sister whispers, glancing over her shoulder.

"What about him? We're just friends, and even if I wanted more–which I don't–he's not interested in me that way." I throw in a shoulder shrug for good measure.

"Well, I think you're wrong, but I guess time will tell. I will say that this dating thing must just be the kick in the ass he needs, Abs."

"What do you mean?"

"Well, if he sees you dating, he just might realize that his feelings for you go way deeper than just friendship." She crosses her arms at her chest and gives me a pointed look.

"Or he may realize that we'll always be friends and he'll be just fine with me dating," I reply, mimicking her pose.

Her smile is the only comment I get. We stare at each other for several moments, my face remaining impassive and stern, while her face becomes brighter and full of mischief. "Levi!" she bellows over her shoulder. It doesn't take long before my friend walks up to where we stand.

"Yeah?" he asks, concern written all over his handsome face.

"You're okay with Abby dating, right?" His entire body tenses. "I mean, you guys are friends and you'd never want to deny her the happiness she deserves, am I correct?"

What a horrible, evil sister she is.

"Uhh, yeah," he says, running his hand through his hair like he always does when he's nervous or upset. "Sure. Abby's happiness is the only thing I want." It's like the words bite him as he says them.

"See! Levi wants you happy like I do. Schedule those dates with all of those guys you've been talking to."

"Guys?" Levi asks, turning those hazel eyes my way.

"Oh, yeah. Lots of guys. Tons of them. She's been inundated with date requests lately, and has been a little nervous to go. I think she should reply to them all. Every one of them. Don't you?" she asks my friend, her face dripping with sweetness.

Levi, on the other hand, looks like he's caught between horror and anger. Both emotions battle for the lead, and I'm not sure which one is out front. "All of them?" he whispers hoarsely.

"All. Of. Them." I stare, dumbfounded, as my sister manipulates my best friend.

"I mean, you don't want to seem too eager," he says, rubbing the back of his neck with his hand.

"Maybe, but you don't want to let any of the good ones get away either. I mean, *you* date lots of different women, and I might be wrong, but it seems like the girls that are the most *eager* get moved to first in line." Lexi smirks at him because she knows she has him. Levi never has to work for a "date." Women are always throwing themselves–and their panties–at him.

He looks as uncomfortable as a hooker in church as he runs his hands repeatedly through his hair. There's a flush to his cheeks and he's struggling to keep his temper in check. Why, I'm not sure, but it's something that I don't miss nonetheless. Unless there may be something to what she was saying earlier...

"I guess if she wants to date, she can. I mean, she should. She should be happy," he concedes, looking completely defeated, yet trying to put on a brave smile. But I see it. I can tell it's fake.

"Good," Lexi says, turning to face me. She's smiling widely, while I can only stare back at her completely in awe and shock. "As soon as you get back tonight, you should message them all!" she exclaims.

I can't answer her, so I just raise an eyebrow. There's also no need to worry about Levi seeing my response since he's staring a hole into his shoe. Without another word, my ornery sister winks at me, and heads to gather her belongings.

There isn't much speaking between us as we follow suit and head towards our cars. He helps me load my empty slow cooker in the passenger seat and turns to face me for the first time since the awkward conversation in back with Lexi. "I'll follow you."

Direct and to the point.

"Okay." After giving my family hugs, I pull out of the driveway, my best friend hot on my heels.

Chapter Twelve

Levi

I'm fuming.

As I follow behind Abby on our way back to our apartment building, I go over and over the conversation with her twin. I'm pretty sure that it was slightly exaggerated for my benefit–hey, I'm well aware of some of the Summer sisters' tactics. But the thought of one man, let alone a whole slew of them, messaging Abby and wanting a date, makes me crazy. Like batshit, I want to punch something, crazy.

My mind is doing battle against itself. On one hand, I have no right to feel this way except to worry and protect her. On the other, I have every right because, dammit, she's my girl.

But she's not.

But she *is.*

At least she should be.

So maybe it's time I do something about that. Fuck the boundaries of friendship. Fuck the worry of hurting her. Fuck the fear of living a life without her. Fuck it all…and maybe fuck her (no, not the bad way; the good way).

I feel something deep for my friend and maybe it's time to figure out what in the hell that is. Sure, I'm terrified of screwing it up and losing her. But what if I don't? What if that crazy ol' woman is right and there's something bigger and greater planned for her and

I? Am I strong enough to deny both of us the opportunity to figure out what that is?

Hell no.

Time to form a plan. Time to put it in motion. Time to take my girl and show her why there's a thin line between friends and lovers, because all I want to do is jump over that line and run straight to the lover part. I haven't wanted anyone else in a long damn time. Too long, in fact. It's been almost a year since I took a girl home from wherever for a night of fun between the sheets.

As I head towards our place, I realize my plan is simple: make her see that we have more chemistry than friendship. Should be easy, right? Of course not, but I've never shied away from a challenge. And if I've learned anything about my friend in the fifteen years I've known her, it's that this will definitely be a challenge. Maybe my greatest one yet. The end result? Having Abby in my arms permanently? Being able to finally taste the lips I've been dreaming about? Taking that body of hers and making us both reach new heights of pleasure?

Fucking worth it.

* * *

I follow her up the stairs, my arms loaded down with the stuff from both of our vehicles, but my eyes are elsewhere. They're positioned squarely on her firm ass. Do I care if she turns around and catches me? Not anymore. I hope she does, actually. I'm about to make it damn clear what my intentions are, even if it's a slow declaration. Even I'm not stupid enough to jump off the building without a parachute.

We head to her apartment first. Her keys are already in her hand–another safety tip I taught her–and she opens the door wide for me. I set her pot and bag down on the counter before turning her way. "I'll be right back," I say, grabbing my own container and heading towards my apartment.

Throwing my stuff on the counter, I boot up my laptop. As soon as it's up, I click on the app and send her a message. Since I had basically worked out what I wanted to say on the ride home, it didn't take me long. I go ahead and click the button to ignore all of the requests and messages already sent to my profile before powering down. Grabbing the second, smaller container from the counter, I head back over to my friend's place.

Not even knocking, I enter. She's not in the kitchen or living room, so I hang back. Sure, my inner caveman wants me to storm to her bedroom, throw her down on the bed, and ravish her from head to toe for hours–days–on end. But I can't let that prick out right now. Right now, I need the softer, sweeter Levi to come to take the lead.

"Sorry," she says, walking out of the bathroom and pulling her hair back up into another high ponytail. For some reason, I'm glued to the long column of her neck. I've never really noticed before, but those damn ponytails do a hell of a lot more than just keep her hair out of her face. They reveal the sexy curve and arch of her shoulders and neck. My dick nods his approval at the thought of licking a line from her spine up to her hairline.

"You okay?" she asks, her green eyes full of worry.

"I'm great," I tell her, clearing my throat. "Here." I slide the small container across the counter and into her hands. She gives me a look before opening the lid.

"Are these all raspberry?" she whispers, her voice all dark and husky. I instantly think of sex.

Leaning forward, I whisper back, "They are."

"We should eat them now." I don't miss that she leans forward just a bit.

"We should."

"I'll get the milk."

"I'll get the plates."

"No plates," she says as she glances over her shoulder, her hand stalled on the knob for the cabinet. "I like to get messy."

And that's when I practically come in my pants. Leaning forward until our faces are even closer, I return fire. "Oh, a dirty girl. I like that."

Her eyes light up, her breathing hitches. I'm getting to her just as easily as she's getting to me. It's like we're engaging in a game of cat and mouse, or as I like to call it, foreplay. And damn, I can't wait to start really playing with my girl.

She doesn't say a word as she heads over to the fridge and grabs the carton of milk. We both steal little glances at each other as we work in tandem in the small kitchen, each of us doing our part to prepare for our small snack. For me, I throw the crepes in the microwave to heat them up a bit. I'd prefer the oven to help keep them crispy, but time's a wasting. Sure, I could probably just place them on my body somewhere since my blood is boiling, but we're not to the "eating food off each other's bodies" stage yet.

We head into her living room with a plate of crepes and two glasses of milk. Without even asking, she grabs her remote and turns on the History Channel. I have a thing for those car shows that transform old cars into badass hot rods, and I guess over the years, she's just become accustomed to watching them with me.

"You can watch something else, if you want," I suggest, settling on the floor between the couch and the coffee table.

"Like what?" she asks, taking her place beside me. Her knee touches my leg, and she makes no motion to move it. Like the true adolescent that I apparently am, I'm pretty sure I jizz in my pants.

"I don't know. What do you want to watch? Pick anything."

She thinks about it for a while before turning the channel. An old episode of *The Brady Bunch* is on, and there's no missing the smile that graces her lush lips. "Excellent choice," I tell her, pushing the plate of goodness in her direction.

She takes one in her hand, her mouth practically salivating, and turns towards me. "You know I was kidding about eating all of these, right? If I do, I'll gain ten pounds."

"Wouldn't matter. You'd still be gorgeous," I tell her, making sure to keep my eyes locked on hers.

A blush creeps up her cheeks and a shy smile slips onto her lips, making me do a mental fist pump. I watch, hypnotized, while she takes a small bite of her crepe. Her eyes flutter closed and that small smile turns to a much bigger one. "My God, these are so good."

"I could watch you eat them all night," I tell her, taking a bite of my own. "There's no greater compliment to the chef than watching a beautiful woman enjoy your creation."

Her eyes open and land on mine. There's a bit of confusion blazing in her emerald eyes; I'm sure it has something to do with the fact that her best friend is practically hitting on her. There's also

119

excitement swirling around. I know she doesn't date much, so I'm assuming she doesn't hear compliments much either. That both thrills me and pisses me off since she deserves to hear nothing but high praise. Now, I just want to be the one saying them.

Crumbs of the flaky crust and a smudge of raspberry are smeared along her bottom lip. Twitch, twitch goes my dick in my pants, but I ignore the impatient bastard. Instead of humping her leg, I lean forward and swipe her lip with my thumb. Her eyes widen as she watches me, a burst of warm breath hitting my finger. Without breaking eye contact, I stick my thumb in my mouth and lick off the sweet fruit.

She shudders.

We're both silent as we watch the show—well, I guess technically, I watch her—and eat our second dessert of the night. I'm very much aware of how close we are on the floor. In all honesty, we've probably sat this close a million times over the last decade and a half, but tonight, it feels different. It feels right.

I'm yawning by the time the clock hits nine-thirty, a gentle reminder that I didn't get much sleep today after working all night. Part of me wants to ask her to snuggle up on the couch together, but I don't want to push my luck. Though, I wouldn't mind waking up with her tits as a pillow and her pussy all but plastered to my leg. Nope. Not gonna happen tonight, asshole. Remember that story of the jackrabbit and the turtle? I'm determined to be the damn turtle, even if my wayward cock is gunning for the starring role of jackrabbit.

"I'm beat. I'm gonna head out," I tell her, unable to stop another yawn from slipping out.

"Okay," she says, jumping up and grabbing the container of crepes. She follows me into the kitchen. I set both glasses in the sink, while she finds the lid. "Here."

"No, those are yours," I tell her, walking over to where she's standing.

"Are you sure?"

"I made them for you."

Several heartbeats of silence wash over us, our eyes eagerly searching the other. We're this mix of confusion and need and anticipation. But do you know what I don't see? What I don't feel? Uncomfortable. Sure, there's sudden feelings blended in that weren't always there, but it doesn't scare me or make me want to move to Taiwan like it might have a few months ago.

I step up close, invading her personal space, and grab the strand of hair hanging over her ear. "Promise me something, okay?" Her bright eyes don't waiver as she nods her head. "Promise me that you won't say yes to one of those dates until you really, really want to. Don't just say yes to date. Say yes because it's the only answer you can give. Say yes because it feels right. Can you do that?"

Again, she nods.

Leaning forward, I place a kiss on her forehead, just like I've done many times before. Only this time, I let my lips linger a little longer and soak in the feel of her skin, the scent of her hair.

"'Night, Abs," I whisper, glancing down and getting lost in those hypnotizing eyes.

"'Night, Lee," she croaks out, her voice very hoarse.

Using every bit of strength I possess, I turn and head towards the door. I'm not gonna glance back to see what kinda emotions are on her face, shining in her eyes. I'm not gonna do it.

But before I can close the door, separating us for the night, I turn towards her. I'm rewarded with the faintest smile on her lips that radiates joy and warmth. There's also no missing the fact that her eyes are glued on my ass again. This time, I wait until she looks up, knowing that I caught her. Not giving her a chance to be embarrassed, I throw her a wink and walk out the door.

I head across the hall.

To my lonely apartment.

To dream about what my next step is in this plan.

A plan to get my girl.

My best friend.

Chapter Thirteen

Abby

So there I am, staring at my best friend's butt, and he turns and catches me. Cue the blush! Could this be any more embarrassing?

I lock up my apartment and turn off all the lights before heading back to my bedroom. There's no need to shower before bed, especially in light of the diddle shower I took at my sister's house only a few hours ago. You know the one, right? Yeah. Didn't think you'd forget that. Lord knows I haven't.

Stopping at the doorway to my bedroom, I glance around and take it all in. Modest sized bed with pretty blue and green bedding. Delicate, yet sturdy furniture that shows a hint of wear and tear. Light filtering curtains because I love to wake up to sunlight. Basically, nothing like Levi's room. His is all dark and masculine with hard edges and a drawer full of condoms. There isn't a condom to be found in my room.

Sad, isn't it?

I bypass my room and head towards my office. Moving the mouse, the screen fires to life, the app tempting and taunting me. What the hell, right? I'm not going to find Mr. Perfect if I don't at least check to see if he's into Internet dating.

My profile pops up, along with two messages. I click on the first one, received earlier in the day. Hammer&Nails sent me a note, more basic details of his life. Is it weird that the first thing I think of when I see his username is Ryan? I mean, I know without a doubt that it's not Ryan, but just the thought of hammer and nails makes me think of my potential future brother-in-law. And that's kinda disturbing.

I reply to his note, asking for more details and giving him more of mine. It's very pleasant to talk to him, but I don't feel anything earth-shattering when we communicate. Am I supposed to feel that? Or something? Maybe that'll come when we meet face-to-face.

And that makes me think of the things Levi said before he left, asking me not to date just to date. To wait until I knew he was the one to spend my time and energy meeting. I guess, that's good advice, right? I mean I really don't want to go on date after date just to find the wrong guy after wrong guy. See? I'm no good at this. Isn't that what dating is?

God, I'm hopeless.

I find the second message from SimpleMan and my heart rate kicks into overdrive. Excitement races through me, and a broad smile spreads across my face as I click on his message. See? Isn't this what I'm supposed to feel?

SimpleMan: *So, I spent a part of the day with a friend of mine, which might be one of my favorite things in the world to do. How about you? Do you have a friend or two that mean the world to you? And I really need to know what your favorite dessert is.*

AngelEyes: *Let's start with dessert, please! My favorite is a fudge brownie. Plain. Simple. Traditional. Though, I've recently discovered a love for raspberry crepes. I love anything raspberry, in fact. Especially eating them whole over ice cream. And as far as the friend goes, I do. Besides my five sisters, I have a friend. A great friend, actually. Honestly, he's probably my only true friend outside of family. We've done everything together since we were ten. Tell me more about yours.*

I click send before I can second-guess myself, and I'm pleasantly surprised to find him online right now. The bubbles appear on the message, so I sit back and wait for his response.

SimpleMan: *A guy friend, huh? That's pretty cool. My friend is simply amazing. There's no other way to describe her. Yep, it's a her. We've been friends for a while too. Sometimes, spending time with her is the best part of my day. Do I need to worry about your friend finding me and kicking my ass? Guys are territorial and weird like that.*

If he only knew. Levi is super protective of me. I also can't help but wonder about his female friend. It's not unheard of, obviously, but it's rare that a guy and a girl remain friends without crossing the line. Or has he crossed the line? Maybe they were lovers first and determined they were better as friends? The green monster of jealousy rears its ugly head suddenly.

AngelEyes: *No, you don't have to worry about him. As long as you're a good guy, he won't cause you any harm.*

SimpleMan: *Good to know.*

AngelEyes: *And your friend?*

SimpleMan: *No worries about her. If she ever met you, I'm sure she'd like you as much as I do. Well, if I get to meet you, that is.*

A million thoughts flood my mind, and they all lead to one question. I set my fingers on my keyboard, only to remove them as if it were to bite me. I bet I do this three times before I finally decide to just go for it.

AngelEyes: *Should we meet?*

His reply is instantaneously.

SimpleMan: *In due time, Angel. In due time.*

* * *

Almost two weeks later, I decide to use one of my accrued vacation days and get out of the apartment. AJ's still off on summer break, though she finds herself spending more and more time at the school, prepping her classroom or holding a cheer practice, as July gets closer to August. Since her birthday is tomorrow, we decided to head to the mall for a little shopping and to get some lunch.

We pull into a small deli chain with the best baked mac and cheese ever. My mind instantly goes to Bri, who always tries to order mac and cheese everywhere she goes. After placing our order at the counter, we find an open table by a window. The sun is bright and the reflection is fierce, but the view isn't bad.

"So, how's work?" she asks.

"Not bad. I'm almost finished with the first round of edits on a new book. I should be wrapped up with my notes and suggestions by Tuesday or so and I'll be able to send them to the author," I reply, stirring my blended raspberry smoothie.

"What's the book about? Is it kinky?" Her eyes light up at the thought.

"Not really. I mean the sexy scenes are pretty detailed, but it's no Fifty Shades. Grandma has the Blue Ray, by the way. I found out the hard way when I stopped by the house to drop off a flyer for the food drive and she was sitting in the living room watching it. She was actually eating popcorn and saying all of the lines along with the characters."

"Yeah, Jaime told me she has, like, multiple copies. It's a little disturbing," she replies before taking a drink of her iced coffee.

"Agreed. Have you talked to Lex lately?"

"She stopped by earlier in the week on her way from the salon. I'm worried."

"Me too."

Our order number is called and before I know it, I'm about to gorge on half a turkey Panini and mac and cheese. Before I take a bite, I grab my phone and snap a quick pic. I ignore the looks I'm getting from my sister and hit send after typing out a brief message.

Me: *Enjoy your leftovers. I'll have some mac and cheese for you.*

Setting my phone down, I dig in. The cheese is still gooey, stringing from my spoon to my bowl. "This is the best stuff ever," I mumble before shoveling a heaping spoonful into my mouth.

"It's almost better than sex," AJ groans as she does the same, chewing slowly as if savoring the bite.

"I barely remember," I grumble, keeping my attention on my spoon as if it was the most interesting spoon on the planet.

"How long?"

Shrugging, I give her an honest answer. "Two years-ish."

"Two years? Your vajayjay is gonna close up forever if you don't use it," she tells me with a straight face.

"That's not how it works, and you know it. You're a teacher for Christ's sake. And besides, it's not like things down there don't…happen, it's just that there hasn't been an actual penis in that vicinity in a long time."

"Vibrators?"

And cue the blush.

"Nothing to be embarrassed about. I use them all the time too. I haven't dated much lately. The last guy, you remember Seth, don't you? Well, we went out a few times and he was more interested in my feet than my vagina."

"Your feet?"

"Yeah. Kept wanting to rub them, which would have been nice except it was a little creepy. The one time we did have sex, he begged to suck on my toes."

Horrified, I gaze over at my sister. "What did you do?"

"Kicked him out of my bed and blocked him on Facebook. He tried calling a few times, but I never picked up. Eventually, he got the message," she says shrugging her shoulders.

We both go about our lunches, cleaning our plates and all but licking our bowls of excessive cheese. When the food is all gone, we start to gather up our trash. She's behind me, checking her phone, when I stop at the door. AJ glances up, worry marring her exotic features. "Toes?" I ask seriously before breaking out in a giggle.

"I know, right? So gross."

Oh, I can't wait to tell Levi about this one.

At the mall, we head straight to her favorite department store. We're about the same size, but our tastes are way different. I like modest and things that are comfortable, and AJ is under the impression that if it hurts, it must look good. You know, shoes, underwear (she's a thong girl and I've never been able to get used to them). The lower the neckline, the more she wants it.

Yet, during her job, she's all plain pastels and paisley prints. She's as straight-laced as they come when she's in teacher mode. But after school? Watch out. She's all about showing off her assets, which would be a fantastic pair of 32D boobs and a butt that I would kill for. Yeah, I may have nice legs, but my boobs barely fill a C cup, on a good day.

She instantly goes towards the bright and bold colors, while I find myself leaning towards a soft purple tank top. The neck is collared and there's a peephole that stretches from your throat down to just above the cleavage. It's a bit more revealing than I normally go for, but with the delicate color and the flowy material, I might be able to overlook the way the shirt gives a peek at the girls.

"Oh, you should get that," AJ says behind me. When I turn around, I see her arms already loaded up with things to try on.

"You think?" I ask, running my hand down the soft material once more. It's sheer with a shimmer overlay. There's just enough material to not have to wear something underneath to keep everyone from seeing your bra.

"Definitely. Try it with this skirt." I glance over and AJ's handing me a black flowy shirt in the similar fashion of the top. It's gorgeous.

And short. Not hooker short, but definitely not the knee-length ones I have at home. This one hits mid-thigh.

"You have killer legs. Show them off," she says, handing me the skirt. "Trust me."

Famous last words. Last time I trusted one of my sisters, I ended up singing karaoke solo to Madonna, while pretending to have a cone bra. Did I mention that was last year?

"Fine, I'll try them on. Doesn't mean I'm getting them," I tell her, snatching the skirt from her extended hand. She doesn't say anything, just smirks before grabbing another pair of denim capris.

As I'm heading towards the dressing room, I find myself in the lingerie section. Normally, I would bypass the entire area. Comfy cotton bras and low-rise panties all the way. Simple. But a light colored turquoise lace demi bra with matching panties draws my attention. The color is striking.

"Oh, that's gorgeous. You should get that too. The color is light enough that you won't see it through the shirt," she says holding up my purple top.

"You think?" I ask, running my fingers along the coarse lace. "I'm not a fan of thongs, though."

"So, there are other styles," she reminds me. One-handed, she starts digging through the different varieties and styles. "You're not getting these," she adds, tossing the ones similar to my normal style aside. "You're gonna live a little. Oh, what about these? Payton says boy-cut shorts are the most comfortable panties out there. I'm partial to my thongs, but I have to admit, they do look comfy. Plus, they cover all of your bits and pieces."

"True," I say, glancing at the delicate pair of panties. They're lace in front and satin in back. There's just enough material to cover my butt cheeks, which is important to me when it comes to panty purchases. Grabbing the pair she's holding, because I know she already found my size, I head for the dressing room.

Fifteen minutes later, we're both heading out with a bag of our purchases (her bag bigger than mine). Across the way is the local body and bath store, so I follow behind until I'm inundated with a wild mixture of fruits and flowers. Part of me wants to get my standard flavor–it's comfortable, you know–but the other part is daring me to be bold and try something new. AJ gets this sweet Asian scent that smells exotic and rich. I usually go for the vanilla or apple scents, but bypass those and head down to where she's standing. The one that draws my attention has flowers on the front, but with a hint of something musky. It reminds me of Levi. No, not that he wears anything resembling flowers, but because of the deep, heady musk. A shiver runs through my body when I think about how good he smells. God, he could just finish with a run and I'd still want to slide my nose along his entire body, drinking in his scent.

See what this stupid crush is doing to me? It makes me want to smell his sweaty body.

But I can't help feel that way, especially after our night together watching *The Brady Bunch* and eating crepes (which I finished off two days later). He was, I don't know, attentive in a way he's never really been. When our eyes locked, I swear the earth shifted or something. And when he touched my lip and licked off the goo with his own mouth? I almost orgasmed right there.

We've texted or seen each other every day since and I still get this crazy feeling when he's around. His eyes never leave mine, and I swear he's all but drinking me in. The other night when he went to leave, I walked him to the door (like I usually do). When we got there, he did that thing again with my hair where he holds a strand of it in his big hands and sort of just feels it. His eyes were intense and I'm pretty sure I wasn't even breathing. His forehead kisses linger longer, or at least they do in my mind, and I got the biggest panty-wetting smile when he finally headed across the hall.

See? Confusing.

"What's got you all tied up in knots in your own mind?" AJ asks beside me.

I contemplate on how much to say to her, but she's my sister, and I tell them almost anything. "Levi."

She glances over at me, her eyebrow raised. "Go on."

Setting a bottle of lotion and body wash of my new scent in the basket with her stuff, I turn to give her my full attention. "None of this leaves us." She takes her finger and makes an X over her heart.

"Things are weird between us."

"Weird how?"

"Well, not really in a bad way, but I might be reading the situation wrong. It's not like I have a lot of experience with this kinda thing, you know? Anyway, it makes me wonder if our feelings for each other might be going deeper than friendship."

"You mean you both want to screw each other's brains out?"

"God, AJ, it's more than sex," I whisper. "And we're not even...there. It's more of this feeling I get around him. At first I thought it was a stupid crush, but then he started to look at me...differently. Like he wants to eat me for breakfast, lunch, and dinner."

"Oh, he wants to eat you, all right."

"Would you stop with the sex? I can't even think about going there with him," I tell her, even though I've thought about it a lot lately.

"Okay, okay. So what's the big deal? You're friends who flirt? Maybe you should go out and see if anything more sparks."

"I can't just walk up to him and say, 'Hey, Levi. I know we're friends and all, but would you like to take me to dinner so we can see if this crazy feeling I have when you're around is mutual?'"

"Why not? Girls ask out guys all the time. Hell, I ask out guys all the time."

"Yes, but you're a vixen. I'm boring."

"You are not boring," she says, as we walk to the counter and set our purchases down.

"I've got this. We'll call it the birthday present I haven't bought you yet," I tell her as I give the sales lady my credit card. "Anyway, I can't do that. It would be weird."

"It would only be weird if you let it. Besides, how do you know that he's not going to ask you out?" she asks as she takes our bags from the lady.

And that's when the panic starts to set in. What if Levi asks me out? Am I supposed to say yes? What happens if we go out and realize we're only supposed to be friends? Do you know how hard it is to find real friends in this day and age? What happens if we ruin our friendship with one single date?

"Whoa, cowgirl, slow your horses. I can practically see your brain hemorrhaging with worry. Don't go there. Just relax and see what happens. I'll be honest, I and all of our sisters think there's something more than friendship brewing between you two." I raise my eyebrow. "Oh, don't act so shocked. You two were practically dry-humping in the mud a few weeks ago. Anyway, don't let fear rule you, okay? You owe this to yourself and to him to give this a shot, if the opportunity arises. And I really do think it will. Just sit back, relax, and enjoy the ride. Don't get all tied up in your own head."

"Easy for you to say. You're all carefree and easy."

"I'm not that easy, despite what Lexi says," she quips with a smile.

And just like that, the conversation turns away from the seriousness of Levi and back into the familiar, laid-back feeling I always have with my sisters. There's no stress, no worry, no deep thoughts; at least none that usually center around me.

Just the way I like it.

Chapter Fourteen

Levi

My plan has been in place for a week now, and I'm really just getting into the execution phase. I've been spending time off and on with Abby, while still maintaining my work schedule and my band practice schedule. It's Friday night and I've been thinking about what I want to do for the last several days. Time to put the plan into motion.

Grabbing my phone, I shoot off a text.

Me: *Plans tonight?*

She responds right away, even though I know she has spent the day with one of her sisters.

Abby: *Big date with* The Brady Bunch.

Me: *Not anymore. Be at my place at seven.*

Abby: *Why?*

Me: *It's a surprise. No questions, no excuses. Be here. Wear something comfy.*

Abby: *You're so weird. Not even a hint?*

Me: *You like my weirdness. Not even a hint.*

Abby: *Fine, I'll be there. How comfy? Yoga pants and a no bra kinda comfy? *winky face**

Me: *Whatever floats your boat, angel. Just be here.*

Abby: *Seriously, how comfy is comfy?*

Me: *Comfy.*

Abby: *You're completely impossible sometimes.*

Me: *Another of my endearing qualities you love so much.*

She doesn't reply for a while, but I'd be lying if I said I wasn't watching for those little bubbles on my phone to appear. Just when I start to get a little sweaty, I finally see them.

Abby: *It's more of a high tolerance because I've known you so long.*

I laugh, almost picturing the way she'd smile at the phone while she typed that response.

Me: *I appreciate your high level of tolerance. Seven.*

Abby: *I'll be there. In my comfy clothes.*

Smiling, I set my phone down and throw on some running shorts. If I'm going to spend a few hours with my gorgeous best friend without touching her, I might as well burn off some of this excess energy and sexual frustration with a run. If I had my way, there'd be a lot more of the sexual part and less tension. But that's not gonna happen. I'm bound and determined to do this right and not jumping into bed with her is key.

Even if it kills me.

After running, I end up calling Tucker and having lunch. We're on the rig together this weekend, so I'm sure he's fucking around today like me. Though, I doubt he has the same plans as I do tonight. Tuck's more of a love 'em once and leave 'em kinda guy. You know, like I used to be.

I meet him at the hotdog stand by the Bay, one of our favorite joints in town. It's popular amongst residents and visitors alike. He's already there, waiting in line to order when I arrive.

"Hey, man. Watcha want? I'll buy today and you can get tomorrow night," he says as I step up beside him.

"Three Chicago dogs and a bottle of water."

When our order is placed and we're given a number, we head over to find an open picnic table. There's someone at every one, so we pick a table with a couple on one end and take the other end for ourselves.

"Big plans tonight?"

"Abby's coming over," I tell him, kicking back and extending my legs beneath the table.

"When are you gonna quit pussy-footing around it and just take her out on a real date?"

"What makes you think I'm not leading up to that tonight?" I taunt him, my eyebrows raised.

"No shit?"

"Well, it's not an official date, but it's a start."

"So you just snapped your fingers and she fell in line?"

"Fuck no. When has Abby ever just fallen into line?" I ask, really trying to think of an instance and coming up empty.

"True. She's always had you by the balls, man," he says with a laugh.

"We'll just see how tonight goes, all right?"

"I hear ya. Just be careful." He gives me a straight, serious look. "I know she means a lot to you, and you're afraid of fucking that up."

"Tell me how you really feel, Dr. Phil."

"Shut up. All I'm saying is go all in or not at all. That chick has always meant more to you than any other. Treat her right or you'll lose her."

He isn't telling me something I don't already know. It's weird to hear it come from another friend, though. I thought I had been doing a better job of hiding the foreign feelings I've had for her recently. Apparently, I'm a piss-poor actor.

"I know. I can't wait for something like this to happen to you one day," I tell him, scarfing down my second dog.

"Not gonna happen. Why settle down with one piece of ass when you can have as many as you want?" His smirk reaches from ear to ear.

"Oh yeah, it's definitely gonna happen. I can't wait."

"Fuck you," he retorts, throwing his empty wrapper at me.

"Fifty bucks says you'll be proposing by this time next year."

"You are off your rocker, dumbass. Ain't no way in Hell."

"We'll see," I reply, giving my third hotdog my full attention.

If only Tucker knew I've been watching how he interacts with Heidi, an ER nurse at the hospital. He tries to play it off as casual, but he's not fooling me. His eyes are always seeking her out or they're following her ass around the emergency department. The fact that he hasn't slept with her is enough to prove my point. Tucker lives his life by his balls, and if he's not sleeping with someone and the interest is there, that's telling.

Ol' Tucker's gonna go down hard.

Soon.

* * *

Five 'til seven, there's a short knock on my door before it opens. Even if I hadn't heard her enter, I'd know she was here by the way the room shifts and my body reacts. I'm already carrying a club in my pants and she hasn't even entered the kitchen yet.

"Hey," she says as she steps around the corner from the front entry.

"Hey. I hope you're hungry," I tell her, setting the rest of the silverware down on my kitchen table.

"Starving," she responds, setting her keys and phone on the counter. "Ever since I got your text this morning, my stomach has been growling."

"Well, I hope your stomach is impressed with dinner tonight. I've got salmon and vegetables on the grill and rolls in the oven."

"What's this?" she asks, pointing to the tall cake pan on the counter.

"Dessert."

"Yeah, but what is it?"

"You'll have to wait and see."

"What is up with you and all this secrecy?"

"It's not secrecy, it's a surprise. There's a difference."

"If you say so."

"There is. One implies defiance or willingly withholding information. The other is only intended to temporarily withhold a detail with the intent of sharing. A proposal? Surprise. An affair? Secret."

"Nice examples, Mr. Morgan. So which are you doing tonight? The proposal or the affair?" she asks with a smile, but I don't miss the way something flitters across her face.

"Neither tonight, angel. Just dessert. And I promise you'll find out soon. That's why it's a surprise. I have every intention of telling you."

"So what else is going on? This is an awfully fancy set up tonight," she states while taking in the use of all of the utensils in the place setting.

"I just wanted to treat my girl to a delicious meal to congratulate her on finishing another manuscript."

"I'm not actually finished, though. That was just the first draft," she says, helping herself to the wine I keep in the fridge just for her.

Reaching into the cabinet for the glass, I hand it to her. There's no missing the way our fingers touch and sparks practically fly through the air. My entire body flares to life with that one little touch. It makes me crave her that much more.

"Doesn't mean I'm not proud of you," I tell her, holding the glass while she pours.

She takes a seat at the table, slowly sipping her white wine. Casual small talk is easy with her and tonight is no different. She asks about emergency calls I was on this week and tells me about the books she's working on. Even when dinner is ready, we communicate and move side by side in the kitchen as if we're an old couple who's been married for twenty years.

"So, I have to ask," I say, stabbing my mushroom with my fork. "Are you wearing a bra under that shirt?"

"What?" she asks, choking on her small bite of fish.

"I'm just trying to determine what stage of comfort you're in for dinner tonight."

"I'm not answering that," she quips, trying to fight a smile.

"What if I told you I'm not wearing underwear?" I fire back.

Her laughter fills the room and my soul. It's healing, a balm for all that ails me, just to hear her laugh. "I bet you never wear underwear," she says, her face flushing a beautiful shade of fuchsia.

Leaning forward, I whisper, "Would you like to find out?"

Those green eyes darken with desire. There's no denying it. This is why I know that taking the next step with her is appropriate. Even though she may not have said the words, it's written all over her face and in her eyes. She wants me. That's not being conceited or anything; it's the truth. Her eyes don't lie.

Abby brings her wine glass to her lips and guzzles the cold liquid. "What if I said yes?" Ahhhh, playful Abby has come out to play tonight.

"Did you say yes?" I ask, raising an eyebrow in challenge.

We stare at each other for several moments before she smiles. "Maybe some other time, big boy. I wouldn't want that thing to fall out and land in your food," she says, nodding towards the table, just above where my rock-hard dick is throbbing in my pants.

"Maybe some other time," I say, stabbing my fish with my fork and taking my time chewing.

"Maybe." When she takes another long drink of wine, I can tell she's fighting a smile.

After dessert of frosted chocolate brownies, I take her into the living room, where I already have one of her all-time favorite movies queued up. *The Breakfast Club* begins as I sit back and get comfortable on the couch. This time, when I glance over at her, her entire face is lit up like a Christmas tree.

"You hate this movie."

"But I like you, so I'm willing to suffer through the mid-80's detention drama for you."

Leaning back against the couch, she glances my way once more. "Thank you." I just give her a return smile.

"Here, turn and face me and put your feet in my lap," I instruct, patting my leg.

She laughs as she moves, placing her bare feet on my thigh. You thought my dick was hard before, you should see it now! Even her laughing at me can't squash this massive boner.

"What are you laughing at?"

"This just reminds me of something AJ said earlier today. She went on a few dates with this guy who ended up with a foot fetish."

"Really?"

"Yeah, he wanted to suck on them," she tells me.

Grabbing a hold of one small foot, I give it a gentle squeeze, using my thumbs to dig into the arch of her foot. Her loud moan fills the entire room as the most erotic sound I've ever heard. And I'm not even fucking her. Could you imagine if I was? Jesus, the noises I could evoke from this petite, sexy woman is enough to give me wet dreams for life.

"Feel good?" I ask, my voice sounding deep and husky.

"That's amazing."

I don't say another word–shit, I couldn't even if I wanted to. I keep rubbing one foot and then the other, massaging it and working my way up her calf. There's a thrill racing through my body just at touching her. Could you imagine what it would be like to finally get her naked in my arms? Yeah, I almost come in my pants.

"And I didn't even ask to suck on them," I tease before swiping my finger over the arch of her foot, causing her to kick out. My girl is ticklish, this I know all too well. I've enjoyed tickling her on many occasions over the years.

Unfortunately this time, when she kicks, she kicks downward. Straight into my balls. Balls that were already swollen and blue are now…well, more swollen and bluer. I groan out a huff of air, bending down and all but cradling my throbbing balls in my hand.

"Oh my God, I'm so sorry!" she exclaims, jumping up and sitting right next to me. "What can I do?" she asks, completely serious and full of worry.

"Angel, as much as I wouldn't mind you touching my balls, now's not a good time. I'm on the verge of throwing up and they're suddenly not in the playing mood."

Another blush sweeps up her neck and lands on both cheeks. "I'm so sorry," she whispers.

"I forgive you. Just give me a moment to collect my thoughts."

"Do you want something? Frozen peas? Tylenol?"

Laughing through the pain, I risk a glance at my best friend. "I'm alright, but I think you should turn and lean your head on me. Put those feet down on the other end," I say, grabbing a pillow to set on my lap. Mostly so I can protect my balls, but also so she can't feel the raging hard-on I still have, even after the shot to my twins.

"Are you sure you want me near you?" she teases, turning and getting ready to rest her head on my lap.

"I'm sure. But see if I ever offer to suck your toes for you again," I say before laughter spills from my chest. She takes a swing at my chest, but misses, hitting the pillow that's thankfully covering my junk.

"Oh my God, I almost did it again," she says, horrified.

"Come 'ere, slugger. Lie down before you make it so I can't have kids one day."

And just like that, she's lying on my lap, putting pressure on my throbbing nuts just beneath the pillow. I ignore it, however, and just relish in the feel of her against me.

We watch most of the movie before she starts to doze off. It's the perfect opportunity to drink her in, memorizing every curve, arch, and plane of her body. My hand has been rubbing her arm lightly since before she fell asleep, but I can't seem to make myself stop. Nor can I stop looking at her sleeping form against the brown pillow on my lap. She's angelic, breathtaking.

And I want her to be mine.

It's getting late and as much as I'd love to just curl up on the couch again and fall asleep with her against me, I know it's not the right thing to do. So I gently say her name and move that soft hair from her cheek to behind her ear. Her skin is soft, oh so very soft and I let my finger trail down her neck one time. Following the collar of her shirt, my finger traces her shoulder and around to her upper back.

She shivers against me and I know she's awake. Yet she doesn't say anything or move.

So I continue to touch her exposed skin with the side of my finger, down the hollow of her throat and into the top of her chest. I stop before I get anywhere close to her tits, even though I wouldn't mind copping a feel. But it won't be like this. When I cop a feel, she'll be fully awake and begging for it.

"Angel, wake up. It's already after one."

"It is?" she asks through a yawn.

"Yeah, you should head home and crash. You have AJ's birthday celebration tomorrow."

"I wish you were going," she whispers, still not opening her eyes.

"Me too." And that's the truth.

Slowly, she starts to sit up, moving those sleepy green eyes my way. I stand up first, reaching down and helping her off the couch. She stands directly in front of me, our bodies close enough to touch. She looks tired, yet so alive at the same time. I'll be honest, I'm digging that look on her face right now. It's raw and hungry.

Together, we walk towards the door. I wait until she grabs her keys and phone, her hand automatically retrieving the key to open her door.

"Thank you for dinner," she whispers.

"You're welcome, angel. Sleep tight," I say, reaching up and grabbing that dark brown strand of hair that always falls in her face. Gently, I move it behind her ear, trailing the tip of my finger against her cheek as I go. I fucking love touching her. I can't get enough.

She doesn't say a word, just stares up at me with those big green eyes that make my heart feel like it's salsa dancing in my chest. Before I even realize I'm on the move, I've got her pinned between my body and the door. Abby inhales sharply, but not in a way that conveys fear or worry. No, this is in shock, yes, but also in desire. Raw need and lust flush my entire body rapidly, the same look that's reflecting in her eyes.

Pressing her into the wooden door, I lean ever so slightly into her body. "Go out with me."

Her breath hitches against my lips. "We go out all the time."

Shaking my head, I let my hand slide from her jaw into her hair. "Not as friends. Go out with me."

"*Out with you* out with you? Like a date?" Her words hitch at the same time her body arches against me.

"Yeah, like a date."

Her hypnotic green eyes search mine. I hope she sees my resolve, my loyalty, and my passion for her in the depths of my hazel ones.

"I'm not sure that's such a good idea," she whispers hesitantly.

"I think it's the best idea I've ever had. I think we should go out, as a couple and not just friends. I think we owe it to ourselves to see what's been happening between us lately. I know you feel it. It's written in your eyes, angel. Go out with me."

She searches my face more, her mind clearly weighing the pros and cons. I'm just about to give her more to add to the pro list, when she surprises both of us. "Okay." Her mouth falls open and her eyes widen after she says it.

"No taking that back," I quip, moving my hand from the hair behind her ear down her neck. "Next Saturday night. I'll be off and can take you on the date you deserve."

She closes her eyes and leans her head slightly into my hand. When she opens them again, she asks, "Are you sure?"

"Never been more sure of anything in my life," I tell her honestly.

"Then I'll see you Saturday night."

"Oh, you'll see me before Saturday, sweetheart. I'm still your best friend, Abs. You'll still be inundated with my stupid texts and horrible jokes. I still expect you to watch car restoration shows and *The Brady Bunch* with me. Just because I'm taking you out next weekend doesn't mean our friendship ends. We're just enhancing it," I tell her with a smile, to which she comes back with her own.

"Enhancing it. I like that."

"And I like that you said yes." Forcing myself to take a step back, I let go of the hold I have on her, breaking the connection. "I'll talk to you tomorrow."

"'Kay."

"'Night, Abby."

"'Night, Levi."

Smiling, I watch as she steps out of my apartment and crosses the hall to her own. She slides her key into the keyhole and takes a step inside, but doesn't completely close the door. Instead, she glances back my way, a small smile playing on the corner of her lips.

Fuck, I can't wait for next Saturday.

The day I finally make my girl mine.

Chapter Fifteen

Abby

Me: *Code Blue!*

Lexi: *WTH does that mean? Are you dead?*

Me: *No, but I need you.*

Lexi: *On my way.*

That message was sent not quite ten minutes ago, and she's here. My twin doesn't waste time knocking, but I never expected her to. Instead, she barges through my front door and races towards where I'm standing in the bathroom, wearing only the new bra and panty set that I purchased last Friday with AJ.

"Are you oh-" she stops dead in her tracks in my doorway. "Wow, look at you. What's going on?"

"I have a date," I whisper, saying the words aloud for the first time since Levi asked me just over a week ago. Well, it may be the first time I said them out loud, but it's not the first time I told someone.

"A date? I thought you were bleeding to death or had fallen and couldn't get up!" she exclaims.

I knew I should have told her that it wasn't a life or death emergency, but as I stood in front of my mirror, wearing sexy lingerie for a date that I'm having with my best friend, well, I just kinda panicked.

"I'm sorry, but I just freaked out a little." My eyes cast downward, sheepishly, and I'm not sure if it's embarrassment from getting her all worked up or from the fact that I'm still standing in my undergarments, preparing for my first date in a really long time.

"Okay, so a date. Is it one of the Internet guys? You said last week there was one you were talking to and really hitting it off with." God, I'm so confused. I really like SimpleMan, and the thought of going on a date tonight makes me feel like some sort of cheating floozy.

"God, this is such a mess," I tell my twin, dropping down on my bed and covering my face.

"Start at the beginning. Don't leave anything out," she directs, coming over to sit beside me.

Exhaling, I begin. "Okay, so this may not come as much of a shock to you, but I kinda sorta have a teeny, tiny crush on Levi."

"No shit," she huffs with a laugh.

"Anyway," I say, drawing out the word. "Well, the whole reason I decided to do the online dating thing was because I saw another woman leaving his place the morning after our Frisbee golf night. I guess you could say it made me sad, so I decided to try to date a bit more."

"More? As if you were doing that before?"

"Do you want to hear this or not?" I quip, giving her a stern look. She gestures with her hand for me to proceed.

"I've spoken with a couple of guys there, but nowhere near the dozens you told Levi that day at Jaime's. Really, it boils down to one particular guy that I've been communicating with a lot. Almost daily."

"Okay," she hedges, looking confused.

"Well, lately, things have gotten a little…intense with Levi. He's been touching me a lot more, in a total non-creepy way, mind you, but I don't know, his fingers would linger on my arm or he'd touch my hair more. And there was this look in his eyes that made me think that maybe the crush wasn't so one-sided."

"Duh."

Giving her a look, I continue. "So, last Friday night, he, well, he asked me out. On a date. Like as more than friends."

"Yay!"

"But what if we're only hurting our friendship? What about SimpleMan? I've been talking to him a lot and then Levi asks me out and I say yes. What does that make me?"

"A desirable woman, Abs. You're not committed to either one, right?" Shaking my head, she goes on. "Then until that happens, there's nothing for you to worry about. You can talk to them both and maybe casually date them. Just be upfront about it. Let them both know what your ultimate goal is, which is to find the person you're supposed to spend forever with, right? Well, just mention that as long as it's casual, you'll be seeing other people. It's not hard."

"It's not?"

"Of course not, silly. And this SimpleMan met you through a dating site. He's probably doing the same thing."

"He is?" I ask, never really thinking about it from the other side.

"Sure."

Before I can think much more about it–or put on clothes–I hop off my bed and run into my office. My computer is still booted up from checking email, so I quickly open the app and bring up my last conversation with SimpleMan from this morning. Positioning my hands over the keyboard, I start to type.

AngelEyes: *I just wanted to let you know that I have a date tonight. I'm super nervous. I know we just met, but I felt like I needed to tell you. I'm having a great time chatting with you and getting to know you, and even though nothing has gone further than that, I still thought I should at least tell you.*

Send. Nerves flow through my body as I wait a few moments to see if he replies. If not, I'll just check back after I get home tonight. Home from my date. My date with Levi.

Suddenly, bubbles.

SimpleMan: *First off, you have nothing to be nervous about. I'm sure whoever is lucky enough to score a date with you knows how fortunate he is that you turned your angel eyes his way. *winky face* And besides, I have a confession too. I also have a date tonight. I'd be a liar if I said I wasn't nervous.*

AngelEyes: *See!? Even you're nervous and you just told me not to be!*

SimpleMan: *Yes, but I'm a man and men are notoriously stupid. Fingers crossed I don't do anything dumb or obnoxious tonight.*

AngelEyes: *I'm sure you'll be fine. You're always very nice and respectable with me.*

SimpleMan: *Not a bad thing, but not always what a guy is going for, angel.*

AngelEyes: *laughs* *Anyway, good luck tonight. I hope you enjoy your date.*

SimpleMan: *You too, Angel. I'm sure he knows already how lucky of a bastard he really is. Check back later for date updates?*

AngelEyes: *Sure *smiley**

"Well, isn't that just the nicest. I bet he's great in bed," Lexi says dreamily behind me, obviously reading over my shoulder and having no issues with it.

"I haven't even thought about it," I snap, shutting down my computer.

"Levi's gonna be here in like thirty minutes."

Suddenly, the reality of the situation slams me upside the head. Fine, that was my sister. "Ouch!"

"Are you gonna wear that out tonight? I mean, you look smokin' hot, but I never pictured you for the lingerie peep on the first date, Abs."

"Of course I'm not wearing this," I exclaim as I turn and run into my bedroom. Grabbing the new tank top and skirt I bought last Friday with AJ, I start to dress.

"That's new?"

"Yeah, AJ talked me into it that day we went for lunch and to the mall."

"She has excellent taste. I might have to borrow it."

"For what?" I ask over my shoulder while heading in the bathroom to start my makeup. "It's not like you're the one dating."

Glancing over her shoulder, I see her shrug.

Uh oh.

"What?" I ask, turning my attention to her, waiting her out.

"Things are just...not good."

"With Chris?"

Tears appear in her eyes. I know how much Lexi has invested into her marriage, but something has definitely been off lately. The others have noticed it too. It's not like we talk about her behind her back, but we've all been very concerned lately. She wants a baby, Chris seems unwilling to get checked so that can happen and focused solely on building his investment business.

"Yeah." Her voice is hushed and hoarse.

"Are you...thinking of leaving him?" I ask her, my own tears threatening to fall.

"Yeah," she whispers again.

Without saying a word, I pull her into my arms and hold her tight. Between everything with Meghan over the last several months and now this with Lexi, I've seen more sadness amongst my sisters than I ever want to see. Well, except for when our mom died.

We hold each other until the tears subside and we're both left sniffling. "I can't believe I just did that to you," she says, wiping her eyes and her nose on a Kleenex.

"What?"

"Dumped that on you. Here you are all excited about your night with Levi, and I bring all of my heavy baggage over to weigh you down."

"In case you forgot, I wasn't exactly in fine form when you arrived. I was freaking out. What about you? Are you gonna be okay? I can cancel with Levi and hang out with you." And I would. I'd give it all up tonight to be there for her if she wanted.

"Oh hell no! You've been waiting for months for this moment. Hell, years," she says. "I haven't made any definite decisions, okay? Promise me you'll go enjoy your evening and won't give me a single thought."

She looks at me with a look that lets me know she won't buy my adamant denial that I'm about to give her, but of course, I say it anyway. "Fine. I won't think about you at all."

We stare at each other for several seconds before we both burst out laughing.

"You are going to knock him dead tonight, you know that, right?"

"I'm not so sure about that. I'm terrified I won't be able to get past the fact that he's my friend."

"I bet you'll be thinking about him naked by the time the appetizer is ordered," she quips with a smile. My cheeks feel warm suddenly, and I try to hide my face. "Oh my God, you've already thought about him naked!"

"Of course I haven't."

"You are the worst liar ever. Ever, Abs. I bet he's packing some serious heat, if you know what I mean," she whispers conspiratorially and gives me a wink.

"You're awful and sound just like Grandma."

Lexi laughs and says, "No, if I were Grandma, I'd have big handfuls of his ass before the door closed."

"True," I say with a laugh as a knock echoes through my apartment.

"Oh my God, he's here!" I exclaim, taking in my makeup-less face and my clothes-less body.

"Go get ready," she says, pushing me into the bathroom. "I'll keep him company until you're ready."

Before she can walk away, I pull my twin into my arms and squeeze her tight. "I love you, Lex," I whisper against her face.

"I love you, Abs."

And then she turns and heads towards my door, and I slip into my bathroom to finish getting ready.

For my date.

With Levi.

* * *

Listening to the hum of Levi and Lexi talking from the other room has done nothing for my nerves. In fact, you could say it has done nothing but elevate them a zillion notches. My hand practically shook while I put on my makeup, and I had to apply deodorant three times. You know, just in case. Slipping on the light purple tank top and slimming skirt, that I actually bought thinking I would never wear, suddenly makes the entire situation so real.

I am going on a date with Levi.

I know, I know. I'm not trying to fixate on that little fact, but I can't help it.

Slipping on my favorite pair of black wedge sandals, I glance in the mirror one last time. My makeup looks good, especially in light of the fact that I rarely wear more than a little mascara. The outfit is flattering and shows a little more of my legs than normal, but even I'll admit my legs look slim and a mile long in my sandals.

"You got this, Abby," I mumble to myself, taking a few deep, calming breaths. "It's just Levi; you've known him since you were ten."

Yeah, you've known him for fifteen years, but you've never gone out with him, I remind myself as I step up to the closed door. More deep breaths, in and out. Grabbing the door, I turn the knob and step into the hallway. Their voices are more pronounced now as I round the corner of the small hallway and step into the kitchen.

My sister is talking, but I have no clue what she's saying. My eyes instantly zero in on Levi, who's standing there in a pair of dark jeans that hang perfectly on his hips and a black shirt that hugs his arms and chest. His hair is styled a bit on top, but still gives that carefree look I love. Well, love to run my fingers through. I practically start to drool on the spot.

"Wow, you look amazing." His words infiltrate my brain enough to draw my eyes from his chest to his face. I'm shocked by the intensity that's there. He has a smile on his lips, which only softens the passion in his eyes a little bit. That look is one I'm not used to seeing on my friend's face, nor anyone else for that matter.

"Thank you. You look pretty nice yourself," I say softly.

"Well, I feel like the third wheel in the opening scene of a porno. Since I'm pretty sure you're not going to ask me to join in– not that I want you to–I'm going to head home," Lexi says with a forced smile. I can still see her hurt.

Walking up to her, I give her another hug and whisper, "Are you sure you're all right?"

"Fine, Abs. Don't worry about me. Go have fun with Levi," she says back before placing a kiss on my cheek. "Bye, Levi. Be nice to my sister or I'll have to hunt you down and do painful things to all of your bits and pieces."

Gasping, I glance over at my friend who's shielding his manhood with his hand. "Understood. You don't have to worry about me," he tells her with a smile.

My eyes are drawn back to my friend as my sister walks out the door, whistling a happy tune. Levi's eyes are fierce, yet excited as he walks over to me. No, walks isn't exactly the right word. Stalks, is more like it.

Levi lifts his hand and moves a soft curl from my cheek to behind my ear. "You really look amazing."

"Thank you," I croak.

His fingers linger just a little longer than usual on my hair, his eyes searching mine. He must be happy with what he sees because he smiles widely and asks, "Ready to go?"

Not trusting my words, I nod. Bending down, he links his fingers with my own, and pulls me towards the door. Opening the door, he allows me to exit first, but still doesn't drop my hand. Together, we take the stairs down three flights to his truck.

Deep breath.

You can do this.

Chapter Sixteen

Levi

I bet I haven't been this nervous a day in my life. Sure, I was worked up on my first ambulance call. Sure, I stared at that blank sheet of paper for what felt like an hour when I took my EMT class. But this? Terrifying.

The only thing that settles my racing heart is how beautiful she looks. Lexi tried to distract me while we waited for Abby to finish getting ready, but it almost did more harm than good. But now? Calmness washes over me as I look over at her stunning face, wearing just a bit more makeup than normal. What really holds my attention now is her outfit. Purple flowy tank top that dips low in the front, granting me a sliver of cleavage for my viewing pleasure. And that skirt. Fuck. It makes me so hard I bet NASA could see the outline of my cock from space. The skirt is shorter than she usually wears, hitting about mid-thigh, which pleases me greatly.

And let's take a moment to give praise to those legs. Holy. Shit. Has she always had legs that make a grown man sit up and beg? Long, lean, and with a hint of a summer tan. Perfect fucking legs to have wrapped around my waist–or better yet, my neck.

"You really look amazing," I tell her, moving hair behind her ear.

"Thank you."

I feel like a shmuck. A complete clueless loser who has no idea how to talk to women. Maybe it's the fact that I'm finally seeing her–I mean, really *seeing* her. From the way she's blushing right now at my compliment, to the light colored polish on her toes, I'm seeing a whole new Abby Summer right now, and it's exhilarating.

"Ready to go?" I ask, taking her hand in my own. Electricity bolts through my body, making it hard to reel in the gasp that almost slips out of my mouth. Everything with her is practically charged, sexually almost. There's this new thrill that hits me every time we touch, and you can bet your ass my cock notices.

She nods, almost as if she can't find her voice. I watch as she closes her eyes, takes a deep breath, and steels her back. When she opens her eyes, it almost knocks me to my knees. She looks so strong, so fierce, so stunning.

We take the stairs slowly down to the ground floor and into the late-July air. It'll be August soon, which means the summer tourist season will be drawing to a close. Those who stay at the small bed and breakfasts and the hotels along the Bay, will be leaving in a few weeks. Personally, I'm ready for it to slow down a little bit; the ambulance has been hopping all summer long.

Keeping my hand on her back, I lead her towards my truck. We could probably take her car, which would be easier for her to get in and out of in that skirt, but I want her in my space–wearing that skirt. And it won't hurt any that I get to be chivalrous enough to help her in and out, right?

When we approach my truck, she gives me a look. "I'll help ya," I offer, a naughty smirk playing on my lips.

"Do you say that to all the girls?" she asks with a smile.

"Nope, only you." And that's the truth. I've never really thought about it before, but I don't necessarily date. Not in the official capacity. I've taken plenty of girls home from bars and gigs, but most of the time I'm more interested in getting them to a bed than trying to be all gentlemanly with my truck. I know, I know. You're thinking, "Damn, Levi, you're a dick." Yeah, I can be, I admit. But never with Abby.

Never.

"Turn around." She glances over her shoulder again before turning and facing me. I smile, bending down and grabbing a hold of her slender waist. Abby places her hands on my shoulders for balance as I lift and set her inside my truck cab. It's a quick exchange, one I wish had lasted a hell of a lot longer than a few seconds, but I don't want to maul her within the first ten minutes.

When she's safely inside the cab, I give her a wink and shut the door. Then because I'm all smooth and shit tonight, I all but run around the front of the truck and hop in the driver's seat. She offers me a tentative smile as she waits for me to start up the truck.

"So, where are we going?"

"I thought we'd do dinner down along the Bay and then I have a special stop we're making on the ride back."

"Sounds good," she replies, but I can still hear the anxiety in her voice. I need to remedy that real quick.

"Tell me about your day."

"Well, I worked for a bit to catch up on a big project that was sent my way. It's a multi-book deal for an author I worked with about two years ago. She was planning to self-publish, but ended up talking to her contact at Stonewell and sent in the manuscript. It was amazing, so we jumped on a deal. The problem is that she was planning to self-publish next month so the entire process is being pushed up to the top of our to-do lists. I have until Tuesday at noon to get the first round of edits done."

"Wow, that's pretty rushed," I say.

"Yeah, and I won't be able to work on it much tomorrow because we're helping Payton move."

"Oh, yeah. Lex reminded me earlier. I'll be ready to go at eight with my truck. Wanna just ride over together? You know, since we're going to the same place."

"That's fine," she says, but I catch the hitch in her voice. Glancing over, I see a shy little smile on her lips that she's trying to hide, and a blush creeping up her neck. God, I love it when she does that.

"I'll be over at seven-thirty. I'll even bring that fancy coffee shit you like." My girl loves those caramel lattes from the coffee house uptown. I'm actually kinda excited to run over and grab her one before our day of moving boxes and furniture for her oldest sister.

"I would be forever in your debt," she quips.

We make small talk the rest of the way to the small coastal restaurant about forty minutes south of Jupiter Bay, that I've been dying to try. Abby doesn't seem too bothered by the fact that we drove all the way down here for dinner, but it's close to our next stop.

"I've heard of this place," she says as we pull into the packed parking lot. "Grandma and Grandpa come here every now and again. She's always raving about the seafood."

"Some of the girls in the ER were discussing it not that long ago, and when I was planning our night, I thought it would be the perfect place to bring you." Again, she blushes that adorable shade of red. It makes me want to keep saying and doing things to make her blush. And maybe someday soon I'll be able to do that *other* thing to really make her blush–or flush, I guess is more accurate.

Yeah, I know. I'm a dirty bastard. Sue me.

"You've never been here?" she asks as I come around the truck and open her door.

"Nope."

My hands are already wrapped around her waist as she shimmies towards the door, holding her skirt down as she goes. When I know it's secure, I pull her out of the truck and against my body. Our eyes lock as she slowly slides down, her chest pressed firmly to my own. I'm one hundred percent certain she can feel the boner in my pants before her feet even hit the ground. Her eyes widen and darken with arousal, and there's no missing the way her tongue darts out and wets her soft pink lips.

I groan.

"I'm sorry," she mumbles, dropping her eyes.

"For what?" I ask, yet to let go of her waist.

"For, well, you know," she whispers looking down at my pants.

"Angel, don't ever be sorry for that. *That* happens a lot when you're around, whether you want it to or not."

"It does?" Her eyes light up in a way that says she can't decide if she should be embarrassed or turned on.

Bending down, I whisper in her ear. "All. The. Time." She gasps. "Come on, let's go grab our table before they give it to someone else because we missed our reservation."

"Are you sure you're able to walk in your condition?" she quips, a gorgeous smile plastered on her face. Oh, she thinks this is funny, does she?

"I'm perfectly capable of walking like this, but if you're offering to help me out with my problem, I won't deny you the pleasure." The words are out of my mouth before I can even stop them.

Shit. Damn. Fuck.

Expecting to see her eyes popping out of her head and a horrified look on her face, I risk a glance in her direction. What I wasn't expecting to see was humor. "Did you really just say that?" She fights to laugh.

"Shit, Abs, I'm sorry. Sometimes I forget I'm with you. You don't deserve to hear me talk like an ass."

"So if this was anyone else but me, you would have said that and not batted an eye?"

I take in her curious face. She's my best friend, right? No lies. "Yeah, I probably would have. You know my past, Abs. I've been known to have one thing on my mind and that's it. But not with you. You're different. I don't want you to get creeped out by my perverse mouth, okay? Just pretend I didn't say that."

I start to walk towards the door, but she hasn't moved. Dread fills my gut as I realize I've killed the date before it even really got started. She's going to ask me to take her home now, I'm sure of it.

"Levi?"

"Yeah." My voice is hoarse and full of remorse.

"Can I ask you a question, and you'll answer it honestly?"

"Always."

"What you said, you'd say that to any other girl, right?"

I swear I'm choking. There's an imaginary noose wrapped around my throat, slowly suffocating the life out of me. "Yeah."

She takes a step forward, closing the distance between us. "Then I want you to say whatever you want. I want this to be the real Levi and Abby, okay? Don't baby me or hold back because of me. Okay?"

I nod, unable to speak over the lump in my throat.

Then, she steps even closer until our bodies are touching again. "Besides, I kinda liked it when you said that dirty stuff." Her eyes are hooded and dark, and my state of arousal shoots through the damn roof.

"Yeah?"

"Yeah."

Reaching around, I wrap my arm around her lower back. "I can do that, but promise me if it ever becomes too much, you'll tell me."

"I want to see more of the dirty, lax Levi. He's kinda sexy and turns me on a little." Her face is flaming red, but dammit if it isn't the sexiest moment ever.

"God I want to kiss the fuck out of you right now," I tell her, tightening my hand on her lower back.

"In public?" Her words are breathy and come out in little pants.

"Hell yes."

"Promise me someday you'll do that?"

"That's a promise I can definitely make, sweetheart. How about we head inside and eat before we give all of the patrons a show and I throw you down on the ground and ravish that sexy little mouth of yours."

She pants again, desire flooding her emerald eyes. "Are you sure? I kinda like the second part of that."

I run my finger from her forehead, down her cheek, and move her hair behind her ear, before taking her chin between my finger and thumb. "As amazing as that sounds right now, our first kiss isn't going to be public. It's going to be somewhere very private where I can kiss you until you're gasping for air and beggin' for more."

"Now that sounds like a kiss."

"I promise you, sweetheart. When I get finished with you, you won't even remember a kiss before it. Mine will be the only one you think about, remember, dream of."

"Something tells me I'm in over my head with you, Levi Morgan."

Glancing down at her and giving her a smile, I respond, "Me too, Miss Summer. Me too.

Placing a kiss on her forehead, I pull back and head into the restaurant. Time to give my girl the best first date in the history of all dates.

* * *

Her head whips in my direction, her eyes full of excitement as we pull into the massive parking lot that's barely housing a dozen cars. I drive my truck towards the building, but park far enough back that some asshole in a Prius can't slide into the space beside me and door ding my truck. It's wide enough that I usually choose to park away from the jerks who'll squeeze in a spot that's a foot too short, just to get as close to the front door as possible.

"Really?" she asks when I throw it in park and shut off the ignition.

"Really."

"But you hate the bookstore."

"Not true. I just never had any use for it back when you were going all the time. I had all the pretty girls doing my homework for me," I quip, unbuckling my belt.

"You had me doing it," she says, doing the same.

"Like I said, pretty girls." Throwing her a wink, I hop out and head over to assist my lady in need. And like before, I use the opportunity to touch her, sliding her down my body in a way that makes me want to throw her over my shoulder, find the nearest hotel, and have my way with her until we're both boneless and lethargic.

"If memory serves correct, I think you also used Sheila Kissee for her language arts skills," she says, the corner of her mouth tilting upward.

"Oh, she had skills, but language arts wasn't one of them," I laugh.

I'm barely able to block her hand as she swats me across the chest. "You're bad," she says, returning my laughter.

"Come on, angel. Let's buy books."

She stops and looks me square in the eye. "That may be the most romantic thing anyone has ever said to me."

"I aim to please, sweetheart. Let's go." There's no need to lead her towards the massive bookstore. No, not anymore. My girl is practically sprinting towards the front door, eyes alive with excitement.

Stepping inside, I follow as she leads me towards the romance section. "I could come here every day and never get tired of it." She gazes starry-eyed over the shelves upon shelves of paperbacks, sliding her hand gently over the spines of the books. "I always thought there was something magical about the library in school, and I'll never forget the first time I came over here and saw one of the books I worked on." Her eyes are alive and have a far-off dreamy look.

"Show me." Those two words hold a whole new meaning than they normally would coming from my mouth, but with just as much anticipation–hell, maybe more.

I follow behind as she leads me further into the romance section. There are covers of every color, with half-naked men and scantily clad women; some locked in an embrace that screams, "We're about to fuck." This is my kinda book.

"Here," she whispers, running her finger down the spine before pulling it from the shelf. *Nightly Calling* by Emma Jane Sloan. "This was my first solo edit," she adds, opening up the book and touching the spot that says her name.

"Very cool, angel," I say, grabbing the book from her hand and flipping it over. "So, is this porn?" I ask, glancing at her with a knowing look.

"It's romance. It's a love story."

"With sex."

"The book isn't about sex."

"Yeah, but there's sex in it."

"So?"

"So, you read about sex," I state bluntly, holding the book in my hand. Stepping closer, I whisper, "I bet it turns you on." Her gasp echoes through the rows of porn (fine, romance) books. "Admit it."

Turning and facing me head-on, those intoxicating green eyes stare straight at me–or into me, might be more accurate. "Fine. Yes, sometimes the scenes turn me on."

"Damn, that's hot," I whisper, closing my eyes and picturing it.

"What are you doing?" she whispers back.

"Shhhh. I'm imagining you getting turned on in that office of yours, reading a dirty sex scene."

"Stop!" she exclaims, hitting my shoulder. We both burst out laughing, big dopey smiles on our faces.

"I'm just kidding you," I tell her, grabbing a piece of that silky hair and pushing it behind her ear. Leaning forward, I add, "I'll wait to picture that tonight when I'm alone in my bed."

Her eyes widen and her mouth practically drops to the floor. I love knowing that I evoke this kinda reaction from her. It makes me feel like it's for me, and me alone. Almost like a super power, you know? No, I have no idea why guys always resort to their childhood and superheroes. They're fucking cool, all right?

"Come on, sweetheart. Show me more."

Chapter Seventeen

Abby

We end up spending almost two hours at the chain bookstore, staying close to closing time. When we leave, I have three new books to add to my bookshelves, and Levi has two. Both books are ones I edited: my first one and my most recent. He even promised to get all the ones in between, but I won't hold my breath. The only books in his apartment are the ones with naked women pictured in them.

The ride back to town is light, fun, and easy. Sure, he's my best friend and we obviously get along, but this is more than that. There's chemistry and this now-familiar sexual tension filling the cab with each closing mile towards our building. When we reach the outskirts of town, words seem to evaporate completely. I keep stealing glances his way, and so is he. It's an erotic slow dance towards something bigger than either of us could be prepared for. Sure, probably sex, but it's more than that.

Much more.

When Levi parks his truck in the back of the lot, he unbuckles his safety belt and shuts off the truck. Without the hum of the diesel engine, the silence in the cab is almost eerie. "Wait there, and I'll come around for you," he says, his hazel eyes looking darker than normal under the glow of the moonlight.

Unable to speak, I nod. He makes quick work of jumping out and coming around to the passenger side. As he has all evening, he's there, opening the door, and waiting for me to slide closer. At first, I was all about making sure all of my bits and pieces were covered by the skirt. You know, don't wanna show off the goods on the first date. Though, that's probably what Levi's used to from other women.

By the time I slide out for the final time tonight, I don't care much about the placement of my skirt. My body is humming with anticipation, my heart beating out of my chest with nerves. Will he kiss me? Should I invite him into my apartment when we get upstairs? If I do, is it expected that I'll have sex with him?

Again, I'm completely out of my league on this whole dating thing. Panic starts to set in as I think about ruining the date. I've done so well all night, but now, at the end of the night, I'm going to mess it all up. He'll run across the hall screaming. He'll never want to speak to me again. I'll lose my friend.

"Angel, I'm not sure what just happened there, but you suddenly look like you just lost your puppy." My eyes fly up to his and the impact is instantly calming. "Breathe, sweetheart. I don't think you've taken a breath since you got out of the truck," he adds, caressing my cheeks with his big hands, never once letting his gaze waiver.

Exhaling deeply, I keep my eyes on his. "That's better. What just happened there? You were smiling when I opened the door, but by the time I had you on the ground, you looked terrified."

"Just getting trapped in my own head," I mumble, choosing to be vague but honest. Levi knows me well enough to be able to see right through any lies.

"I was afraid of that." Wrapping his arms around my back, he pulls me in close. So close I can feel the firmness of his chest and *other* parts against my body. "Come on," he adds, leading me towards the apartment. The entire way, he never lets go of my hand.

We're silent as we walk up three flights of stairs, my feet starting to protest with each step I take. I'm not used to wearing heels or wedges for any significant length of time in light of the fact I work from home. Heck, most of the time, I'm still in yesterday's clothes until about noon. Totally gross, by the way.

When we reach our floor, I'm mentally contemplating what I'm supposed to do. Do I walk to my door and hope he follows? Go to his door? He answers the unspoken questions for me when he leads me towards my door. My gut drops to my shoes when I realize he's ending our night out–our date.

Reaching my door, I grab my keys from my purse, not realizing that I didn't have them already in my hand the way I was taught. Dread fills my body, replacing the desire I had just minutes ago.

Before I can insert my key, however, Levi turns me to face him. "Confession time. You ready?" I'm shocked he whips out our old game we used to play when we were younger. When one of us would call for a confession time, we each had to confess something that the other didn't know. It's been years since Levi and I have shared a confession, and I'm not sure why he would pull it out right now.

"Okay." I'm not sure if that word comes out a question or an answer.

"I'll go first. I had a really great time tonight."

"You did?" My voice sounds shaky, even to my own ears.

"Yeah, I did. Actually, great isn't even the right word. What's better than great?" he asks, arching his eyebrow upward and giving me an easy smile. "Your turn."

"Um, okay, well, as you know I haven't been on a lot of dates, though for a while, they were always just first ones. I guess what I'm trying to say is that this was the best one I've ever had." His face lights up, his smile widens. "And, I guess if I was still confessing, I'd say that I was really nervous about tonight, but even more so about now."

Levi reaches forward and caresses my cheek. "I was nervous too. For the date, but not now. Know why?" Unable to find words, I shake my head. "Because being with you in any setting–on a date or otherwise–feels like the most natural, easy thing in the whole world. Because it's you."

My heart just literally stopped beating and my lungs seize up. I'm sure that my face, right now, is comical–mouth hanging open, eyes the size of saucers. But his eyes don't hold the humor I would expect. Instead, they darken and start to smolder. My entire body shivers, but not from any cold air. It's from his look; I feel it clear down to my soul.

"Are you still nervous?" he whispers, leaning into my personal space, but not moving his hand from my cheek.

I try to speak, but it comes out a croak. You know, like a frog. I basically regress to an aquatic amphibian. Kill me now.

"Don't be nervous," he whispers, inching closer and closer until our lips are a mere whisper apart. I can feel his breath fanning against my dry lips. My tongue slips out, sliding along my bottom one. His eyes dart downward as if he's transfixed on the movement.

His free arm wraps around my back, pulling me flush against his body. I'm pliant and move easily, letting him lead. I wouldn't know what to do in this situation if it were to slap me upside the head. See what I mean? I'm wrapped in my best friend's arms, probably about to be kissed by him for the first time, and my mind is reminding me ever so unpleasantly that I have little to no experience in this kinda situation.

Moving his hand from my cheek to my hair, he whispers, "Abby, I want to kiss you. I want to kiss you more than I've ever wanted to kiss anyone in my life."

"That doesn't sound horrible," I whisper back, mortification sweeping up my neck and staining my cheeks.

He chuckles lightly. "I'm glad because I'd hate for you to think it was horrible."

"No, I think it sounds really nice. Wonderful, actually," I tell him honestly.

Slowly, he lowers his mouth the rest of the way, our eyes lock on each other as our lips touch for the first time. It's almost euphoric. My entire body practically melts into him, and that's before he licks along the seam of my lips. And holy crapola, when he does that, I'm pretty sure fireworks actually explode nearby.

The first taste of his mouth is heavenly. Our tongues begin to slide with ease against one another, each stroke kindling a fire that's burning deep inside me. He must feel it too, because his hands tighten in my hair (heck no, it doesn't hurt), and he moves me as close as humanly possible to his body. So close that even air can't pass between us.

That kiss ignites. My hands slide up his chest and wrap around his neck, pulling him until my breasts are plastered against him. It's the first time I've ever wished my clothes would magically disappear. I'm lifting my leg, without even realizing it, wrapping it around his leg, seeking out his touch.

Levi turns us until I'm against the door. One hand slides up the outside of my thigh, gripping and pulling me into him. My hands move upward as I angle my head, allowing him to take the kiss straight past deep and into the category adjacent to pornographic. His hair is just as soft and thick as I remember, and I can't stop myself from grabbing handfuls of his sandy-blond hair.

The result is a groan and a flex of his hip into the V of my legs. The friction causes my own moan to slide from my lips and into his mouth. We're half a second away from getting it on in the hallway of our apartment building, and I couldn't care less. I'm rooting for it, actually.

Suddenly, like a splash of cold water, Levi let's out a frustrated growl and removes his mouth from mine. We're both panting and breathless, entwined around each other as if we were one body.

"Confession time," he whispers, nuzzling my nose with his. "Best. Fucking. Kiss. Ever."

Again, I find myself speechless. My eyes have a hard time focusing under heavily hooded lids, but I can see the faint smile on his lips. My heart races with excitement, my blood boiling with desire. It's everything I ever imagined this kiss to be.

And then some.

I'm just about to ask him to come inside with me when he speaks again. "I should let you get inside."

Ice. Water.

My face must convey my shock and disappointment, because he quickly opens his mouth. "No, no, no. *Not* because I don't want to come inside with you, because, angel, I *really* want to come inside with you." He smirks at the double implication. "I told you from the beginning that you were different, and I'm going to prove it."

"So you won't sleep with me tonight?" I ask, shocked and a little hurt.

"I won't sleep with you tonight because it was our first date, and you're so much more than a first date lay. You're…everything."

I soften against him as he keeps me pinned against my front door.

"But the second date?" he whispers, licking the shell of my ear. "The second date is fair game, angel."

Gazing up at him, I say boldly, "Confession time. I'm really, *really* looking forward to the second date."

Levi closes his eyes and moans. "You're gonna kill me."

Setting my hiked-up leg back down on the ground, Levi runs his hands up my neck and caresses my cheeks. "I mean it. Tonight was the best date I've ever had and that's because it was you. It never felt weird, even when you had your leg wrapped around my waist, rubbing that sweet pussy against my hard cock." Oh God, cue the blush! "It felt anything but awkward. It felt amazing and so fucking right."

"It did," I confess.

"So I'm going to end our night with a much shorter kiss, I'm going to send you into your apartment, and I'm going to eventually fall asleep with the biggest, cheesiest grin on my face, and I want you to know that it was *you* who did that to me, Abs. You."

My own cheesy smile breaks out, and I can't help it.

"Good night, Abigail."

"Good night, Levi," I whisper before he brings his mouth back down to mine.

The kiss is much shorter, though it still causes sparks to fly. My body is numb, weightless with giddiness as he slowly releases me and opens my door. I feel the void of his body as soon as we're apart, my body yearning for his touch, his closeness. "Night," he whispers one last time before I turn and enter my apartment.

Before I close the door, I whisper my own, "Night." His eyes never leave mine until they're separated by the wooden door.

My fingers automatically lock both the knob and the deadbolt. I listen for his door, but it doesn't come right away. I stand there, my back against the door, and listen to him breathe against the opposite side of the door. I can practically feel him. After several minutes, I finally hear movement. I stand still, refusing to move a muscle, even to look through the peephole. Eventually, though, I hear his door open, and after several more heart-stopping seconds, it finally closes.

Sagging completely against the door, the smile on my face feels as big as the sun. I'm sure it's just as bright too. I glance around my apartment, making sure that everything is all right, before heading down the hallway. Instead of heading for my room though, I find myself walking towards my office. My computer boots up quickly, and before I know it, I'm staring at the PerfectDate app.

Open.

My emotions are all over the place, my body wound tight. Bringing up the messages, I click on his name.

AngelEyes: *Best. Date. Ever.*

Three words that speak of nothing but the truth. Smiling, I ignore the other messages and log out.

I practically float from my office and into my bedroom, removing my outfit and tossing it into my hamper. After a quick trip to the bathroom to remove my makeup and brush my teeth, I slide beneath my covers, the never-ending smile still firmly on my face.

Tonight, I went out on a date.

Tonight, I had the most wonderful time.

With Levi.

My best friend.

* * *

"Pick it up more, wussy!" AJ hollers, holding up the other side of the kitchen table.

"I am! Stop yelling at me," I grunt as I try to steer the table through the back door.

We've been moving all of Payton's belongings from her little house over to Dean's place. What doesn't go there is heading to our childhood home where our dad is going to store it until we have a sale. But I'll be honest with you, the way I see Lexi eyeing some of the furniture, I wouldn't be surprised if she isn't making mental notes of what might be available should the need arise.

And after yesterday's conversation, I'd say the need might arise rather quickly.

That thought just depresses me. Chris is an all right guy, but he's definitely changed over the years. He was always very driven to be a success, but in the last three years, I'd say his relationship with my sister has deteriorated tremendously, which breaks my heart.

I want her to be happy and if that was with Chris, then so be it. But it's not. At least not anymore, and that tears me up inside. For now, I'll just be there and support her, knowing that when the time is right, she'll make the hard decisions she's meant to make.

"Quit daydreaming about Levi with his shirt off and help me maneuver this thing out the door." AJ glares at me from across the table, twisting and turning it so that it fits through the doorway without dents and dings.

Her words register. I practically drop my end of the table, turning my neck, almost painfully, to see what she's talking about.

And there he is.

Levi and Ryan are both shirtless and using an appliance cart to move the refrigerator from the kitchen. The man looks absolutely scrumptious in loose fitting jeans that hang dangerously low on his hips and work boots, the fitted gray tee that he was wearing earlier is hanging out of his back pocket. I literally, just stop and stare. Gawk, is actually a more accurate term.

His muscles flex in his back as he helps maneuver the large appliance through the doorway. What pulls my attention is the large phoenix tattoo across his back that moves with each stretch of his muscles.

"Really?" AJ mumbles behind me, pulling my attention back to her.

"What?"

"You act like you've never seen him naked," she says with a smile.

"I haven't!" I defend. And that's the truth. We've seen each other in swimsuits and sleepwear. Yes, I know he has a large tattoo on his back and one on his chest, not to mention several on his arms. Yes, his body is lean and hard and has more ripples of muscles than most men. Yes, I've fantasized about what he would look like without the pants, but I've never actually seen him naked.

"You're such a liar. I saw the way he wanted to gobble you up like Thanksgiving dinner earlier," AJ quips with a smirk.

"She's right," Levi whispers against my ear, causing me to jump. The heat of his flesh sears my entire body and he isn't even touching me.

"Of course I'm right," AJ retorts before setting her end of the table down on the porch. Dean is there, wearing his shirt, I might add, and grabs her end.

"Allow me to help," Levi says, bending over and kissing my exposed shoulder. He takes the table from my hands, allowing me to step aside and out of the way. Effortlessly, he moves the table until it's out the door. Before he's out of sight, he throws me a smile and a wink.

"Seriously, I can't believe you two haven't hooked up before now," AJ says, stepping up beside me.

"Why do you say that?"

"You two have been doing the sexual tension tango around each other for years." Leaning forward so that no one can hear, she asks, "How was the date?"

"How did you-" I start, but know it's fruitless.

"How do you think? Lexi told Grandma who took out a message in the church bulletin this morning."

Gasping, my eyes fly towards my sister's green ones. "What?!"

"Kidding. Jeez, calm down. She did text us last night and told us all that you two finally got your shit together."

"And that's big news?" I ask, hating that my siblings were all communicating about me, but knowing that it was inevitable.

"Of course it is, silly. We've all seen it forever now; we've just been waiting on you two to catch up," she says before grabbing one of the lamps sitting on the floor and heading back out the front.

Levi and Dean load the table into the trailer that'll go to my dad's place, while Ryan meets them around the back with two of the chairs.

"Well, how was the sex?" Lexi whispers excitedly behind me.

"For the love of God, we didn't have sex," I tell her, spinning around to find her, Jaime, and Payton both there with smiles.

"Whatever," Payton grumbles, sarcastically, as she grabs one of the last few boxes in the living room.

"It's okay if you didn't, Abs. I didn't sleep with Ryan on our first date," Jaime says, picking up another box.

"Yes you did, hussy! You spent the night with him," Lexi chimes in.

"That was the second date," Jaime defends before walking towards the door. "Our first date was just a kiss. The most perfect kiss ever."

My face blushes as memories of last night's kiss parade through my mind. That kiss was single-handedly the best kiss of my entire life. It was the Super Bowl and World Series all rolled into one. No other first kiss could ever possibly measure up, which just sucks because every time I kiss someone for the first time, I'll think of Levi and how wonderful his kisses were.

But what if there never was another first kiss?

Call it wishful thinking, but even I'm not naïve enough to know that's probably not true. Nothing ever happens like in the love stories I read day in and day out. Levi and I are friends, sure, but not destined to be together or anything. Even though he makes me feel alive and invincible, even just from a single night of kisses, doesn't mean he's the one I'm destined to spend the rest of my life with.

But, boy, wouldn't that be amazing?

Blushing again, I turn back and face my sisters. They're all wearing matching grins. "What?"

"Tell us," Payton encourages, stepping forward and eliminating the gap.

Three sets of eager eyes stare back at me. "It was...amazing."

"Like your body was going to burst into flames?" Payton asks.

"Mmhmmmm," I hum with a coy smile.

"If by the way you're blushing is any indication, I'd say it was better than amazing," Jaime says.

"And you didn't have sex with him? Have I not taught you anything?" Lexi grins over the box in her arms and heads out the door.

"Ignore her, Abs. You go at your own pace. Only you and Levi will know it's right, if it's right." Payton clearly slipped into the big sister role effortlessly.

"Thank you, Pay," I say before she can slip out the door.

"But my vote is for marathon sex. I bet that man could go all night long," she hollers over her shoulder before slipping outside herself.

"My only advice is that whenever it happens, make sure you're not in public. Indecent exposure won't look good on you, Abs," Jaime contributes before following the others outside.

I'm left alone in the living room with only a couple of packed boxes and my thoughts. Yeah, of course, I've imagined what it would be like to sleep with Levi. Recently, it seems to be all I can think about late at night when I'm lying in bed alone. But something tells me the things I've pictured won't do the real Levi Morgan's sexual magnetism, justice.

Man, is it hot in here?

Before I can head out the door with my own box, strong arms wrap around my waist and stop my progress. His lips are warm and soft as he places a tender kiss on the back of my neck. Shivers slide down my spine and strike at my extremities. My breathing is shallow and my body is swaying back in his direction.

All of this from the slightest touch of his lips.

"Were you talking about me?"

"Maybe," I whisper. My eyes flutter closed as his lips linger at the base of my neck.

"What were you talking about?"

"Nothing much."

"It must have been something for Lexi to walk out and tell me she was disappointed in me." His hands don't move, his lips don't move. I don't move. I close my eyes and feel.

"She's just being Lexi," I murmur, my breathing labored, all of a sudden.

"So it was about sex?"

Laughing, I glance over my shoulder and meet his twinkling hazel eyes. "You know her well."

He snorts and I feel his hands flex on my lower stomach. "I do, but I know you better." His eyes flare with fire that resembles the same heat he had last night right before he kissed me. "I know you are excited, yet nervous to have me this close to you. I feel it, see it, know it because I know you. You want to see what else is there between us, but you're still scared.

"Me too, angel. I'm terrified I'm going to fuck up the best friendship I've ever had, or will have. But do you know what?" he asks, his eyes unwavering. Unable to respond, I shake my head. "My need to find out what has developed between us is greater. It's like a craving I can't quench. You're my craving."

"As long as you keep kissing me like that, I don't think you can screw anything up." And that's the honest to God truth. The man kisses like I'm the very air he breathes.

"That I can do," he says just before spinning me around and placing his lips on my own. It's a tender kiss, but still contains the euphoric spark I've come to associate with him.

His lips move gently against mine, slow and seductive. The tip of his tongue slides gingerly along the seam of my lips, coaxing my mouth open. His breath mingles with my own, minty and hot. He smells and tastes just as he did last night, only now with a hint of sweat. Honestly, the slightest whiff of him turns me into a puddle of hormonal mush, all wanton-like and ready to strip off my clothes.

Levi pulls me against his chest, his hard muscles flexing beneath my fingertips. And lest I forget to mention that his chest isn't the only *hard* thing pressed against me at the moment. Good God, this man is pure sin.

"There's still a bed in Payter's room if you two need a few minutes!" The statement is practically shouted, echoing through the near-empty house. Levi and I jump apart, my left foot catching on one of the remaining boxes in the living room.

"Grandma!" I exclaim, my balance shifting and twisting my body. Before I go down, his arms are wrapped around me, pulling me back against his body.

"Oh, don't Grandma me, young lady. I saw that tonsil hockey you were engaging in with that young man. In fact, I saw quite a bit of it. He has good moves," she says with a wink and a sweet smile. My face, on the other hand, burns with mortification.

"You are so embarrassing," I whimper, burying my face in his bare shoulder. My entire being is flooded with his scent once more, and it ignites my blood. I'd wiggle in nice and close if it weren't for the elderly lady five feet away, probably videotaping.

"Maybe so, but I'm not the one swapping spit in your sister's house with your entire family milling around. You should be thankful it was me who found you and not your grandpa. He's looking for any excuse he can get to find out Levi's intentions."

"His intentions?" I ask at the same time Levi says, "My intentions?"

"Sure, sure, intentions. You should have heard him when he cornered Dean one afternoon at Brian's. The poor man was red for two hours."

"My intentions are pure," Levi says, tightening his hand around my waist. "Well, mostly," he adds. I glance up just in time to see his wink at the little ol' lady behind me.

"I knew I liked you for a reason," Grandma coos behind me, adding to the humiliation. "Well, that, and that ass you could bounce quarters off of."

Before I can even formulate a reply, she's gone, leaving us alone.

"Come on, Levi. We've got bedroom furniture to move," Ryan says as he walks in the front door and gives me a smile. I haven't missed the fact that strong arms are still wrapped around my body.

"Gotta get back to work," he whispers against my ear before sliding his hand up my arm and to my cheek. In a move I've come to expect, he gently slides a strand of hair behind my ear. His lips peck my lips, soft and sweetly.

"Awwww." Turning slowly, I find four of my sisters standing in the doorway, big cheesy grins on their faces.

"Let's get to work," I mumble as I pull myself away from Levi's warmth. I blush horribly while he throws me another wink and turns to follow Ryan down the hallway to my sister's bedroom.

"Come on," I tell the girls. "Let's get back to work."

Chapter Eighteen

Levi

I'm sweaty and hot and could definitely use a cold shower, but that still doesn't stop me from reaching over for Abby's hand as we head home from Dean and Payton's place. She gives me one of those shy grins that I've come to love the shit out of. Just one glance at it makes my heart start beating crazy-fast in my chest.

It's a scary feeling, but I don't let myself freak out over it. Not now. Not when sitting beside her, with her hand in my own, feels so fucking right.

And I ran from this? Hell yes, I did. This feelings shit is big-time scary, but I'm not going to let it pull me down. There's no room for doubts anymore. It's like standing on the diving board. I've already committed to the jump, so there's only one thing left to do: jump. And that's what this is. A big leap of faith and trust, but if I'm going to step out of my comfort zone and into the relationship zone, then I'd only want to find Abby on the other side.

She's my calm. My solace.

It's a short drive to our building, so before too long, I'm pulling into the parking lot. She waits until I can come around and help her down from the passenger seat, something that I've come to love in light of recent events. Her body molds to mine as I help her, the scent of vanilla and a bit of sweat hitting my senses like a freight train.

Abby gives me another grin, her green eyes shining as the day turns to night. Taking her hand again, we head towards the front door of our building. Another couple from our floor is coming out, and after exchanging a few pleasantries, we're heading towards the stairwell.

She has her key out before we hit the landing for the third floor. I follow at a very close distance, craving that nearness. When the door is open, she turns, those emeralds sparkling up at me like diamonds caught in the sun.

"I have to work next weekend, but we have a gig at The Beaver Friday night. Go?" I ask, stepping forward and running my hands up her bare arms. I'm rewarded with a shiver.

"Oh, um…" she hem and haws around, the wheels in her gorgeous head spinning faster than a hamster wheel. "I don't know."

"What's wrong?"

"Nothing," she insists quickly. Too quickly.

"Why don't you want to go?"

She looks to be sputtering to find the right words, and eventually just stops trying. Abby stares at me, wordlessly.

"Confession time." I know she'd never lie to me during a confession. It's part of the pact.

She closes her eyes for a moment, and I start to wonder if she's going to speak. It only takes a few seconds before her eyes open and she's staring straight at me. "Okay, so you know I've kinda had a crush on you for longer than a few weeks, and well, it was too hard watching you go home with other girls after your shows. That's why I haven't gone much lately." Her eyes divert from my face, but there's no way to miss the look of hurt etched in those eyes.

"I haven't done that in a year," I tell her honestly.

Irritated. Oh, my little firecracker is definitely looking at me like she wants to bite. And yeah, I might like it, but I don't want her to do it because she's pissed at me. "You're not supposed to lie during a confession. It's against the rules," she reminds me.

"I would never lie to you. I haven't."

"I saw that girl slipping out of your apartment a few weeks ago, Levi."

Think, Levi, fucking think!

Then it hits me.

Jessa.

"Oh, no! That was Dexter's sister. He ended up hooking up with Crystal when I wouldn't so I gave her my spare bed for the night so she wasn't scarred for the rest of her life, listening to her brother have sex."

Relief seems to transform her face as she relaxes a bit. "Oh."

Stepping forward, I rest one hand on her shoulder and use the other to stroke her cheek. "Confession time," I say. "I haven't been with a woman in about a year because I've been hung up on my best friend."

She seems completely fucking surprised by my confession, and we can't have that now, can we? "You didn't know? I'm sure I've done a shitty job hiding it."

"I didn't know," she confesses sweetly.

"You don't have to go Friday night. I don't want you to feel uncomfortable, but I need you to know that I'll be going home solo. You don't have to worry about that."

"You want me to go?" she asks.

"Fuck yes," I tell her. "I love it when you're there, and besides last month, I haven't seen you there in a while."

She nibbles down on that lush bottom lip, making me want to suck on it. And I will; I just need her answer first.

"Okay, I'll go," she whispers, giving me a warm smile.

"Will you go with me? It doesn't take too long to set up and tear down. But I'll understand if you don't want to be there that long. It can be a long night," I say, pulling her against my body and wrapping my arms around her waist.

"Sure."

Hell yes. I've got big plans for my girl Friday night. Big plans that involve good music and hopefully very little clothes. I wouldn't sleep with her last night because it was our first date, but all bets are off on Friday. If the offer is there, I'm taking it.

And taking her.

As I bid her good night, I can't help but smile as images start to parade through my mind. One with her and me and nothing but the sheets. I wonder if I'm being too presumptuous with how I picture the night ending, but then I recall the fire in her eyes and the bite of her nails as she held me close, grinding that sweet body against mine. She wants me just as bad as I want her. I feel it.

Oh, yes. It's happening Friday night.

* * *

My computer lights up, the app taunting me with a new notification. I've been home only long enough to jump in the shower and rinse off before firing up the laptop and grabbing a beer. I shed the towel, not a stranger to walking around naked. I just learned the hard way to make sure the front door is locked when I do. Dexter and Andy walked in on me one night, and even though it didn't bother me as much, they say that some things are better left unseen.

Apparently, neither of them has ever seen a dick piercing.

After the initial shock wore off, we played a riveting game of twenty questions, all focused on my cock. It was...educational. In fact, I'm pretty sure by the end of it Dexter was heading to get his done. No, I don't know for sure since I don't make a habit of questioning my friends about their genitals.

Sitting down on the couch with my beer and laptop, I pull up the dating site. I decline all of the other messages and connection requests and click on the one message I'm expecting. We've talked a lot over the last couple of weeks via this stupid site. No, she still doesn't know it's me, but I promise to tell her soon.

Bringing up the message, I instantly smile.

AngelEyes: *I think I have a second date lined up already.*

SimpleMan: *Yeah? That's great news. I think I'm in the same boat.*

The bubbles appear, so I sit back and wait for her reply. I can picture her now, in her office, sitting at her desk and nervously biting on that luscious lower lip of hers until it's bright pink and plump. That's the exact spot I want to suck into my mouth until she's moaning my name.

AngelEyes: *Is it weird that we're on a dating site and talking about dating other people?*

SimpleMan: *No way. We're both here because we want to find our someone, right? Well, part of that is meeting new friends and giving them encouragement.*

AngelEyes: *I guess you're right. Tell me about your date?*

Well, shit. It's not like I can tell her where I went on my "date." That'll blow my cover, and quite possibly my friendship.

SimpleMan: *Dinner and then we hung out.*

True. Vague. That'll work.

AngelEyes: *Nice.*

SimpleMan: *What about yours?*

AngelEyes: *Dinner and he took me to my favorite place in the whole world.*

SimpleMan: *Paris?*

AngelEyes: *No *smiley* He took me to the bookstore.*

SimpleMan: *Wow, sounds like the guy really wanted to score points with ya! Did you get a goodnight kiss?*

AngelEyes: *I don't kiss and tell. *winky face**

SimpleMan: *Well, that pretty much tells me you did. If it weren't for the beating around the bush, the smirky wink emoji would've given it away.*

AngelEyes: *Not telling. What about you? Did you kiss her?*

SimpleMan: *What, you don't kiss and tell, but I have to?*

AngelEyes: *You don't have to. I was just curious.*

SimpleMan: *Well, I will tell you that it was the best kiss of my life. Hands down. *inserts flaming emoji**

AngelEyes: *Yay! Good for you.*

SimpleMan: *And I don't get anything?*

AngelEyes: *Didn't I tell you last night it was the best date ever?*

SimpleMan: *Kiss, Angel. I need deets about that kiss.*

AngelEyes: *Life. Altering.*

I throw my fists in the air like I just won the fucking Super Bowl. And in a way, I did. Never have I been complimented more than in the direct messages I've had with Abby in the last twenty-four hours. And believe me, I've had a lot of compliments. But I couldn't tell you what one was. This one? I'll remember Abby's words for the rest of my life.

We sign off an hour later, promising to be in touch later in the week. It didn't even occur to me in that time that I'm still butt-ass naked. Shutting down my laptop, I head to my room and climb into bed. My dick was starting to throb like some perv as I pictured her on the other end of that Internet conversation, so it's no surprise to me that I'm unable to squash the fantasy of her getting up from her computer and going to bed. Naked.

My cock is in my hand moments later, jizz seeping from the tip and providing my own lube. It's a quick finish, one I'd normally be embarrassed about. But not when it's Abby I'm fantasizing about.

When sleep finally claims me, it's with a smile on my face and her on my mind.

Chapter Nineteen

Abby

He's been on stage, rocking it hard, for the last three hours. His eyes continually seeking me out, offering me the biggest of smiles with each look. They take a fifteen-minute break each hour, and he keeps coming back to the side-stage where I've been watching the show, anxious to spend a few uninterrupted minutes with me.

No, uninterrupted isn't the right word. Because we are definitely interrupted. Fans–and by that I mean girls–flock to him like he's covered in honey and they're bees. He pays them no attention, though. It baffles me because Levi has always received, and eaten up, attention from those in possession of a vagina, like it was candy. He never met a woman he couldn't charm, that's for sure. But tonight, I don't see any of this flirty banter, his sexy winks, or his wicked smile that makes the panties just slide off.

He only has eyes for me.

At the beginning of the fourth and final set, Levi steps up to the mic. The crowd goes wild. Girls are out of their mind, screaming and fighting their way to the front of the small stage in the garden of The Beaver. I keep myself as far away from the crowd as possible. I've never been a fan of big groups of people–especially horny, crazy girls who are trying to gain Levi's attention.

I'm happily stationed beside the stage, out of the way, while nursing a Sprite, when I hear my name. I hear it loudly. When I realize it's coming from the microphone, I glance up on stage and see Levi's hazel eyes focused on me. In fact, I see a lot of eyes focused on me. Oh, God. So many eyes.

"Come on, pokey. Get up front. If I'm gonna sing your song, I want to see you sing the words with me," he says with that gorgeous smile that seems to steal my air.

I don't move, hoping he'll leave me in peace in my dark, hidden nook, away from the action. "Don't make me come back there, Abs. If I have to come and get you, I'll have the crowd chant your name." His smirk disarms me, making me offer a smile in return. The crazy thing is I know he's dead serious.

Slowly I get up and walk towards the corner of the stage. When the cluster of staring, drunk women refuse to move an inch, I head towards the back, away from the screaming horndogs up front. Turning around, I risk a glance up to the stage and find those same eyes following me.

"I love this song," Levi tells the crowd. Again, the women practically orgasm right there in the grassy courtyard. "I love it because it's my best girl's favorite song." The noise level reaches an ungodly pitch, making me cringe. You'd think he just professed his undying love to each one of them. "This one's for Abby."

And then he starts strumming his guitar, and sings the first line.

I'm hypnotized as he starts the Jeff Healey tune. The crowd starts to sway to the music, but my eyes are riveted to the man on stage. He's larger than life when he's up there, his guitar in his hands and a mic in front of his face. I know he doesn't usually like to sing, but has one of those voices that's deep and husky. He pretty much makes ovaries burst every time he opens his mouth.

I sing along with each line, each word, our eyes locked from opposite sides of the garden.

When he finishes, I find myself holding my breath, waiting. And then he does it. He points and offers me the most perfect, panty-wetting smile I've ever seen. My heart beats wildly in my chest, a beat that's alive and fierce.

"You guys are so sweet. I'd never be able to only be friends with a man like him," a girl says beside me, sipping her fruity drink. She looks like she's barely eighteen, let alone old enough to be in the bar. The girl's wearing barely-there clothes and too much makeup that makes her look like she just stepped off the street corner. Instead of acknowledging her comment, I give her a small smile and return my eyes to the stage. Levi has already moved back, ready to finish up their show by playing guitar.

"I mean, there must be some reason he doesn't want to sleep with you, right? He sleeps with everyone, from what I've heard. In fact, I'm hoping to catch up with him later after the show. You should try to show more skin and wear makeup. Guys don't want girls who dress like they're heading to the library every day," she says, not taking her eyes off my best friend, her predatory smile shining only for him. She keeps talking, but I have no clue what she says.

My heart stops beating and my vision blurs as I stare at my out-of-my-comfort-zone orange toenail polish. Her words keep repeating over and over again in my head, vocalizing my biggest concern and fear. What's wrong with me?

I pretty much gave him an open invitation to sex me up after our date, but he turned me down. He said I was too good for first date sex, but what if it was more? What if he just can't bring himself to sleep with me? I mean, I know he woke up that morning with a massive hard-on, but don't they always do that? It probably wasn't me at all, but just a common reaction to waking up and breathing.

I'm not sure how the rest of the show goes. My mind reels, replaying every moment and every conversation we've had over the last three weeks. Keeping back in the shadows, I wonder for the ten thousandth time if I'm making the biggest mistake of my life trying to explore this attraction I have for Levi. The man can have anyone he wants. Why would he want me?

"Because you're gorgeous and caring and real and everything I never knew I wanted from you."

Shocked by the words I hear, I slowly turn and find Levi's eyes blazing with an intensity that I rarely see. He's always so fun and laidback, rarely getting worked up. Now, his eyes are alive with a fierceness that causes my heartbeat to quicken and if I'm being completely honest, a little turned on.

"What?"

"Why would you ask that?"

"Ask what?" It's a lame question, but I can't help but try to stall a bit as I try to figure out how he knew what I was thinking. Unless, those thoughts weren't in my head...

Taking a step forward until our bodies are so close, he reaches up and grabs a strand of my hair. It slides effortlessly through his fingers as his eyes bore into me with such passion. "Why are you doubting that I would want you?"

Shrugging my shoulders, I drop my eyes back down to my toes, suddenly embarrassed by my insecurities.

"You listen and listen good, Abigail. I've never met a more beautiful woman, inside and out. I can honestly say I'm a better person just by being near you. If you want to know why I would want you, and my words still aren't enough, then I guess I'm just going to have to show you," he says moments before his lips claim mine.

The kiss is…yeah. Amazing. Consuming. Amazing. (Worth saying twice.) Levi urges my mouth open with his, possessing and dominating me with his killer lips and wicked tongue. Our mouths mold together like sex, deep and hard, giving and taking. We breathe each other in as our wild hands roam over each other's bodies.

He's sweaty from being on the small stage, his shirt molding to his muscular body as if it were made specifically for him. My core throbs with a reckless desire I've never felt before. Gripping his t-shirt at his back, I grind my body, shamelessly, against his hard front. I'm rewarded with a groan that I swallow, because I refuse to remove my lips from his.

Before I realize what's happening, I'm moving. Well, we're moving. My lips tingle, my breathing erratic, and my legs wobbly. I can feel eyes on me as Levi leads me through the garden, where groups of people are milling around, and straight out the gate that leads to the parking lot.

When we reach his truck, he presses me against the cool metal and takes my face in his. "Do you feel it?" he asks, breathing hard against my face.

"I feel something," I quip, rubbing my hip against his impressive erection.

He doesn't reply right away, but the corner of his mouth still tips upward. "That's funny. Do you feel the heat we create? Do you feel how crazy my heart is beating in my chest just by being around you? How I can't think straight or keep my hands to myself? Do you feel my eyes on you when you're in the room? My God, Abs, do you feel how much I want you?"

There's only one answer to all of his questions. "Yes," I whisper, nodding my head. "I feel it. All of it."

"Thank fuck," he says just before devouring my lips once again. They're swollen and quivering with each second that passes. Unfortunately, the kiss ends too soon. "Come on," he growls, practically yanking the passenger door off the truck like some Hulk moment. And I'll be honest…it's fucking hot. Yes, I said fucking. It's okay to say it when you've just been kissed the way I have been.

Levi practically tosses me up into the truck like a rag doll. "Buckle up." His voice is raw and edgy, like he's a millimeter away from reaching his breaking point. A part of me wants to give him a gentle shove, see what he's like when he loses control.

We're both silent on the ride back to our building. My hand is firmly gripped in his, and every time I glance over, I can see the hardness in his jaw, the subtle tick of his mouth. He looks tense, irritated, but I'm sure he's not.

He must feel my eyes on him because he quickly turns over and looks at me. My body ignites all over again as he directs that fierceness on me. He scans my face, my eyes, and then drops down to where very minimal cleavage is showing with my blue top. His eyes continue to roam downward to where my shorts meet bare leg. I made sure to shave tonight and added lots of yummy scented lotion. My legs reflect the moonlight and it isn't until he growls again and I feel his hand tighten around mine that I realize just how hot it is inside the truck cab.

"What about your stuff?" I whisper, my voice almost unrecognizable.

"One of the guys will pack it up for me," he answers, glancing back up at the road.

"Oh. Do they do that often for you?" He glances back over again and studies my face with a critical eye, but he doesn't answer my question.

Levi whips into the parking lot, practically on two wheels, and finds the first available parking spot. Actually, he takes two spots because he's definitely not between the yellow lines. He's out of the truck as if it was on fire and stalks around to the passenger side. I tense, wondering what exactly I said to make him seem so upset.

When the door is open and my seat belt is removed from my body, I'm pulled gently from the truck and wrapped in his arms. He's practically panting against my face as he runs his nose against the shell of my ear. "No," he rumbles.

"No?" I gasp as he takes my ear lobe into his mouth and bites.

"No, I've never done that before. I've never needed to be with someone so bad that I leave my guitar and my equipment behind for one of the guys to take care of. I've never run out of a gig, ignoring my responsibilities, because I was so fucking desperate to be with a woman that I felt like I was going to die if I didn't have her. You. You make me so fucking nuts that I can't think straight, can't even see what's around me. You are all I see, all I want, and all I fucking need."

A gasp slips from my mouth moments before he claims it with his own. His kiss is feral, and every instinct I have takes over. I wrap my arms around him, grinding my body against his, craving more and more of his touch. Levi lifts me in the air and pins me against his truck, my legs instantly wrapping around his waist. The hardness of his erection presses firmly into my aching core, my body alive and yearning for more.

For the second time tonight, we're moving before I can even comprehend the effort. I'm still wrapped around him like a jungle cat, his lips furiously taking everything I have, as he steers us towards our building. Thank goodness it's dark outside; I'm sure we're a sight to be seen.

My back bumps into the building and my hip catches the handle on the door, causing me to jolt against Levi. Our mouths pull apart as we gape at each other, all labored breathing and wild eyes. "Maybe we should wait until I get you upstairs," he says flexing his fingers on my butt, and for the first time I realize where his hands are actually located.

"Maybe you should hurry. I hear firefighters have great stamina when it comes to stairs," I jibe, tightening my legs around his body even more.

"Oh, Abs, you have no idea how good my stamina is," he retorts with a side smile.

Inside, the fluorescent hallway lights shine brightly and I can easily see his hair wild from my eager hands. He starts to take the stairs–two at a time, mind you– and I start to giggle as I bounce against him. Levi holds on tightly as he runs up three floors, never once straining or showing any sign of fatigue.

"Wow, you do have great stamina," I whisper against his ear, smiling as he growls deeply.

Levi doesn't slow down until he's standing in front of his door, his key magically appearing in his hand. "I want you in my bed." It's not a question, but a statement.

"Yes." That single word comes out a pant, laced with anticipation and impatience.

The door is barely closed before I'm pressed against it. His lips find mine again, willingly and effortlessly. Levi pushes his tongue into my mouth, stroking mine, rekindling that burn I've felt since he kissed me at The Beaver. My fingers slide through his hair, grabbing hold and tugging slightly.

"Fuck, I've wanted this for so long. So fucking long, Abs. I thought I could never have it, could never have you."

Our eyes are locked as I tell him, "You have me."

"You're sure? Because once I have you tonight, I don't think I'll be able to let you go."

Swallowing over the massive lump in my throat, I whisper, "Then don't let me go."

His eyes burn brightly as he slowly walks towards his bedroom. I've been in here before but never like this. Never about to strip down naked and join him in the middle of that bed.

My God, I'm about to strip down naked and join him in bed.

Levi. I'm going to get naked with Levi.

My best friend.

Chapter Twenty

Levi

She looks a bit freaked out, but it's not in actual fear. No, my Abby has nothing to be scared about when it comes to me. I'd never do anything to hurt her.

My knees hit my bed, stopping me in place. "You're sure?"

Her eyes are the brightest green I've ever seen, even dilated and wide. "So sure." I can see her excitement mixed with nerves reflecting in those hypnotic orbs.

Slowly, I lie her down on my bed, covering her body with my own. Honestly, I need to take a step back and collect my damn thoughts. If I don't, I'm liable to embarrass the shit out of myself and lose it in my pants. She has me all kinds of torn up here, ready to explode from wanting her so badly.

Needing to turn it down a notch, I take her lips with mine as my hand wanders to the hem of her top. Gently, I slide the material upward, exposing the warm, creamy skin of her abdomen. When my hand reaches the silky material of her bra, I move my hand around to the side, cupping one perfect tit in my big hand.

You'd think I'd never touched a damn boob before. My cock starts to spasm in my pants, jumping and flexing, begging for attention. I tear myself away from her lips, just long enough to get her shirt up and over her head. There's no finesse to the way I strip her top off, and as much as I try to calm down, I can't seem to do it. I'm too worked up, too excited to be with her.

Using my hand, I slowly slide it down her shoulder, along her arm. Abby shudders against me. Her eyes close, her mouth opens as she pants, and she arches off the bed the closer I get to her tits.

Keeping my eyes locked on hers, I slide my hand inside her bra, feeling her hard nipple press against my palm. "So soft and smooth," I groan, rubbing her nipple with the tip of my finger. Her answering moan lights up my world.

My hand moves downward, heading towards the button of her shorts. Her legs are still wrapped around me, my body nestled perfectly in the V between them. As much as it pains me, I maneuver myself so that I'm beside her, giving myself plenty of room to work with. My eyes return to hers as I flip the button through the hole. The bite of the zipper lowering echoes through the room, mixing with our labored breathing.

I keep my eyes on hers as I remove her shorts. Even with my heart beating like a freight train in my chest, she calms me. Well, calms me until I look down and see the sliver of blue satin between her legs. Wet satin. Closing my eyes briefly, I say a prayer, thanking the good Lord for this gift he has bestowed upon me.

With her shorts out of the way, I'm finally able to feast my eyes on Abby. Yeah, I've slept in the same bed with her (platonically), and yeah, I've seen her in a killer bikini a bunch of times, but this? Seeing her in her blue bra and panties is like all of my fantasies coming to life.

"My God, you're so fucking beautiful." My voice is raspy and low as my hand skims up her smooth thigh. Even in the darkened room, I can see the blush creep up her face.

"Abby, this is a time where I need complete disclosure from you, okay? I want to know what you like and what you want. You need to tell me, all right?"

She nods her head, her eyes wide with anticipation.

"I'm going to take off your bra and panties, okay?" Again, she nods. "Words, Abs, I need to hear you say it."

"Yes," she says, nodding at the same time.

I give her a smile–she's so fucking cute–then get to work removing her bra. My fingers have a slight tremble to them as I reach behind her and unhook the piece of material containing her tits. When they're free, I practically swallow my tongue. We're talking the blue ribbon, gold metal of all tits.

The next part has my cock dripping in anticipation. Grabbing the sides of her panties, I gently slide them down her legs. Tossing them over my shoulder, I'm transfixed at the sight before me. She's splayed out on my bed, naked and panting. There's a small patch of dark curls above her pussy, and my mouth waters just thinking about one little taste.

"I need to put my mouth on you, Abs." She nods frantically, her eyes begging. Sliding my hands up her thighs and parting her legs, I lean in close. "I've been dying to taste you. I've been thinking of it all night."

"Me too," she pants.

"You want me to fuck you with my mouth?"

Her gasp is loud, but so is the moan that follows. "Ye...yes. Please."

Keeping my eyes locked on hers, I lean the rest of the way forward until my tongue can swipe across her swollen flesh. Her

207

scent wraps around me like a blanket, her sweet little body drawing me in even more. Using only my tongue, I lick her from the top of her clit to her sweet little pussy. I'm rewarded with another groan.

Not wanting to waste any more time, I suck her clit into my mouth and run a single finger through the wetness. Her pussy is so fucking tight as I slide in the finger, curling it upward. "Oh," she groans, writhing against my bed, thrashing her head from side to side.

I pick up the pace, sliding a second finger inside her warm body. Latching onto her clit, I suck hard until she's screaming my name out in orgasm. Her body clinches around my fingers, pulling me in farther. Fuck, I wish it were my cock.

When the last bit of her release is pulled from her body, I back up, gazing up at the woman before me. She's sated with her eyes closed, and I'd think she'd fallen asleep if it weren't for the smile on her face.

"I've always wanted someone to do that," she whispers.

"What?" I ask, confused. Is she telling me no one has ever gone down on her before? For fucking real?

"Huh?" she asks, gazing up at me with cloudy eyes.

"What did you say?"

"I didn't say anything."

Crawling up her body so that I'm stretched out beside her, my head resting on my hand, I say, "You did. You said you've always wanted someone to do that. Was that your first time?"

Embarrassment creeps up her neck and reddens her face. "I…well, it's not my first time to have…you know…but it might have been my first time someone did…that."

Instantly hating every fucking clown she's ever dated, I cup her cheek with my hand and lean in for a kiss. "That's a fucking shame."

"Colton, he, umm, never wanted to. The one time I asked him to, he said it was gross."

"Fuck," I breathe harshly, closing my eyes. I'd give anything to knock the shit out of that douche right about now. "Baby, *that* was amazing. Watching you come by my mouth, my fingers, has me so fucking turned on, I'm afraid I'll embarrass myself if I don't get inside you soon."

"Really?" her voice eager and hopeful.

"Hell yeah. I'd do it again if it weren't so imperative to my health that I feel that tight pussy wrap around my cock." Her eyes flare to life, excitement reflecting brightly in those sexy green eyes.

"I'd let you do it again," she whispers, averting her eyes coyly.

"And I will do it again. But not now." I slide on top of her, loving the way her body feels against mine. I'm still dressed, which must be remedied immediately.

Standing up, I quickly lose my shirt. My boots and socks are next, very hastily followed by my pants. I should fucking shower, but I'm not wasting one more second to make her mine. I've already told her this much, but now I make it official. Now, I claim my best friend as my own.

I slip my boxer briefs down my legs and a loud gasp rings out. Glancing up, Abby's eyes are focused on my cock. It's large and jutting straight from my body. The head is an angry shade of purple from all the teasing and foreplay. But that's not what she's staring at.

"What's that?" she whispers.

"That's an Apadravya."

"You have your…it pierced?"

"Yeah. Got it done a few years ago. Hurt like hell and took about six months to heal."

She's blatantly gawking at my cock, studying with openness and curiosity. "Can I touch it?"

"There's nothing I'd love more, but I'm afraid I'm a little too wound tight, Abs."

"Please," she begs softly, her eyes returning to mine. And I know in that moment, I couldn't deny her anything.

Giving her a slight nod, she moves to a sitting position and crawls to the end of the bed. She's checking it out with a critical eye, her hand hovering just below my dick. "Can I?" Again, I give her a shaky nod.

I steel myself for what's to come next, but wasn't even remotely close to being prepared for Abby's touch. Her fingers are gentle and tentative, as if she's afraid my cock might bite her. Oh, and it might, just not in a bad way.

"Wow, that's pretty hot," she whispers absently, and I wonder if she actually meant to say it aloud.

Her warm hand wraps around me and I almost come out of my skin. I start to count backwards from one hundred, praying that I'll be able to control the lust slamming into my body with her slightest touch. Shit, at this point, I have to remind myself to breathe.

Gazing down, I'm in awe at how beautiful she looks. Sure, she's staring at my dick like it's a fudge pop, but there's something that resembles wonderment in her eyes. Her fingers gently slide along the head until she reaches the ball on the underside.

Breathe, Levi. Just breathe.

Her fingers continue to touch the piercing, the hypersensitive head about to explode off my body. She wraps her other hand around the base of my cock, gently squeezing as she toys with the ball on top of the head.

One hundred, ninety-nine, ninety-eight...

"I want to lick it." Those hypnotizing eyes clash with mine, and I swear mine about bug out of my head. Is she serious? She's not just a fantasy anymore; she's fucking everything.

"As much as I'd love that, sweetheart, you do that and it'll be game over for me," I say as I help her stand up. "Later," I add, taking her lips with my own. "You can touch and lick as much as you want later. But first, I need to have you. All of you."

Laying her back on my bed, I place tender kisses down her neck, over her collarbones, and down to those glorious tits. Her legs wrap around my waist, lining us up perfectly. Before I say fuck it and slide home, I reach over to my nightstand and grab a condom.

"How does that work?" she asks shyly.

"Very carefully. I just have to be careful not to rip a hole in it." Ripping open the packet, I spread the rubber wide open over my expansive head and gently roll it down into place.

Sliding back over top of her, I position myself at her pussy. She's still soaked, my sensitive head sliding effortlessly through the wetness. "Are you sure?" I ask one last time, needing to know this is what she wants.

"I'm sure. Though I'm not sure it'll fit. You're a little…ummm, bigger than the others." Her face bursts into flames, and I practically growl as jealousy slams into my gut. I know she's been with other douchebags, but the thought makes me see red. Someone else touched my Abby. *My Abby!*

Looking for a redirect, I bring my mind back to the task at hand. She's with me now, and that's what I need to focus on. "I promise it'll fit. It's going to feel amazing. We'll go slow, okay?" She nods in reply before wrapping her arms around my neck.

She looks tense so I make sure to go slow as I gently push inside of her. Just an inch and I can already feel the death grip her pussy has on me. Keeping my eyes focused completely on hers, I slide in just a little more, the two little balls of my piercing sliding easily along her walls. Jesus, she's so damn tight.

"Relax, sweetheart," I whisper against her ear.

Needing to pull her attention away from the size of my cock, I nibble on her ear before raining open-mouthed kisses down her neck. Her skin tastes fucking fantastic, and before I realize it, I'm seated all the way inside her.

"Oh God," she groans, arching up into my body, hers taking every millimeter of my dick.

Shitdamnfuck!

One hundred, ninety-nine, ninety-eight…

"Please don't stop," she whispers as I pull almost completely out, making sure to keep the apa against her internal walls.

"Never, Abby. I'm pretty sure I'm never gonna want to stop fucking you," I answer before slamming into her with a little more force. I'm rewarded with another moan, her muscles tightening around me once more.

My hands go to hers, gripping them tightly above her head. My body starts to move on its own, sliding almost out of her pussy and slamming back inside. With each thrust, her eyes become wilder, her body climbing higher and higher.

"When you come, Abby, I want my name to be the only word spilling from your gorgeous mouth," I tell her as I slam back home, angling my hips so that I hit that magical sweet spot deep in her pussy.

Her eyes are cloudy but bright as I continue to piston my hips. When her orgasm starts, I feel it all the way down to my toes. She grips my dick so tight, my eyes cross. At this point, holding out any longer isn't possible and I slam into her hard, chasing my own release. The piercing slides against her tight walls, sending a flood of sensation straight to my balls. My spine tingles and I can't hold off any longer.

"Levi," she chants over and over again, her flushed face shining, her perfect mouth forming the most brilliant little O.

Slamming into her one last time, I let loose a year's worth of sexual tension with a roar as I come and come inside my best friend. My Abby.

Unable to hold myself up, my arms finally give out as fatigue sets in. I roll to my back, pulling her with me, craving her skin against mine. She moves easily, her body completely pliant and sated. My dick is still twitching inside of her, bringing a smile to my face.

"Can we do that again?" she asks, smiling against my chest.

A laugh rumbles from my chest. I can't help it; I pull her in tight, nestling her even closer than before. "You're gonna have to give me a few minutes, sweetheart. I might need some time to recoup after that."

"Feels to me like you're already ready to go," she says, wiggling against my still-erect dick. I'm pretty sure I'm dealing with a twenty-four seven hard-on at this point. Now that my cock has gotten a taste of her sweetness, he's going to be eager and ready to go all the damn time now.

"You trying to kill me?" I ask, maneuvering her until she's straddling me. Damn, she looks phenomenal sitting on top of me.

"I just wanted to see if that Apa-thing is as good the second time as it was the first," she says coyly, her face flushing once more.

Gripping her hips, I hold on as she kneels above me, my cock falling from the comfort of her body. I almost groan in protest. But then she's reaching into my nightstand and realization sets in. I remove the used condom, knotting the end and placing it in the garbage. I watch helplessly as she removes the rubber from the package and stretches it over the head of my dick. She does it expertly, as if she's covered my erection a million times before.

Returning to her position above me, she takes a hold of my length, lines herself up, and slides home. Our collective groans fill the night when I'm completely seated within her. It feels just as fucking amazing as it did the first go-around. But then she starts to move. And holy shit, does she move. Who am I to deny her this research?

"I think it's starting to feel just as good as the first time," she gasps as she drops down hard.

Groaning, all I can do is grip her hips and hold on tight. "Go ahead. Be my guest."

* * *

I'm pulled from a deep sleep and reach for Abby, but find only cold sheets. My mind clears instantly with realization that she's not in bed with me anymore. After getting busy a second time, we both passed out, exhausted and very well sexed. But now? She's not here, and for fear of sounding like a girl, it kinda bothers me.

But then I hear the music.

And not just any music, but a guitar.

Getting up, I grab my boxer briefs and slide them on before heading out to find the green eyed, brunette who's the source of the music. I already know where she is, so it only takes me a moment to walk across the hall and find her in my guest room. The sight of her sitting on the twin-sized bed, wearing my black t-shirt causes all of my blood to rush to one concentrated place.

I stand in the doorway, watching her strum my favorite instrument. The song she's playing takes shape, one that I've heard a thousand times before on the radio, but never heard her play.

I taught her to play a few years ago after she returned from college. Abby was a natural, picking it up easily. She's actually very musically inclined. She can play guitar, but can also sing. Her voice is angelic as she starts at the refrain and sings, even if she won't share it with the world because she's too shy.

I'm so lost in thought, the sweet words to the Enrique Iglesias song running through my mind, that I don't realize right away that she stopped. When I glance up, her eyes are locked on mine. I can't help but smile.

"Did I wake you?" she asks turning and resting the guitar on her leg.

"Nope. Whatcha doing?" I ask, joining her on the bed. Situating myself so that she's between my legs, I reach around and reposition the guitar on her lap.

"I couldn't sleep so I thought I'd play for a few moments. I hope that's okay."

"Of course it is," I tell her, leaning down and placing a kiss on her bare neck. "You can play my stuff anytime you want; you know that."

Reaching around her, I strum the guitar, starting the opening rift to my favorite song. It's the first song I learned how to play. Well, besides Row, Row, Row Your Boat, but I don't tell anyone that shit.

We sit in silence for a few lines of the song, neither of us moving. Well, she can't exactly move considering she's holding my guitar and my arms are wrapped around her while I play.

"This song reminds me of that dating app." She whispers the words so softly that I'm not sure she intended to say them out loud. The hairs on the back of my neck stand up.

"Oh?" I hedge, continuing to play, but very softly.

Turning her head, green eyes clash with mine. I can tell right away, she's torn between telling me about SimpleMan and not.

Abby clears her throat before continuing. "Yeah, there's a guy that I met on there. His name is SimpleMan. Says it's his favorite song."

"You're telling me about talking to another man? While sitting naked under my shirt? Should I be jealous?" I quip with a slight smile so she knows I'm just teasing.

"No, it's not like that. We've just talked."

"Talked, huh?"

"Yeah, talked. He's kinda like…well, he's like you. He's a friend."

This would be the perfect lead-in to telling her that I am SimpleMan, but my mouth doesn't move. At least, it doesn't move in the way it should. Leaning forward and nuzzling her hair with my nose, I rest my lips against her bare skin. Calmness settles within me, my heart slowing down to a natural beat.

"Hopefully not completely like me," I say before trailing open-mouthed kisses down the side of her neck, to her shoulder blade that's peeking out from my shirt. Her gasp is the only words I need.

No, I don't confess the things I should, but I will. I'll tell Abby that I'm SimpleMan, along with my reasons why, but I can't do it when she's distracting me with my favorite instrument and her nakedness. We've played together before, but never this intimately. Never have my arms been wrapped around her so tightly, her tits, though covered with my shirt, pressed against my Gibson. Never has my cock been so freely able to press into her ass, ready to go another round or two.

"Seeing you play my Gibson while wearing my shirt is sexy as fuck."

"Yeah?" she pants, gripping the guitar with white knuckles.

"Hell yeah," I tell her, pulling the shirt down to bare more of that smooth, creamy flesh. "The only thing that would make this better is if the shirt would suddenly evaporate into thin air." My tongue trails a line from her shoulder blade to the bumps of her spine.

Sensing where I'm going with this, Abby gently lifts the instrument off her lap, careful with her hair so the strap doesn't get caught. When it's safely set aside, I crawl around her, pushing the shirt up and over her head as I lay her back on the bed. She's gloriously naked again, my new favorite way to see her.

"Mmmm," I mumble as I nudge her legs apart with my own and get nice and close to the Promised Land. My dick is weeping tears of joy as it thumps heavily down on her lower stomach.

"I don't have a condom with me," I tell her, chastising myself for not being prepared. I was a fucking boy scout, dammit. We're always prepared.

"It's okay. You don't need one. I...I trust you," she confesses, her sweet words striking my soul with the weight of a thousand elephants.

"I trust you too," I reassure her. "I wasn't kidding when I said I hadn't been with anyone in a year. We get tested every year at the hospital for work. I'm clean."

"Me too. It's been...a while for me."

I cover her body with my own, reveling in the feel of her soft skin completely against mine. I know in this moment that things have changed. I'll never look at her without seeing the look of pure lust in her eyes. I'll never be able to hear her voice without recalling what it was like to hear her say my name as she came on my cock. I'll never again feel as alive as I do when she's in my arms.

My Abby.

Chapter Twenty-One

Abby

Levi covers my body with his own, the coarseness of the hair on his legs tickling my overly sensitive skin. My heart is pounding in my chest, I'm sure the neighbors can hear it.

"You're sure? I don't want to look a gift horse in the mouth, but I want to make sure you're really okay with this," he says softly, running his hand along my jaw and pushing a strand of hair behind my ear.

God, I love it when he does that.

"I'm sure. There's no one I trust in this world more than you," I confirm. His eyes smile down on me moments before his lips claim mine. And holy cow, do they claim. Each kiss is more possessive, more dominating than the one before.

Wrapping my legs tightly around his waist, I feel the pierced head of his erection press against my wetness. A gasp slips out from the onslaught of sensations it creates. Not to mention the fact that I haven't gotten this much action even in the few weeks' worth of dating Colton.

Without saying a word, I feel him flex his hips and slide into my body, stretching me just as much as he did the previous two times before. I try to relax, to allow my body to adjust to his incredible size, but that piercing moves against the walls of my girly parts and causes my body to go haywire. Whoever said those things heighten the feelings during sex definitely knew what they were talking about.

Our eyes remain locked as he reaches for the guitar leaning against the side of the bed. Taking the instrument in his hand, he places it above my head, never once faltering in his hip movements.

Yeah, he's that talented.

"Reach up," he tells me, gently thrusting into me. Placing my hands above my head, he sets the neck of his favorite guitar in my hands. "Grab it." And of course, I do. "Don't let go," he adds before giving me a wicked smile.

Then he starts to move. He's slow but deliberate, precise each time he fills me, completely. I'm hypnotized by the way his eyes watch me. He scans my face, his eyes lingering on my eyes, before falling slowly down to where we're joined together. The way his hazel orbs flare with heat as he watches causes me to flex and tighten around him. My grip on the guitar turns white-knuckle taut as I gaze down and see what he's watching.

When his eyes return to mine, they're soft and full of unspoken emotions that remind me of something deep and heartfelt. I'm sure it's just the sex that has that look on his face, but I can't help but wonder if that look means more than the typical friendship vibes I usually get from him.

"Damn, that's fucking sexy," he says, flexing his hips expertly, his eyes locked on where I grip his guitar. His hands trace my arms from my shoulders all the way up to my hands. When he gets there, he wraps his hands around mine and holds me tight.

Words that I shouldn't say spill to the tip of my tongue, threatening to let fly everything that I'm feeling. We crossed over the friendship line and are toying with a relationship, but this? This is so much more than just caring for someone.

I'm falling in love with him.

Hell, I've always been in love with him. Way before I even knew what love was, I've felt a connection to Levi. What started off as friendship, early in our youth, has slowly blossomed into full-on love. I know it; I feel it.

I just don't know what to do with it.

I can't risk saying it and scaring him off for good. Levi's skittish about this whole relationship thing in the first place, but to throw labels and titles and big words like love around? That's suicide for us. So, I bite my tongue and hold in the words I long to say and just revel in the way he makes me feel.

Levi's piercing hits my G-spot, and I practically see stars. I've heard all about this mythical, magical place, but never experienced it firsthand. With Levi, he's shown me over and over again that it really does exist. And right now, the small barbell of his apa piercing is rubbing me in all the right ways.

I feel myself clenching around him as I get closer and closer to an orgasm. I'm lost in a sea of wonderment when he bends down, whispers words of how gorgeous I am in my ear and plays with my nipple with one hand. His other hand remains locked on my hands, holding on to me as if he doesn't ever want to let go.

"Only my name," he whispers, flexing his hips and rotating them in this delicious way that makes me see stars.

"Levi," I whisper just to see how his face lights up again.

I'm rewarded with a small smile and a deeper thrust. Words evade me as I climb higher, my body tightening around him, taut like a guide wire. Panting, I explode, my eyes glued on his as I detonate like a bomb. He holds his breath as he watches me come, but continues to move inside me. His jaw tightens, his mouth a thin line, yet he continues to watch. Euphoria fills me completely as he finally lets go, releasing himself inside of me with a grunt and the whisper of my name.

He collapses, his weight pinning me to the mattress. His skin is hot and sweaty and sticking to me, but I don't mind. My entire body is dead weight, even if he wasn't on top of me. Smiling against his shoulder, I give him gentle kisses. Unfortunately, my own shoulders start to burn, and it's then that I realize my arms are still pinned above my head by one hand.

Wiggling my hands to gain blood flow, Levi lifts his head and glances up. "Oh, shit. Sorry," he says sheepishly before letting go of my hands and moving the guitar to the side. Taking my hands in his own, he shakes my arms and moves my fingers, placing a kiss on the end of each of my ten digits.

As exhaustion starts to settle in, I find myself cocooned in the security of his arms. He pulls me snuggly into his chest, my legs tucked between his. I'm wrapped in comfort as my eyelids droop and eventually close. Levi's hold on me never relaxes, even as he starts to drift off to sleep.

My last conscious thought is not how amazing this feels–and wow, does it feel pretty spectacular–but how will I ever go back to sleeping solo after this.

* * *

Sisters' night isn't going the way we planned. It's not a good day for Meghan, as tomorrow would have been Josh's birthday. She tried to cancel our plans, but we're a lot more tenacious than to allow her to sit at home alone, drowning in her tears and wallowing in her misery. This is the first special occasion without him, and his birthday nonetheless.

Meghan's trying to be strong, but the tears just keep coming. That's why we're at her house instead of doing one of the other activities we had planned for tonight. Payton ordered pizza with all of our favorite toppings, Jaime brought six different quarts of ice cream, and AJ and Lexi brought booze. Lots of booze. And me? Well, before Levi went to work, he made me a batch of his famous spinach dip with fresh, warm bread.

"You guys should go out and have fun. This isn't what these nights are for," Meghan says between sniffles. She's sandwiched on the couch between AJ and Payton, each of them taking turns filling up her plate or her glass when either starts to empty.

"No, these nights are for whatever we need, and tonight, we need this. I'd rather be here with you, holding you while you hurt, than getting drunk in a bar and failing at playing putt-putt golf," Lexi adds from her seat beside me.

"Agreed," we all say in unison.

"Someone tell me something good. I need to hear something that'll make me smile," she whispers, her desperate green eyes bouncing from one sister to the next.

"Okay, so Brielle might have started to call me…Mom last week," Payton says, her eyes alive with happiness.

"What?" we all ask at the same time.

"That's amazing," I tell her.

"It is. She asked Dean if he thought I would be okay with it. Dean told her the only way to know for sure was to ask me. It took all of the strength I had not to cry when she asked. Her voice was so strong and steady, and I'm pretty sure she held her breath when she waited for my answer. Of course, there was only one answer to give her, and before we were done talking, she called me Mom; you know, just to try it out." Payton, our oldest, fearless sister, has tears swimming in her eyes and leaking down her cheek. Funny that it took a five-year-old girl to bring her to her knees.

"That's beautiful. You're going to be an amazing mother to that little girl," Lexi whispers, tears in her own eyes.

"Well, ummm...I might have found a receipt in Ryan's work pants this morning. A receipt from Casberry's," Jaime tells us.

"Casberry's Jewelry?" I holler way too loudly. (Bad, alcohol. Bad.)

"No, Casberry's Egg Farm," Jaime retorts with a look. "Yes, of course, Casberry's Jewelry."

"Well, maybe he bought you some great earrings to go with the necklace he got you for Christmas," AJ says, levelheadedly.

"In August? My birthday was months ago. If he were going to get me them, wouldn't he have done it already?"

"It's totally an engagement ring," Meghan whispers beside Payton. "He looks at you as if you hung the moon and the stars. That kinda love? Well, it's once in a lifetime." Her face falls slightly and tears fill her green eyes, but she offers her a small smile. "Believe me, I know. What you have with Ryan is what I had. He loves you so much that he'd crawl to the end of the earth just to make you smile."

The lump in my throat feels suffocating.

"Payton," Meg says, turning towards our oldest sister as the tears start to fall. "You'll be next, I know it. Dean knows exactly what kinda amazing woman he has with you. Not only do you love him unconditionally, but his daughter too." Tears brim Payton's eyes before slowly sliding down her cheek.

"And you," she says, turning her attention to me.

"Me?" I ask, my throat clogged with so much emotion. "Don't give up on Levi. I know you keep saying you're just friends, but I'm here to tell you you're not. He loves you, even if he doesn't know how to say it or show it."

"Actually..." I start, not quite sure if this is the right time to tell them, but unable to keep it to myself any longer. "Levi and I, well, we've sort of been...seeing each other."

"Of course you have," Meg says, giving all of my sisters a real smile.

"And you two. Your happy ending is coming too." Meg stares straight at Lexi and AJ.

Lexi diverts her eyes, trying to hide her pain. But I see it, and I can't help but wonder if she's any closer to reaching a decision about leaving Chris. Last time she was at my place, she was seriously considering it, and I know when she's ready, she'll make the right choice.

AJ snorts and rolls her eyes. "Not me. I'm pretty sure I'm going to be single forever. The last guy I slept with was so bad I fell asleep, Meggy."

"You fell asleep?" I ask, recalling how boring sex had been with Colton years ago. But Levi? There's no way I could even comprehend how someone could fall asleep when you have someone like Levi delivering the best orgasms of your life.

"Yeah, Dexter definitely isn't all he's cracked up to be," she snorts, rolling her eyes.

"Dexter? Levi's drummer Dexter?"

AJ looks a little sheepish and a whole lot mortified, but she confirms, "Yeah. He was awful." Suddenly, we're all laughing, and laughing hard.

When the laughter dies, we all look around at each other, drinks in hand and tears drying in our eyelashes.

"You'll find it again, Meggy. You have the most beautiful heart of all of us, and you're destined to love. I know it's hard to think about it now, but you'll find your happiness again." Payton's words cause that lump in my throat to swell in size.

"My love died in a car accident six months ago, Pay. I honestly can't even imagine feeling that kind of love again. And that's okay. No one will ever measure up to Josh," she whispers, closing her eyes as memories of her lost love plague her mind.

"You don't have to think about that now, Meg," I say, getting up and crouching before her. "Someday, you'll find someone who'll consider himself the luckiest man in the world because he gets to love you. It might not be now and it might not be easy, but I believe with all my heart that you'll have your happily ever after." Glancing around at my sisters, I add, "We all will."

The next thing I know, I'm surrounded by five pairs of arms as we shed tears and hold each other in only the way sisters can do. We comfort each other in our times of sorrow and celebrate when the time calls for rejoicing. We're a mixture of happy and sad, but that's the way life goes.

"I love you," I whisper to no one in particular.

"Love you too," they all repeat one after the other.

We embrace each other for several minutes, wiping our tears of joy and grief. When we're left with nothing but smiles and sniffles, Lexi turns to Jaime and says, "You realize Grandma's going to want to plan your bachelorette party, right?"

Again, we all burst into giggles, each of us smiling so big it hurts. After a few moments, the laughter dies down and Meghan turns to me. "I kinda want to hear all about Levi and Abby."

My face burns with a brutal flush, but their eager and hopeful eyes encourage me to speak. "Let's just say, it was so hot, it felt like my body was touching the sun," I start to a chorus of girly giggles.

"And then he grabbed his guitar…"

* * *

The fogginess in my head keeps me from glancing at my alarm clock, but seeing the sunlight filter through the cracks of my eyelids, I can tell it must be mid-morning. My head throbs with the aftermath of a night in with my sisters. I know I drank more than normal, but the conversations were a tad heavier than our usual sisters' nights.

Dean delivered me to my building somewhere around one this morning, helping me into my apartment before securing the lock and heading out to take his girlfriend home. They were probably doing dirty things to each other before they even got out of my parking lot. That's what happens when you're in love and can't keep your hands off each other.

I never really saw that with Lexi and Chris, but I can justify that with being away at school when they were deciding to move in together immediately after high school. And Meg and Josh were a little less PDA and a lot more cutesy hand holding and kissing discretely in their coupledom. Understandably, I never really saw the appeal of wanting someone so bad that you'd risk a public indecency charge just to give road-head.

But now? With Levi? The thought of driving down the road and needing to taste him, bring him to the point of explosion just because we can't wait another five minutes to get safely home, definitely holds some appeal. In fact, I might want to try the whole blowjob thing on our next outing.

Needing to cross my legs to ebb the desire I suddenly feel, I'm startled when my leg encounters a much hairier one. Before I can scream out for help (you know, because there's an ax murderer snuggling me in my bed right now), I'm pulled into strong arms and a muscular bare chest. Familiarity slides down my spine, sending all of my senses on high alert.

And then his scent hits me. He smells like woodsy soap and mint toothpaste, and my already overly sensitive body is suddenly aching with need. My hands slide up his bare chest, caressing each abdominal muscle that God graced him with. He tenses beneath my touch, but relaxes just as quickly, as if he knows who's touching him, even in sleep.

His eyes are closed, a peaceful look etched on his gorgeous face. His sandy blond hair is askew from sleep or going to bed with wet hair. My fingers itch to slide through those soft locks.

Levi must sense my wakeful eye, and slowly cracks open his own. I'm rewarded with a soft smile and the happiest hazel eyes on the planet. "Hey," he mumbles, pulling me into his arms.

"How'd you get in here?" I ask, sleepily, as he draws me deeper into his embrace.

"The spare key I made you give me so I had it if you ever forgot yours," he mumbles, running his nose along the shell of my ear.

"Oh. That's convenient."

"Mmmhmmm. Is it okay that I'm here? I didn't like the idea of sleeping in my bed alone."

Well, if that doesn't set my heart a flutterin'.

"Yes. I like that you're here," I tell him, his arms wrapping even tighter around my abdomen.

"Did you have a good night with your sisters?" he asks quietly, closing his eyes once more.

"Yeah. What time did you get here?" I ask, unable to keep myself from touching him any longer. My hand goes to his hair and there's no missing the way his eyes flutter dreamily when I toy with his shaggy locks.

"Got off at six. Showered at my place, but I couldn't sleep. Crawled over here about seven."

Glancing over his shoulder, the clock on the wall reads eight-thirty. "Go back to sleep. We can talk more later."

"Stay with me here?" he asks, pulling me even closer into his body until I'm not sure where I end and he begins.

"Always," I whisper, continuing to play with his hair until he drifts off to sleep.

Then, like some crazy high school stalker, I watch him sleep, taking in every flutter of his eyelids and movement of his uber sexy mouth. A few times he whispers, but I can't understand what he says. Before I can stop myself from going there, I wonder if he's dreaming about me. Lord knows I've had plenty of nights where I dreamed of him.

After another thirty minutes, my bladder can't take it any longer, and it's very necessary that I get up. It's almost physically painful to slip out of his arms and scoot undetected out of bed. He reaches for me, even in deep sleep, but doesn't wake up. It's easy to get lost in watching him; well, until I realize I'm about to pee my pants.

I take care of business in the bathroom and brush my teeth before heading into the kitchen. I'm surprised when I reach the coffee pot, mostly because I didn't prepare it before bed last night—or this morning. Whatever. There's only one person who could have done it, and that thought causes those butterflies to take flight in my stomach and warmth to spread through my body.

Smiling, I start the coffee maker and throw a slice of bread in the toaster. There's a small pile of mail on the counter, and after tossing away all of the junk, I have three new bills to pay. My toast pops up, slightly on the burnt side to Levi's dismay, and I grab a jar of homemade apple butter. Levi and I made a bunch last fall after someone brought in several buckets of fresh apples from their tree, into the hospital. The result was a dozen jars of cinnamony apple butter that goes perfectly on an English muffin or toast.

I make a mental note to check into getting more apples, since I'm halfway through my last jar.

Instead of heading into my room to watch Levi sleep like a completely hopeless loser, I grab my coffee and toast and head into my office. I finish off my toast while my computer fires up, and before long, I'm staring at my desktop. Emails await me, this I'm sure, but it's the dating site app that I find my mouse hovering over. Two clicks later, and the site pops up on my screen.

Ignoring the new "matches" the system has chosen for me, I bring up the message screen. Not surprising, I find one from SimpleMan. Instantly, I recall Friday night when Levi started to play the song, his arms wrapped around me. Funny that they have the same song, right? I mean most people when they have their pick of any Skynyrd song either pick "Sweet Home Alabama" or "Freebird."

Clicking on his message, I smile.

SimpleMan: *It's early in the morning and I'm just heading to bed. Hope you have an amazing day, Angel.*

Just going to bed?

The message was sent at 6:56am.

I wonder what kind of job SimpleMan has? When we were getting to know each other, he said something about public service but he's never really said what that is. Maybe he has a job like Levi's where he works odd hours.

Weird, right?

Shaking off the strange feeling settling into my gut, I type out a reply.

AngelEyes: *Just heading to bed? What do you do exactly? My day will consist of laundry, lunch with my family, and maybe dinner with a friend. Sleep well, Simple.*

Uneasiness stirs in my stomach causing my coffee to not settle well. Heck, that could be from the drinking last night too. Shutting down the app, I bring up my email. After scanning through and deleting the junk, I send two replies to my boss regarding my current project before logging off completely and heading towards the living room.

Unable to stop myself, I gawk openly at the man sleeping in my bed. I still have this odd feeling that I can't shake as he softly snores against my spare pillow. Why, I'm not sure, but something tells me I'm missing something. Something big–and not in the good way.

I just wish I could pinpoint what.

Chapter Twenty-Two

Levi

It's midafternoon when I finally pull myself from the deep coma I was in. Work was fucking brutal last night with several minor accidents, one fatality involving a truck, and even a few water incidents, thanks to the overload of tourists still trying to get the most out of what's left of their summer vacation.

My head is fuzzy but I can tell instantly where I am. This bed is softer than the one I normally sleep in and carries the scent of a certain woman who gives me more boners than a Penthouse magazine.

And speaking of boners…

In typical guy fashion, I scratch my nuts and gaze around the room, searching for the woman who might be able to help me with my little problem. She left the curtains closed and a glass of water on the nightstand. The apartment is quiet; the only sound is the gentle hum of the air conditioning and the ticking of the clock on the wall, which tells me she's not back yet from lunch with her family.

Grabbing the glass of water and chugging half of it before hopping up, I head to the bathroom on a mission. Even in here, I'm assaulted with a rich vanilla scent that reminds me solely of her. Smiling, I grab her toothbrush and paste and scrub the grossness off my teeth. It doesn't even weird me out that I'm using her brush.

The kitchen is clean and tidy, the coffee pot already washed and sitting in the drying rack. I take the glass pot and fill it halfway with water before dumping it in the maker. It's something I've done a million times for her, but for some reason, it feels a little more domesticated now.

There are a few bills stacked up on the counter right next to the place I imagine bending her over and sliding between those luscious ass cheeks. In fact, it was around three o'clock this morning when that naughty little image entered my dirty brain, rendering me completely bone-ified for the next hour. Do you know how hard it is to drive around in an ambulance with another dude when you're sportin' wood? Hard. Wood. Get it?

Anyway, I've been fighting a raging boner since the early hours of the morning, and there's only one woman who can satisfy my craving. Snuggling against her this morning was killer, but I was too exhausted to do anything about it. Now, don't get me wrong, if my girl had wanted a little early morning nookie, I'd have risen to the challenge. But since she was still out cold, I took the opportunity to cuddle in close and pass the hell out.

Her fridge is kinda bare, except a couple of chicken breasts and some veggies she picked up for dinner tonight. I love to grill and I can't wait to show her a thing or two with those breasts. (The chicken's, not hers.)

Digging in the fridge, I find that apple butter she loves and some fruit. I'm sure she has something in the cabinet to throw in the toaster. I just need a little something to tide me over until dinner since I missed lunch with her family.

I hear the key in the lock and the door start to open before I can pull my face out of the refrigerator. "Glad you're back. I've got a little problem that only you can take care of," I quip, smiling at myself, as I think about spreading her out over the counter.

"I'm pretty sure, whatever that problem is, I am the last person you want to assist you." Turning to face the door, I'm statue-still, mostly naked, and staring straight at Abby's father, Brian.

"Shit," I whisper harshly.

"Yeah," he says, averting his eyes. Apparently, I'm not the only one who realized I'm standing in a pair of boxer briefs with a raging hard-on in his daughter's kitchen. That pretty much squashes my boner and any future erections I may have for a while.

"Uh, excuse me, sir. Let me grab some...pants." Hightailing it to Abby's room, I find the shorts I was wearing when I slipped across the hall around seven this morning and top it with my wadded up, wrinkly tee.

I don't embarrass easily, but this might not be one of my proudest moments. Realizing that I just propositioned my girl's father for some afternoon dick-play isn't one of my finer moments, that's for sure.

Hanging my head, I make my way back to the front room and find Brian standing pretty much in the same spot I left him in. "Abby forgot her sweater," he says, setting the white short-sleeved little top on the counter.

"Yeah, she always complains about getting cold in the diner," I add, scratching the back of my neck.

"She does."

Awkward silence descends, making this officially the worst impression I could possibly make on a parent of the girl I'm seeing. "So, I bet you're wondering what I'm doing here. In Abby's place and not my own," I stammer like an idiot.

"Not really," he says, making my eyes jump up to his. "Come on, Levi, you and Abby are the only two who haven't realized that there's more than friendship building between the two of you. Sure, it started that way, but you've been slowly dancing around it for a long time."

Unable to speak, I just nod.

"Abby met you when she needed you most. Her mom had just died and our family was a mess." His eyes shine with tears, but he keeps them locked on mine. "It was brutal raising six girls between seventeen and nine, alone. They needed their mom more than anything. Shit, do you know how many nights I begged for the Lord to take me and spare her?" He casts his eyes downward, probably so I won't see the tears fall, but when he returns them to me, I know that's not the case. He's not afraid to cry in front of me. He's lost in the memory and pain of losing his wife.

"If I can butt into your business for a few moments, it'd be to say this: If you love my daughter, don't let her go. Show her every day how much she means to you because if you're not paying attention, it could be taken away from you in the blink of an eye. I lost my love to cancer, Meghan lost hers in a car accident. Those events were going to happen whether we wanted them to or not. What is important is how much we loved while they were alive.

"I'm not saying Abby's gonna be taken from you or anything like that. My point is *love* her. For a day, a year, a lifetime, just love her as long as you can. And when the time is right, tell her. Don't be afraid to say those words because there is nothing greater than the feeling you get when she says it back. By God, son, show her because my little girl deserves the moon and the damn stars. Are you the one to show her?"

Swallowing is difficult, but somehow I get the word out. "Yes."

Brian smiles at me, a real, genuine smile. "Good. I always thought you were. Even when she dragged home a gangly little ten-year-old boy with skinned up knees and crooked teeth, I knew you were the one," he says, rendering me speechless all over again.

"You know, Levi, I've always thought of you as the son I never had. Trish and I tried and tried again, but it just wasn't in the cards. You were at our house more than anyone else, and I'm damn proud of the man you've become."

Jesus, he's going to fucking make me cry like a baby.

"Thank you, sir."

"I know things just got real heavy for us, and I apologize. I didn't come over here to ambush you or anything. Hell, I didn't even expect you, but the opportunity presented itself. My little girl is an amazing woman and I want to make sure the man she loves is worthy. You're worthy, Levi, if you take the chance and follow your heart."

"Love? Abby loves me?" My eyes search his for any sign that he's pulling my leg, but all I see is sincerity and understanding.

Smiling, he says, "Of course she does, son. She's always loved you."

We're quiet for a few minutes, both lost in our own thoughts. He wasn't kidding when he said it got heavy, but it's what I needed to hear. I knew I was falling for her, but until he put it all in perspective, I didn't realize how much she really meant to me. I love her. Fuck, I've been in love with her for years.

"I never thought I'd say this, but do you have any idea how happy I am that it was you who caught me half naked in Abby's kitchen and not Orval and Emma?"

Brian laughs. "Well, I'm not so sure any father wants to find someone in his underwear in his little girl's kitchen, but I see what you're saying. Did I ever tell you about the first time they caught me with Trish?"

Shaking my head, he smiles again, grabs a beer from the fridge for himself and a water for me, and sits down across from me at the table. "We were on our fourth date, I think, when things got a little hot and heavy in my ol' truck. You know how it is," he adds with a sheepish grin. "I never intended for it to go as far as it did, but when you're young and dumb, sometimes things happen. We were parked on the back of her property, about a hundred yards from the house. There were trees between us and I thought, for sure, there was no way they could see my truck from the house.

"Anyway, afterwards, we were barely dressed when there was a knock on the driver's side window."

"Oh shit," I say, fighting the urge to laugh.

"Yeah, not exactly the impression I wanted to make on her parents. Orval just stared at me with this stern look, and Emma started in on Trish. Asked her why she hadn't saved herself for marriage like she did. Then Orval just looked at her and said, 'What are you talking about, woman? You didn't save yourself for marriage. We barely made it through our first date before I had you naked.'"

I can't help it, I die laughing.

"Yeah, poor Trish was mortified, afraid I was gonna run for the hills. And maybe I should have, but I might have fallen in love a

239

bit with those two ol' kooks that night. Emma had just looked at Orval and said, 'Oh, yeah. Never mind.' And then asked if we needed more rubbers."

I guess now we know that kinda thing runs in the family, huh? Poor Jaime and Ryan didn't stand a chance. I can't believe the same thing happened to her parents thirty-five years prior. That's probably why Orval and Emma like telling that story so much about having to bail them out of jail following the cops finding them parked along a field; it reminds them of the time they busted Brian and Trisha.

Sitting with Brian, I find myself listening to story after story, each one better than the last. I can't help but wonder if I've ever smiled as much as I have in the last thirty minutes listening to Abby's dad share moments from his past.

This is just the kinda crazy family I've always seen myself being a part of.

Chapter Twenty-Three

Abby

Before I can insert my key into the lock, I hear laughing coming from my apartment. Giving the knob a turn, I find it unlocked, but I'm more surprised to find my dad sitting at the kitchen table with Levi. My dad is drinking a beer, while Levi takes a sip from a half-empty bottle of water.

"Dad?" I ask, stepping inside and setting my purse on the counter.

"Hey, honey. I just stopped by earlier to drop off your sweater. You left it at the café," he says, standing up to give me a kiss on the cheek.

"Oh."

"And your dad was just telling me about when he was dating your mom," Levi says with a laugh. "Your grandparents were a hoot way back then."

"Well, they were definitely something," my dad replies with another grin. They both stare at each other for a few moments, and I can practically see the private conversation pass between the two of them. I look around, wondering if I stepped into some wacky alternate universe that looks like my apartment, but it's inhabited with aliens. That's the only way to describe the weirdness going on right now.

"Anyway, I should go. I'm sure you two have plans before Levi heads to work."

"You can stay," I stutter, meeting him at the door.

"I have an early flight in the morning. I thought I'd drop by Meggy's and see how she's doing before heading home." The sadness in his eyes is evident.

Meghan attended the family luncheon, but definitely wasn't herself. She was quiet and forlorn and barely cracked a smile, even when our grandparents started their perverse antics over dumpling soup. And why would she be? Today would have been Josh's twenty-eighth birthday.

"Okay, Dad. Give her my love."

"I will, sweetie. Enjoy your evening," he says, placing a kiss on my forehead. Then he turns back to Levi, who's standing beside the table. "Good to see you again, son. We missed you at lunch," Dad says, extending his hand to Levi.

"I'll be there next time," Levi replies. My head volleys back and forth as they continue to talk as if they're long lost buddies.

Dad bids us goodbye once more before slipping out of my apartment, reminding me to lock up.

"That was weird," I say, turning to face Levi.

"What?" he asks, stepping forward and pulling me into his arms.

"What were you guys talking about? I felt like I interrupted something." My hands wrap around his neck as my soft body collides with his much harder one.

"Guy talk, angel," he says before his lips claim mine. The kiss starts sweet, but the moment his tongue sweeps across the seam of my lips, it ignites into something more. My entire body starts to hum with anticipation and excitement. But it also feels like he's using the powers of his magical lips to distract me from something.

Pulling back, I gaze up at his lustful eyes. "Confession time," I whisper, sliding my thumb over his bottom lip.

Levi sighs. "Fine. He might have walked in here when I was wearing nothing but my skivvies, pulling something to eat from your fridge."

I blink once. Twice. "What?" I whisper, sure that I misheard.

"Don't fret about it. We talked. It's all good," he says, trying to continue the kiss we started.

"You talked? About what?"

Again, he sighs and takes a step back. "I might have said something about wanting to use you to alleviate my hard-on." I gasp. "I didn't know it was your dad!" he exclaims as my hands cover my mouth.

"And he didn't kill you?"

"Why would he kill me, angel? We talked and he knows how I feel about you," he says, covering my hands with his own and moving them from my face.

"How you feel?" I whisper, my heart hammering in my chest.

"Yeah, he understands that our friendship has grown into something more. He knows I'm crazy about you and enjoy spending time with you. He realizes that my feelings for you have developed into something bigger than anything I've felt before, and as scared as I might be, I really want to explore that with you."

Lacey Black

"You do?" Is that my voice? Why does it sound like I'm choking?

"I do. Do you know what you want? We don't have to put any labels on anything, but I'd be comfortable saying we're dating. Exclusively."

"Really?"

He smiles down at me. "Why does all this surprise you so much?"

"Well, you haven't exactly been a relationship kinda guy, Levi. In fact, I don't recall you ever having a one, let alone anything exclusive."

"You're right, this is all new to me. Turns out, I'm an Abby kinda guy and as long as I have you, I don't care about all of those labels and bullshit. I just want you," he whispers moments before reclaiming my lips.

This kiss isn't slow or sweet. This kiss is consuming and controlling. His tongue possesses, his lips dominate me. And that's not even including his hands. They slide firmly against my back, down until he's gripping my rear. In one smooth motion, he picks me up, my legs wrapping around his waist. I can feel his erection through his shorts as it presses against the place I ache for him.

"Trust me?" he rasps, kissing his way down my throat.

"Y-yes." I do.

"I want to take you from behind, beautiful," he says, setting me down and helping guide me until I'm facing the cabinets.

Then his hands are on me, gripping and touching me in a way that leaves me so hot and bothered, I'm afraid I might actually die from lust. My shorts and shirt are gone, my panties a distant memory as I brace my hands against the countertop. His very talented hands slide easily over my body until he finds me embarrassingly wet and swollen. I mean, we're talking water left on, I can feel it sliding down my thighs kinda wet.

"God, I love your body," he whispers harshly against my ear moments before I feel the slide of his piercing between my butt cheeks. Just the thought of him being so close to my *ain't gonna happen* area, especially with something as gigantic as his monstrous penis, should leave me clenching and tense. But it doesn't. The feel of that little ball slipping through the wetness and teasing my rear entrance causes my heart to race and my nipples to pebble more.

"Not today, angel. Maybe someday I'll claim that part of you too, but not today," he breathes against my ear as he slides into my trembling pussy.

"Oh God," I whisper, my body as taut and pulsing as a live electric wire.

I feel everything with him. The piercing, the way his body moves inside me, making me feel so full and complete. And then he wraps his hands around mine, entwining our fingers together, and places them back on the countertop. He uses them as leverage and starts to pump his hips, determined and full of raw desire. I cry out in euphoria every time those little balls slide against my G-spot.

Holy mother of God and all things almighty.

"I can feel you clenching around my cock, Abs. Feels so fucking good," he mumbles, pistoning his hips again and again.

My reply comes out a jumbled, mumbled, choppy sentence of sounds. I start to clench around him, squeezing the life out of his penis. (My vagina is such a hussy.) Before I realize it, I'm practically screaming out a release. Nope, no clue what words are actually coming from my mouth right now.

Levi's right behind me (no pun intended) and slams into me with enough force to almost send me crashing into the countertop. But he holds me hostage (in the best way possible), my name falling from his lips before he stills inside of me. I can feel him pulsing and coming, my inner walls milking him for all he's worth.

"Jesus," he groans, bringing his mouth to my shoulder and biting gently. The sharp sting causes me to shudder.

"Wow."

"Yeah," he says, kissing the place that he just marked with his teeth. "I'm just glad I was still able to get it up."

"What?" I ask with a small laugh, turning and looking over my shoulder at his flushed and slightly sweaty face.

"I'm just glad your dad's arrival didn't kill the fantasy." Again, he kisses my shoulder and the back of my neck, moving my hair across my other shoulder and exposing more skin as he goes.

"I'm glad too. It would have been a shame if we never got to experience that. In my kitchen."

"Your kitchen may be my new favorite place. It's a great kitchen."

"It is," I say, breathlessly, as he continues to kiss my neck, his hands wrapping around my abdomen. That's also when I notice he's still rock hard inside of me and moving very slowly.

"One more before I go to work? It's going to be a long, miserable night without you."

"What about dinner?" I ask diplomatically, but praying he doesn't stop.

"Dinner can wait, but having you one more time before work, can't."

And then he starts to move.

And administers no less than two more orgasms.

Chapter Twenty-Four

Levi

By the time I can steal more alone time with Abby, it's Thursday night. A bout with food poisoning at the ambulance headquarters took half the crew out of commission for three days. Thank fuck I'm not a fan of shrimp dip, otherwise I would have been praying to the porcelain God, screaming from both ends, like the rest of those sorry suckers.

I sent a quick text message this afternoon to Abs, letting her know we're going for Chinese tonight. I've been craving teriyaki chicken and fried rice like no one's business, and I figured this was the best way to kill two birds with one stone. Food *and* a little alone time with my girl.

Hopefully some naked time later too.

Even in my exhausted state, I can manage to get naked with Abby between the sheets. Or in the kitchen again. Maybe bent over the couch? Whatever.

I grab my computer and fire up the dating app. I've felt like the equivalent of dog shit all week while working, texting Abby one minute as Levi and messaging her through the dating site the next as SimpleMan. This shit has got to come to an end soon, or I'm liable to get myself caught in something I can't sweet talk my way out of.

The longer the guise goes on, the harder it's going to be to come clean. Yeah, yeah, I should have done it weeks ago when the opportunity kept presenting itself to me, but I'm a big fucking chicken, all right? I don't want to hurt her, nor piss her off, and I'm afraid I'd be doing both when I tell her.

See? Fucking chicken.

I hover the mouse over her picture, that one that gets my heart racing and my blood pumping to one concentrated area in my pants. And because I'm a glutton for punishment, I click on the image and bring up her newest message.

AngelEyes: *What's for dinner tonight?*

SimpleMan: *Chinese. I'm starving, angel.*

The bubbles appear and then disappear, as if she was typing but then stopped. I wait for several minutes, yawning loudly as I get comfortable on my couch, until I see another message pop up.

AngelEyes: *Busy day at work?*

SimpleMan: *The busiest. I'm exhausted.*

AngelEyes: *Maybe you should order in and crash early tonight?*

SimpleMan: *I would but I'm taking my girl to dinner. She's the best part of my day.*

AngelEyes: **smiley face* Good for you, Simple. I'm off to get ready for dinner.*

SimpleMan: *Bye, Angel. Have fun.*

AngelEyes: *Bye.*

Even if it's only four, my eyes are fighting to stay open. I've got two hours before I have to grab Abby and take her to dinner, so I set my laptop down on the coffee table and close my eyes. A two-hour nap is just what the doctor ordered.

* * *

When I open my eyes, it's because my phone chimed with an alert. Reaching blindly into my holster, I pull it out to find two text messages from Abby.

Abby: *Still on for tonight?*

Abby: *Everything okay?*

The first messages came at 6:10, while the second just moments ago. Shit! I'm late for picking up Abby for dinner. Jumping up, I fire off a quick reply as I head towards my bedroom. I've got just enough time to change my clothes quickly and brush my teeth.

Levi: *Overslept. Be there in a second.*

I'm out of my stinky work clothes and into clean shorts and a tee before you can snap your friends. Sure, I'd love to take a shower first, but I'm already late and don't want her to wait any longer than she already has.

Grabbing my phone and keys, I pay absolutely no attention to the rest of my place before flying out the door. I probably left all of my lights on, but I don't give a shit. My girl is waiting.

I don't even have to knock before the door opens; and there she is. She's wearing a light blue sundress that goes all the way to her ankles and cute as fuck silver sandals. My dick takes notice immediately.

"Hey," she says, holding the door open for me.

"Hey, sorry about that. I fell asleep on the couch."

"Long day?"

"Excruciating. Tons of calls and we're still short-staffed. I feel like I haven't slept in days."

"We can do this another night if you want."

"No way," I say, pulling her into my arms and kissing her lips. "I've been dreaming about taking you to dinner all week, and I'm craving Chinese like you wouldn't believe," I add with a laugh. She just gives me a funny look that makes me wonder if I have something in my teeth or on my face.

"Ready?" I ask, pulling the door open and waiting for her to exit. God, I love the way her hips sway and the soft material of that dress hugs her ass.

We make our way down the stairs and to my truck, her hand tucked firmly in my own. It's a short drive to the restaurant, but it doesn't stop me from touching her like it's an Olympic event and I'm battling for the gold. She's my happiness.

"Grandma stopped by this afternoon."

"Yeah? How are they?"

"Fine. She was just leaving the flower shop and decided to bring me poppies."

"Poppies?" I ask, glancing at her quickly before pulling into the parking lot for the restaurant.

"You don't want to know. Grandma insists they look like hairy vaginas but are good luck. So she delivered some to each of us girls apparently."

"Good luck for what?" I ask, jumping out of my truck and meeting her at the passenger door.

"Oh, I'm sure it's all BS. She says Grandpa loves poppies. I believe that's code for something and I'm too terrified to ask more questions for fear I'll need therapy when we're done. I just take them and smile."

Inside, the restaurant is dark and cozy. Even though it's a Thursday night, there are still several tables full. The hostess leads us to an empty booth, takes our drink order, and returns only moments later with two waters.

"This place always has great service," she says absently, taking a sip of her water.

Another server returns, this one a young female with short black hair and a wide smile. "Levi! So good to see you again," she coos.

"Uh, hi." I rack my brain, trying to figure out how I know her, but come up empty.

"Drinks?" she asks, glancing at Abby, the bright smile still plastered on her face.

"Coke for me," Abby responds, glancing my way with a curious look.

"Me too. And two orders of teriyaki chicken, an order of fried rice, vegetable lo mein noodles, and crab rangoons." Looking at Abby, I add, "Anything else?"

"Nope, that sounds good," she replies sweetly.

We make small talk while we enjoy the soup and the rangoons. She tells me about the new book she's editing, while I tell her an abbreviated version of some of the calls I've been on this week. When our meal is delivered, we dive in like we haven't seen food in days. I love that Abby's not afraid to eat real food. She'd take a big ol' cheeseburger over a healthy salad any day, and that's perfect for me.

When the plates are cleared, I reach over and take her hand. Her skin is soft and I can't help but touch it, even if I have to keep it PG in a family-friendly restaurant. "You're the best part of my day," I tell her as I kiss the tender skin right below her wrist. She tenses and pulls her hand away.

"What?" I ask, her green eyes searching mine.

She's silent for several long moments, and I can practically see the wheels in her head turning. "Confession time," she finally whispers.

"Okay, I confess that you really are the best part of my day. Even when I don't see you, I carry you here," I say, tapping my chest over my heart.

Her eyes cloud with tears, but she doesn't say anything. Not for two very long minutes where she scans my face, reading my thoughts, and seeing straight into my soul. "Are you on the dating site PerfectDate.com?" she finally asks, causing my heart to stop fucking beating in my chest.

"Why would I be on there?" I ask casually, tracing a line in her palm with my finger and diverting my eyes to watch the movement.

"I don't know. It's just something you said right now was exactly what my friend said earlier," she says. I feel her eyes burning into me. Jesus, I should tell her. I have the perfect opportunity to confess that I am SimpleMan, but I choose to keep quiet. I don't want to have this conversation in a restaurant full of diners. It's best to come clean in the privacy of one of our homes so that if she screams, yells, and throws things at me, it won't be with an audience.

So instead of answering her question truthfully, I lie. "Nope. Not me."

The words burn in my gut, eating a hole through my stomach lining. The food I just consumed threatens to make a reappearance. I've never lied to her, not like this, not to her face, and definitely not during a confession time. Yet, I can't seem to retract the words. My head is screaming deny, deny, deny, while my heart is shaking its head and telling me I've made a big mistake.

"Okay," she says, offering a small smile, just as our server delivers our check and fortune cookies.

"What the hell?" I ask, taking in the dozen or so cookies on our tray.

"Did you order extra?" Abby asks.

"Nope. Maybe that girl has the hots for me. She's trying to woo me by giving me extra fortune cookies," I say with a laugh, smiling that my comment earns one back from my girl.

"Here, pick one," I say, offering her the tray.

Abby takes one from the middle and cracks it open. She pulls out the slip of paper, a smile on her face, and reads. Then her smile drops. "Oh my God!" she exclaims.

"What?" I ask, reaching for her fortune. "*No glove, no love.* Holy shit, is that a sexual Chinese fortune cookie?" I ask, busting out in laughter.

"I think so," she mumbles, her face an adorable shade of fuchsia.

"Yours is probably better than mine," I say, grabbing a cookie and cracking it open. *"Cover your stump before you hump. Are you serious?* What kinda fortune cookies are these?" I ask through fits of laughter.

We both dive into the cookies, each one opening cookie after cookie.

"Wrap it before you tap it."

"If you want in the heat, better package your meat."

"A sword with armor will never harm her."

"Cover your vein, then drive her insane."

"Before you get spunky, cover your monkey."

Wait, this is my favorite," I say, unable to contain my laughter. *"If you're not going to sack it, then go home and whack it."*

"What kinda fortune cookies are these?" Abby asks, tears rolling down her face as she collects the dirty little fortunes.

"No clue, but I feel like we've been punked."

"Wait," she says, staring off over my shoulder. "Wait a minute," she adds before digging into the naughty fortunes. She must find the one she's looking for because she holds it up, victorious. "This one! Before you get spunky, cover your monkey. I've heard that before," she says, deep in thought. "Yes! Grandma said this one time to Ryan when he started to see Jaime. I'm almost sure of it because I recall how odd it was she called it a monkey during a Sunday lunch." Abby's face blushes, which makes me smile that much more.

"So you're telling me your grandma is behind these? Like Sex Ed 101."

"Oh God, of course! Why didn't I realize?" she says. "I remember her telling us she subbed for a health class back in the sixties. She talked about how she taught all of the boys to put on condoms using a banana."

"Your grandma was a teacher? Wow, I didn't see that coming."

"Actually, no one really knows what she did," Abby says. "She did a little bit of everything when we were young, and by the time she and Grandpa moved into our home to help raise us girls, she just stayed home."

Grabbing my wallet and throwing a few bills on the table for a tip, I say, "I can totally see your grandma schooling the young boys in a sex ed class."

"Ugh, so can I," Abby mumbles as she slides out of the booth and takes my hand.

I maneuver Abby as close to the middle of my truck as I can and still keep her safely tucked behind a seat belt. Her hand settles on my thigh, my heart in her other hand, figuratively speaking, as I steer us back home.

By the time we're almost home, my guilty conscious has me so worked up, I can barely think straight. Why in the hell did I have to lie? And to her face, at that! I'm the biggest fucking coward this side of the Atlantic, that's for sure. I'm a straight up asshole with a capital A, who doesn't deserve her love.

But I have to try to fix this.

As soon as we get back to her place, I'm telling her that I'm SimpleMan. I'll beg and plead with her to see what I did as an act of love. Because motherfucker, I love this woman more than life itself.

She's my world, fucking everything I didn't even know I wanted. And I refuse to go down without a fight. Sure, she's going to be pissed as hell, but I'll make her see. It came from a good place, a place that she may not see right away, but eventually will.

At least, I hope so.

My heart is hammering in my chest as we make our way out of my truck and towards the building. Our hands are joined as we head into the stairwell and walk up three flights of stairs. For some reason, my legs feel leaded, like a death row inmate making their way towards the electric chair.

What am I so worked up about? We're going to be fine. Sure, she'll probably be pissed off at me for a bit, but one day, we'll look back and laugh at this little hiccup in our relationship and share the details with our grandkids.

Grandkids.

That would insinuate having children. And marriage. And a life together.

Yep, I fucking want that, and I want it bad.

Who would have thought: me, Levi Morgan, proverbial bad boy and womanizer, would fall in love with the one woman who has been by his side since he was an ugly little ten-year-old.

But those thoughts don't scare me. No, it's the ones where I try to picture my life *without* her. Those are the images that scare the ever-loving shit out of me. Because in just a short amount of time, I've fallen head over heels in love with my best friend.

Fine, I'm a little late to the party.

You're right.

I've been in love with her before I realized it. Everyone else could see it, but not me. And maybe not her either. That's why I've got to convince her to forgive me for my little FUBAR and ride off into the fucking sunset with me.

Easy peasy.

Well, after I convince her to forgive me for deceiving and lying to her.

Shit.

When we reach her door, words are ready to fly from my mouth like some Indy Car tearing out of pit road, but she stops. She's heartbreakingly beautiful as she gazes up at me with so much trust and love in her eyes. I see it. Love. And I pray she sees the same thing reflecting in my own.

"Listen, I have some things to say to you," I tell her. Abby's face falls in that *holy shit, you're going to break up with me way*. I'm not too familiar with it since I'm not a big dater, but I've seen that look before.

Taking her hands in mine, I bring them up to my lips and place sweet, tender kisses to each of her ten knuckles. "It's not bad," I tell her reflectively, earning a smile in return.

Well, it's not all bad, I think to myself.

"Actually, I have something to tell you that I hope might make you happy."

I love you, I love you, I love you.

I fucked up. Please forgive me.

Just as I open my mouth, my fire pager goes off. The noise echoes in the empty hall, loud and piercing. "Shit," I mumble as I pull the clip from my belt.

"Attention Jupiter Bay Fire. All available units respond to a single level residential structure fire at 1221 Coastal Way Jupiter Bay."

"I have to go, angel. I'm sorry," I tell her, grabbing the sides of her face and kissing her soft lips as if my life depended on it. "Can I come over when I get home?"

"Yes," she whispers, her lips already swollen from my kisses.

"It might be kinda late."

"That's okay."

Placing a shorter, chaste kiss on her lips, I tell her, "I'll shower first and come over. Crawling into bed with you will give me something to hurry home to."

God, I'm such a sappy loser.

Don't care.

"Be safe," she says before kissing me one last time.

I'm moving through the hallway, shooting down the stairs before I even have a chance to look back and see her face one last time. Something pulls at my heart, telling me not to go. To go back and hold her in my arms one more time.

But I can't.

Lives could depend on my response right now, so as much as it pains me, I push thoughts of Abby and the confessions I was about to make out of my mind. I prepare myself to do my job, ready and willing.

Tonight, when I'm through, she'll be waiting. I'll climb into her bed and tell her exactly how I feel. I'll confess the love I've felt for her for what feels like a lifetime, and hopefully, God willing, she'll return the sentiment, and we'll start a new life together. One where I get to tell her every day that I love her, and show her even more. One with her in my arms where she belongs.

Anything else is unthinkable.

Chapter Twenty-Five

Abby

The apartment is so quiet.

Nothing has held my attention since arriving home from dinner with Levi. I turned the television off an hour ago, unable to get into the high-drama reality shows they're airing this evening. I sat down to work, but my mind just wasn't in it. I read the same sentence three times, and when I realized I still missed the misspelling of the word cable, I shut down the program and stared at the blank screen.

The dating app taunts me, so without giving it any further thought, I click on the icon. Instead of skipping over the usual requests I get to introduce myself to others on the site, I click on a few of the faces. Three new guys have liked me, giving me the perfect chance to connect. But I'm not interested.

If I was being honest with myself, I wasn't really interested when I started this whole hoopla. My heart and my head have always led me towards one man; one that I thought was unobtainable until recently. Levi seems determined to prove to me, and maybe himself too, that he's capable of sustaining a real relationship.

And he wants that with me.

I find myself back at my previous conversation with SimpleMan. He mentioned wanting Chinese food and Levi took me to Chinese food. That was just one of the few similarities I've discovered in the last week or so, but when I asked Levi about it outright–and during a confession time, no less–he denied knowing anything about it.

My gut still tells me something isn't right.

Another thirty minutes later and I've tossed and turned in bed, unable to get comfortable. The clock reads nearly ten, and I'm still wound tight. Finally, I jump up and head for the kitchen. Grabbing a bottle of water from the fridge, I glance through the peephole like a crazy ex-girlfriend and wonder if he's back yet.

Of course he's not back yet. He said he'd come over.

Unable to stop myself, I grab the spare key to Levi's apartment that he keeps here for the same reason he has one of mine. Maybe I'll just head over and wait for him to get home. I know he said he'd come to me after a shower, but wouldn't it be a nice surprise if he found me already in his bed, waiting? That sounds way better than sneaking over and sniffing his pillow, huh?

A wide smile crests my face as I slip across the hall and enter his place. There's a light on above the sink, but I still manage to smack my knee into his coffee table. It must be moved out further from the couch. Rubbing the tender flesh on my leg, I plop down on the couch, worried that I'll have to limp my way into his bedroom.

Levi's laptop is sitting on the table and the jarring of the table must have woken it up. It's bright in contrast to the darkened room, and after a few moments, my eyes adjust enough to focus on the screen. And not just any screen.

PerfectDate.com.

I'd know it anywhere, even if I didn't see my own profile name at the top of the message screen.

AngelEyes: *What's for dinner tonight?*

SimpleMan: *Chinese. I'm starving, angel.*

AngelEyes: *Busy day at work?*

SimpleMan: *The busiest. I'm exhausted.*

AngelEyes: *Maybe you should order in and crash early tonight?*

SimpleMan: *I would but I'm taking my girl to dinner. She's the best part of my day.*

AngelEyes: **winky* Good for you, Simple. I'm off to get ready for dinner.*

SimpleMan: *Bye, Angel. Have fun.*

AngelEyes: *Bye.*

I cry out, my hand covering my mouth as I read the screen a second, then a third time.

All this time.

Since the very beginning.

Levi is SimpleMan.

SimpleMan is Levi.

He lied to me.

The tears are falling before I can stop them. I feel them hit my hands as they hold the laptop, the wetness doing nothing to mask the numbness taking over my body.

I scroll up, gazing through tear-filled eyes at every conversation I've had with SimpleMan over the last month. When I reach the beginning, I click on his profile, bringing up the photo of the guitar. Now that I get a good look at it, I can tell it's his Gibson. His favorite.

Oh, Levi. What have you done?

Unable to control myself, I search his profile for any signs of his online activity. I'm shockingly surprised to not find anything else. No messages, no other connections, no meetings set. Just AngelEyes.

What does this mean?

Standing up, I set his computer back down on the coffee table. I may not know why he's done this, but I do know one thing as plain as the nose on my face: he lied to me. I specifically asked him this evening, after I noticed the similarities, if he was on this site. He said no. He said he wasn't, and I believed him.

I. Believed. Him.

Anger races recklessly through my entire body. Pacing back and forth, I contemplate my next move. I want to play him at his own game, just the way he played me. He toyed with me, making me believe there was something more between us. But there wasn't. There were games and lies and heartbreak.

My heart aches at the thought of losing him, but how can I remain friends with someone who would so easily toy with my emotions? I can't, that's for sure. Levi's not the person I thought he was, not by a long shot.

Grabbing my phone, I snap a picture of his laptop, our last conversation clearly visible in the photo. My heart hammers and my mind swirls as I glance down at the key still in my hand. With shaking hands, I set the key on the table, right next to the laptop. Then, I grab my phone and head towards the door.

Slowly, I gaze around the apartment I've spent almost as much time in as my own. The laughs, smiles, meals, and yes, arguments we shared as friends. Gone. They evaporate like puddles in July. Here one minute, gone the next.

Making sure the door is locked behind me, I give it a pull and close myself off from Levi for good. God, my heart hurts so bad. Wiping more tears from my face, I let myself into my own place and walk numbly into the living room. I don't allow myself to wallow in my misery just yet. No, when I fall apart, it isn't going to be here.

With quick resolve, I make my way to my room and pack a bag. I have no clue what I even throw in the old, worn suitcase, but I fill it with some of my belongings and head across the hall to my bathroom. I grab my toothbrush and hairbrush, choosing to leave my makeup behind. It's not like I'm going to feel like getting all dolled-up anytime soon anyway.

Before I head out, I make my way to my office. I send a quick message to my boss, taking tomorrow off as a personal day. Without checking the rest of the emails, I sign off and bring up the dating app. Grabbing my phone, I upload the photo of Levi's laptop and attach it to a new message. My words are short and sweet, and hopefully to the point.

Then, to make sure this mess never happens again, I deactivate my profile page and sign off for good. Swiping at more tears, I close down my entire computer and head towards the door. Without so much as a glance back, I'm out of my apartment and heading down the hall. As a sign of defiance, I press the call button for the elevator, and am pleasantly surprised it arrives just a few moments later. Like a man walking the plank, I step into the car and head down to the lobby.

With my bag tucked securely in my trunk, I slide inside the car that I used to love so much. Hell, so much used to give me joy, but now everything seems tainted. Everywhere I look, I see signs of Levi, and then I think of his deception. Now I'm probably going to have to sell my car, leave my apartment, and move to Guam just so I can get a little peace. Because if I know anything about my best friend, it's that he'll never give me a moment's amity–even subconsciously.

I pull my car from my parking spot and head towards the only place I can picture showing up so late at night. No, that's not true. Any one of my sisters would welcome me with open arms, even in the middle of the night.

More tears threaten to fall as I drive through the mostly deserted streets of Jupiter Bay, heading towards my childhood home. As I pull into the drive, the front porch light turns on even before I'm out of the car. When I reach my trunk, a warm hand wraps around my shoulder before reaching down to grab my luggage.

My dad wraps his big, strong arm around my shoulder and escorts me into the home where I grew up. The familiar scents, photos, and furniture are too much for me, and as soon as the door is closed, I burst into tears. He never says a word, just holds me tight while I cry.

I'm home.

I'm surrounded by the only man I can trust not to hurt me. I thought there was another one I could trust just as much, but he proved me wrong. Thinking of Levi causes a physical pain in my chest, like someone is cutting me wide open with a butter knife.

"Come on, sweetie. Let's get some rest. We'll talk in the morning," Dad whispers, placing a kiss on my forehead.

He leads me up the stairs and into the small room I shared with my twin sister growing up. My head hits my pillow moments later, but sleep evades me. My mind whirls with memories of my time with Levi; everything from casual dinners, to cooking lessons, to making love.

There's no way I'll get any sleep tonight.

And why would I want to, when every time I close my eyes, I see his hazel eyes and his killer smile.

Welcome to Hell.

Chapter Twenty-Six

Levi

It's late.

Or early, depending on how you look at the clock.

It's just after one in the morning, and I'm dog-tired. I'm suddenly extremely grateful for the mini nap I took this afternoon when I had the chance. Otherwise, I would have started to struggle when we hit the third hour of battling that blaze. The older home went up quickly, and when we arrived, threatening to take the houses on both sides. We were able to keep it from spreading completely, but it was damn close there for a while.

Now, all I can think about is scrubbing this nasty burnt smell off of my body and crawling into bed with Abby. I'm sure she's sound asleep by this point, but that doesn't matter. I crave just the touch of her skin against my own and to hold her in my arms.

With renewed spring in my step, I let myself into my apartment, throwing my bag over to the side to take care of later. Taking a few steps into my place, I'm surprised when I slam my upper shin into my coffee table. "Son of a…" I holler. "What the hell?"

Limping slightly, I make my way to the end table and flip on the lamp. Soft light bathes my living room, and I'm finally able to take in the room. I recall moving the table a bit when I propped my legs up to take my nap. My computer is open, and the movement of hitting the table must have woken it. Hell, I didn't even log out of that dating site before I snoozed.

Grabbing the computer, preparing to power it down, a photo catches my attention. Upon further inspection, the photo is of my own computer sitting on my coffee table. This exact screen.

Mother of fucking hell, what is this?

The picture was sent at 10:10pm from AngelEyes. From Abby.

"No, no, no, no!" I exclaim, roughly setting my computer back down on the table and not caring. That's when I see something shiny sitting beside my discarded laptop. Picking it up, my gut tightens painfully, my throat closes shut.

A key.

My key.

To this apartment.

She left it behind after she discovered I'm SimpleMan. She asked me outright if I was on that fucking site, and I denied it. I deceived her. She gave me the perfect opportunity to come clean, not only today, but a few weeks ago, and I didn't take it.

Fuck.

It doesn't matter that I was gonna tell her tonight, not to her. And not to me either, because I've done the one thing I swore I'd never in a billion years do: broke her trust.

And probably her heart.

Because a friend doesn't lie. Even when your ass looks huge in the dress or you have globs of mascara in your lashes, a friend is supposed to tell you the honest to God truth, and I didn't do that.

Needing to make this right–and quickly–I race across the hall. I don't even knock, it's well after one in the morning, and as frantic as I am to get to my girl, I'm not about to wake the neighbor. He's a guy about my age, but still not cool. Using my key, I let myself into her place.

Instantly I feel it.

It feels as empty as my heart right now.

I can tell before I even make my way into her bedroom that she's not here. Desolation surrounds me, pulling me under with its strong current. Her bed isn't made, which tells me she was here at some point. Probably before she came over and found the live bomb with her name, wrapped in a pretty bow sitting on my coffee table.

Her drawers are askew slightly, and I'm just desperate enough to check them. They've been rifled through, and if it weren't for the current situation I left us in, I'd be concerned that something was up. But I know what's up. She's left, and she left in a big hurry.

Her makeup bag is still sitting on her bathroom sink, but her toothbrush is gone. Just like a piece of my soul. It's crazy how empty I feel right now, not knowing where she is or if she's okay. Hell, I don't even know if we'll ever be *us* again.

For good measure, I go ahead and check the rest of her place. You know, just in case she fell in the office or passed out on the living room floor. But she's not here. I pick up my phone and immediately dial her number. Unfortunately, it goes to voicemail right away. After listening to her chipper greeting, the beep tells me it's my turn to speak.

But the words don't come.

So, I hang up and call again. Her voicemail picks up immediately again, but this time, I'm a bit more prepared.

"Abs, I know this looks bad. Call me. Please. Let me explain." I take a deep breath, even though the air seems to suffocate me. "Please, Abs. I need to talk to you. I…I need you. I…" And I almost say it. I almost tell her exactly how I feel about her, but I stop myself. She doesn't need to hear that I love her on a message. "Please."

Hanging up feels like the equivalent to cutting off my own arm because I'm, once again, cut off from the one woman who makes me whole.

Instead of going to my own place, like I should, I make sure her door is locked, kick off my shoes, and crawl into her bed. Her covers are bunched up at my feet, but I make no move to grab them. I'm a smelly mess anyway. But I need to smell her, be close to where she sleeps, where her beautiful brown hair was splayed out, smelling like vanilla, just a short time ago.

Back when things were fine.

Now, they're anything but.

Holding my phone, I send off a text message, then another, and once I start, I can't seem to stop.

Levi: *I know I hurt you, but please call me. Please.*

Levi: *I need to know that you're okay.*

Levi: *If you need time, take it, but don't shut me out completely.*

Levi: *If you give me the chance, I'll explain everything.*

Levi: *I know it's late. Shit, it's the middle of the night, but I'm freaking out here, angel.*

What am I doing? I'm sending stalker-like text messages to my girl at two in the morning. Isn't that what most sane, rational men do in the middle of the night when they fuck up? Oh, and don't forget the begging and pleading; I'm not above that shit, not when it comes to Abby.

Getting up, I rid myself of my t-shirt and pants. They smell nasty from the fire, and even though I know I should shower (Yes, I'm making her bed smelly), I just don't seem to have the energy to take care of that task. Even if the result would leave me smelling great and just like Abby, because there's no way in hell I'm leaving this apartment right now.

Crawling back into bed, I hold my phone like it's the lifeline keeping my heart beating. Her pillow cradles my smoky head, the occasional scent of her shampoo permeates through the stench and brings me the slightest taste of comfort. But the reprieve is short-lived, and before I know it, the trace of her is gone again.

Just like Abby.

* * *

My phone makes a noise, pulling me from the lightest sleep I've ever experienced. It's a text. From Abby. Sent now, at 3:14am.

Abby: *I'm not ready to talk.*

My fingers fly across the screen, my response coming only moments later.

Levi: *I get that, but tell me you're okay. Please, Abby.*

I hold my breath and wait. And wait and wait for those little bubbles. It must be ten minutes before I have my response.

Abby: *I'm fine.*

But something tells me she's anything but. This is one of those times where a woman says she's fine, but isn't. She says there's nothing wrong but is clearly pissed off. No, I may not know these examples firsthand, but I've heard enough married dudes on the fire department or with the ambulance to know that when your woman says *I'm fine*, you've fucked up good.

I want to reply more, but choose to let it be. It's still in the middle of the night, and Abby needs to be sleeping. As for me, there'll be no sleep. My thoughts will be plagued by emerald eyes and the sexiest smile I've ever seen. My fingers will twitch when I think about her hair and my dick won't understand what's going on when it gets so painfully hard for her touch that it might suffer some long-term damaging effects.

No, I'm on my own tonight.

Just me and a big fat fucking case of misery.

* * *

There's a loud beating at my door, one that pulls me from this weird drunk-like fog I've found myself in. It takes me all of one second to realize, even with a throbbing headache and a horrible kink in my neck, I'm not drunk or hungover, not even a little bit.

The pounding continues, but sounding slightly distant this time. The clock reads seven-thirty, which isn't too early for visitors, unless you've been up all night wishing you hadn't lied to your best friend and told her from the get-go about joining the dating site and befriending her on the sly.

Abby.

What if Abby's at the door? Maybe she forgot her keys. We already know she doesn't have my apartment key anymore, but what if she misplaced hers and can't get into her place? She's probably pounding on my door right now for help.

Jumping up, I sprint to the front door, sliding around the corner in my socks and into the kitchen. Throwing the lock on the knob, I rip open the door, out of breath and completely oblivious to the fact I'm in boxer briefs and socks.

There she is. Long brown hair pulled back at the nape of her neck, tight yoga pants, and an oversized t-shirt. She's getting ready to pound on my door again, her hand poised high to strike again, when I cross the hall to stand behind her. I almost wrap my arms around her, but knowing that she could very well hate my guts right now, I opt to reach out and touch her shoulder. "Hey."

Abby whips around, a startled squeak coming from her surprised face, and that's when I realize my mistake. This isn't Abby. It's Lexi.

"Jesus," she scolds, her green eyes hard.

"Sorry."

"Why do you smell like you swam in a fire pit?"

Reaching around and rubbing the back of my neck, I answer, "Uhh, I had a fire last night. Haven't showered yet."

"Is that because you were too busy being a douche to my sister?"

"What?" I ask, surprised by her hostility, yet completely unsurprised by it at the same time. Lexi's always been the slightly more passionate sister. Where Abby has always been quiet and shy, Lexi is a little more in your face and always tells it like it is.

"Maybe you can explain to me why my sister called me up an hour ago, *crying,* Levi, and told me you were the biggest liar in the history of the world." I open my mouth to speak, but she continues.

"And, believe me, *Levi,* I've known my fair share of liars lately." Again, I open my mouth, but she raises her hands, stopping me in my place.

"The one person who's never supposed to hurt and use her did just that. You toyed with her feelings, making her fall completely in love with you, for what? Some sick game? Do you do this with other women? Be all sweet and sexy and make them fall for you? Then toss them aside like yesterday's trash?

"She was crying because of what you did, Levi. *You* hurt my sister, you worthless pile of dog shit, and for that, I'm going to have to cut off your balls and stuff them down your throat. With a nail file!" she practically shouts at me in the middle of the hallway.

"Wow, that sounds painful, dude. Might want to invest in a cup when you're gonna be near that little firecracker." The deep voice comes over my shoulder and off to the left.

Lexi's flaming eyes turn on new prey. "Excuse me?"

"Hey, don't get your panties in a wad, sweetness. I was just warning my man here that his woman was more of a firecracker than I originally suspected," the new addition says. Linkin is leaning casually against his door jam, a wide smile on his face. He's lived next to Abby for a handful of months, and even though we've spoken a few times in passing, this would be the most consistent words we've shared since I met him.

"His woman?" Lexi seethes.

"Whatever you want to call yourself, sweetness. It don't bother me any," Linkin practically coos at my girl's twin sister. Her rage is visibly pulsing through the thick air in the hallway.

"This isn't Abby, Link. It's her twin sister, Lexi," I tell him. He gives me a knowing grin and nod before turning those dark eyes back at Lexi.

"Twins. I like it."

"Unless you want your own balls to be sawed off with a dirty spatula, I suggest you head inside and leave us be," she fumes at the tall man across the hall.

"Feisty. I dig that in a woman," Linkin says with a wolfish grin. Then, to really piss her off, he throws a wink over his shoulder before heading inside his apartment, whistling a happy tune. When the door shuts, we're surrounded in uncomfortable silence.

"Listen, Lex, as much as I love getting my ass handed to me in the hallway, do you mind coming inside?"

"Why are you practically naked?" she asks, following me into Abby's apartment. "And why are you in my sister's place?"

"I'm here because I was worried about her and hoped I could talk to her when she came home," I say, talking over and standing by the counter.

"She won't be home. Not while you're here."

Swallowing the lump in my throat, I walk over and drop down into the closest kitchen chair, and run my hands from the back of my neck up into my hair. "I fucked up, Lex."

"No shit, Sherlock."

Glancing at her, I see the hostility in her eyes ebb, but only minutely. "How much did she tell you?"

"Not much. She couldn't really talk over her crying, you know?"

Shaking my head, I avert my eyes for a moment before returning them to hers. "When she signed up for the dating site, it kinda made me all nutty."

"Jealous?" she asks with a smirk.

"Insanely. I ended up creating my own profile on the site with the thought that it'd be just to keep an eye on her. But then we started talking online, and we were still hanging out all the fucking time, and the lines became blurred. I wanted her."

"Wanted her…" she encourages.

"Like wanted her in my arms, in my bed, and in my life twenty-four seven, kinda wanted."

"Finally," she mumbles.

"I had plenty of opportunities to tell her the truth about the guy she was talking to online, but I didn't. I was terrified that she wouldn't see it as a way for me to watch over her, and keep her safe. The Internet is a crazy fucking place.

"Anyway, it doesn't matter now. What matters is I should have told her and didn't. *But* it wasn't because I was playing some game with her, okay? I would never do that, not to anyone, but especially not to her. I fucking love her, Lex."

"You love her?" she asks, her eyes looking brighter, probably from unshed tears. Damn it with those tears. "Like really, *really* love her?"

"Yeah, I do. I was going to tell her last night. Honest."

"She said you lied in a confession time."

Hanging my head in shame, I admit, "I did. It was stupid, but I was afraid she'd be pissed at me. My brain just told me to deny it, even though my heart wasn't on board. I had planned to confess everything last night and tell her how I really felt, but then we had the fire call, and I had to leave. She went to my apartment and found my laptop. You can imagine what happened next."

Lexi stares over at me, her knowing eyes trying to gauge the sincerity in my words.

"I need to see her, Lexi. If she's not with you, then where?"

Seemingly torn between telling me or not, she finally gives me a bit of relief. "She's at Dad's. She went there last night. After I talked to her, he called me; said she was up crying most of the night, but wouldn't tell him why. Just said someone she loved hurt her." My heart literally tries to crawl out of my chest. "I knew instantly who had hurt her. Besides her family, she only loves one person, and that man was too stupid to see it. That's why I came over here to maim you."

Direct. Hit.

"I see it, Lexi, and I want it. Fuck, I want her love bad, but I don't know how to get her to talk to me right now."

"You can't. She needs some time to think and settle down."

"But I need to tell her the truth. She needs to know that she wasn't some game, that I really do love her."

"And you'll tell her that, but just not yet. She says she needs time, and you need to give it to her."

Time. The one thing that almost pains me to give her, but if that's what she needs, then I guess that's all I can do. I'll be here, waiting (or more accurately, at my own apartment), for when she's ready to talk. It might be a day, maybe a few. God forbid she makes me wait more than a handful of days–that thought is catastrophic.

"I'll give her time. As much as she needs."

"Good."

"Now, what's going on with you? Why were you coming at me like a rabid pitbull who hasn't eaten in a week?"

"Because you're the asshole who hurt my sister," she says matter-of-factly.

"True, but that was more. You basically said all men are liars, which isn't like you. Is it Chris? Did he lie to you about something?" I ask, gauging her reaction. My question hits bullseye, her eyes watering once more.

"Doesn't matter," she whispers.

"It does," I say, kicking the chair across from me away from the table. "Sit."

She does, and without any sass, which tells me this is something that's really bothering her. But when she starts talking, I'm left stunned by her admission. My blood boils and my heart breaks, and for the first time since last night, I'm thinking about someone other than Abby Summer.

I'm thinking of how I can kill Chris Jacobson and make it look like an accident.

Chapter Twenty-Seven

Abby

I had no idea the human body could shed so many tears.

Which is funny considering six months ago, I watched my sister Meghan's world shatter around her as she lost her fiancé, Josh. Those tears never seem to dry. Those tears were constant, day and night, and I almost feel guilty comparing my misery and heartache to something as monumental as losing the love of your life.

Levi wasn't that for me.

He proved it by using me as a pawn in some sick and twisted game of chess. Well, checkmate, Levi. You win.

My mind keeps trying to figure out why. Why did he search me out on that stupid dating site? Why did he befriend me and carry on as if he had no clue who I was for a month? Why would he take me out on dates and make love to me with his stupid magic penis? Okay, no it's not magic, but it is pretty fabulous. And most importantly, why would he lie about all of the above?

My heart and my head are doing battle. My heart tells me to talk to him, that there's more to it than a juvenile game of cat and mouse. My heart tells me *my Levi* would never intentionally hurt me the way he has. My heart tells me that love can overcome anything, even when the one your heart is calling for betrays you.

My head, on the other hand, tells me to rid the world of the no-good, too handsome, lying, cheating bastard. Okay, yes, my head might be caught up in a bit of melodrama, but whatever. He didn't cheat. At least, I don't think so.

See? My head is in a funky place right now. I need to take some time, think about what I really want out of this relationship, and talk to him. Of course, if he doesn't really want a real relationship, then what I want doesn't matter, does it?

Stupid head.

I need my space. As much as I love spending time with my dad and grandparents, they're hovering as if I'm about to go postal any moment and start picking people off with a sniper rifle from the clock tower. And our town doesn't even have a clock tower.

That's why I'm loading up my car to head back to my place. As soon as my bag was packed, I sent Lexi a text message, asking if the coast was clear. I know she was there earlier today. I know she talked to him. She never once pushed me, but just kept saying that when I was ready, I really needed to speak with him.

Maybe it's not as bad as I think? First off, Levi wouldn't still be breathing if Lexi got a hold of him. The fact that she talked to him, and *didn't* rip off his balls like she said she was going to, is telling in itself.

Yeah, there's only one way to find out what has really been going on, but today is not going to be that day. Right now, I just want to curl up on my couch, watching mindless, boring television, and get bloated eating too much Rocky Road ice cream. Maybe eat raw cookie dough for good measure.

"You know, I could go over and speak to the young man, if you'd like," Grandpa says from my doorway.

Glancing at the aged man who acts like he isn't a day over thirty, I can't help but smile. "Oh, and how do you know it's a young man?"

Lacey Black

He enters my bedroom and takes a seat on my bed. "Well, beside the fact that your grandmother came to bed last night cursing like a sailor on a three-day bender at a whore house about the stupidity of the male species? I might be old, sweetheart, but my eyesight is fantastic. It's Levi, right?"

Unable to speak, I nod my head.

"Well, that boy has always been a little slow on the upswing, sugar. Even when he was younger, he was impulsive and reckless. Scared the bejesus out of all of us a few too many times," Grandpa says with a fond smile. "But he's always loved you, even if he didn't realize it until recently."

"Why does everyone keep saying that?" I ask curiously with a humorless laugh. It's not likely Levi called up my grandpa and told him all about his feelings for his granddaughter or anything.

"Anyone in a five mile radius can see it, sweetie. Everyone but you." I start to deny, shaking my head frantically, when he cuts me off. "No, don't even try to deny it. We've all known for a while, but apparently, you're a little slow too. Maybe that's what makes you two perfect for each other," he adds with a chuckle.

"Can I ask you something?" He nods as I take a seat beside him. "What would you do if Grandma lied to you?"

"Without knowing the circumstances, that's hard to say. I guess if it was something she felt like she was protecting me from, then I'd forgive. I love your grandma more than anything, so it would have to be pretty bad for me to walk away. When we married, I vowed to love and protect her, and because of those vows, I'd like to think I'd do everything within my power to make our marriage work, and that includes forgiveness."

"I wish it were just a simple decision," I tell him.

"The things worth fighting for rarely are. Listen, I don't know what Levi did, but I know you'll weigh all of your options and make the right decisions where he's concerned. Just make sure they're not rash ones. Hear him out and then make your choice. Okay?"

"Okay," I tell my grandpa, wrapping my arms around his frail shoulders and holding on tight.

"And if you need help burying the body, you call us. Your grandmother and I are pros at establishing alibis when the time calls for one," he says with a straight face. At first, I laugh, but I'm suddenly not so sure he's joking.

With a warm, comforting hug and my bag in hand, he walks me down the stairs–okay, I might help him more than he helps me, even though he's still amazingly agile for a man his age.

The August sun is still shining high in the sky, even for late afternoon. After my dad throws my bag back into the trunk, I head out and make the short trip back to my apartment. I just pray Levi's on duty tonight so that I don't risk running into him. I'm not sure I'm strong enough not to throw my arms around him and beg him to love me.

Love me the way I love him.

* * *

My pulse hammers in my throat as I walk down the corridor. I want to glance over my shoulder at the wooden door across the hall, but keep my focus straight ahead. My movements are almost sluggish as I stick my key in the knob and give it a twist. Sighing deeply and allowing my eyes to close briefly, the quiet of the hallway surrounds me, choking what little life remains.

I'm not sure which hurts more: the fact that he abided by my wishes and left me alone, or the fact that he didn't.

Stepping inside, I gently close and lock my door. There's no movement, barely any noise from within my space except the ticking of the clock and the sporadic drip from the kitchen sink. Dropping my bag on the floor beside the door, I step further into my kitchen, and that's when I see it: a potted deep purple orchid.

My favorite.

Stepping up to the flowering plant, I can't help but bend down and inhale deeply. It's so fragrant and exotic, and brings an instant smile to my face.

He remembered.

A big part of me wants to run across the hall, throw my arms around him, and vow to forgive him for everything he's ever done and probably will do in the future. But I keep myself rooted in place. My grandpa's right. I need to spend some time alone, thinking about what I want from our relationship and where I see it heading. I need to make sure I know what I want with my life first, then I can take the next step; hopefully, with Levi. Next up would be speaking to him and hearing him out.

It's an easy enough plan; let's just see if I can hold to it.

Retrieving my bag, I head to my bedroom to unpack and start a load of laundry. Stepping into my bedroom, I'm shocked and amazed by the sight. My bedroom is covered in roses. Vases everywhere. On my dresser, on my nightstands, against the walls. The bedspread and floor are covered in dark red petals.

With wobbly legs, I walk over to my pillow where a rectangular envelope sits, perched up by a single red rose. My hands shake as I pull the small postcard-sized card from within. It's hard to read, but not because of his horrible chicken scratch handwriting. No, it's difficult to see through the tears clouding my eyes.

My sweetest Abby,

There's a rose here for every time I've thought of you since last night. A petal for every minute my heart beat for only you. Take the time you need, but know that I am thinking of you, my arms ready to hold you, my lips ready to kiss you, my heart ready to be given to you.

I'm yours.

Always have been. Always will be.

Levi

I burst into tears once more, those big body-shaking sobs that turn even the hardest woman into a little girl.

I'm so confused and angry and sad and happy. How can a man who played a lowdown dirty trick on his best friend write such sweet words that melt my heart until it's a puddle at my feet?

Because he's not that kinda man, stupid.

I know that, in my heart of hearts, Levi didn't mean to hurt me. He couldn't. Not the man who cried with me when I broke my arm in seventh grade, helped pull the rocks from my knees when I wrecked my bike at ten years old, and beat the shit out of Joel Harper for calling me a nerd senior year of high school.

My Levi isn't cruel and wouldn't do the things my head is accusing him of. There's more to the story; there has to be. Fate isn't harsh enough to make me fall in love with my best friend only for him to be the monster he has always protected me from.

With a new sense of purpose, I'm determined to find out why he lied to me. Heading into my office, I fire up my computer. It takes way too long. My anxiety is high as I bounce both legs in anticipation and impatience. As soon as the home screen is up, I log on to PerfectDate.com and reactivate my account. Everything is basically as I left it (of course it is, no one could contact you, dummy).

I find my message thread with SimpleMan easily, mostly because it's one of the only ones there. The final message I sent, accompanied by the photo, stares back at me from the screen.

AngelEyes: *I never expected that the one person to hurt me this badly would be you.*

Typing a new response, I click send before I can talk myself out of it.

AngelEyes: *I don't know why you did what you did, but I want to know. No, I need to know. I don't believe you did it to hurt me, even though that's where my mind originally went. That's on me, and for that, I'm sorry.*

The message bubbles don't appear, but I guess they wouldn't if he is at work. I wait a few more minutes, but still don't get a reply. And I'm sure he's not trolling the dating site, especially after I deactivated my page the moment I ousted him via the dating website.

Or could he be?

No. No, Abby, don't go there. He wouldn't have bought your sister out of roses if he was still manwhoring his way through Jupiter Bay and the western half of Virginia.

Deciding to shut down my computer without checking email, I grab my phone and download the app. Why I never did this before is beyond me? I've never really been big on using my cell phone for anything other than calling and texting. I don't have game apps or social media on my phone that I obsess over all day long, so it's not like my first thought was to download the PerfectDate.com app and turn on the notifications.

Yes! Turn on the notifications!

When it's all set up (and I check my messages four different times just to make sure I didn't miss anything), my stomach growls angrily, reminding me that I haven't eaten much today at all. Grandma made breakfast, but I chose to drink an extra cup of coffee instead of having French toast with fresh maple syrup. Yeah, that hurt. It's usually my fave, but with my guts all distorted like a game of Twister, I didn't have much of an appetite.

Opening my fridge, I'm reminded once again of the man who lives across the hall. There's not much inside the refrigerator that could constitute food, but what I do find warms my heart. Homemade mac and cheese with three kinds of cheese.

Another of my favorites.

Smiling, I take the clear plastic container from the fridge and head towards the microwave, sniffing the ooey, gooey cheesy goodness as I go. After sixty seconds, I stir the spiral noodles (because spiral noodles are way better than boring ol' elbow macaroni noodles), and stick it back in for another minute. When the timer sounds, the perfect comfort food is ready.

Instead of eating at my table, I take the bowl, a bottle of water, and the bag of fresh cornbread muffins I found on the counter (thanks, Levi) into the living room and get cozy on the couch. It's a quiet evening with nothing on TV, but even if I had found something worth watching, I'm not sure it would have held my attention.

A door closing in the hallway has me jumping off the couch. I wonder if it's Levi? I mean, I suppose it could be my neighbor, Linkin, but I usually don't hear his door as notably as I do Levi's. Of course, it could be me just *wanting* it to be Levi.

Sighing, I return to my seat and take a deep breath. If it is him, I don't need to storm the castle like some crazy ex-girlfriend, you know? We have a lot of issues to work out before I just fly across the hall and climb him like a tree. Jump him like a pro basketball player. Ride him like a cowboy. You get my point, right?

Now do you see why I'm so confused? I hate him, I want him. I push him away, then want to be wrapped in his arms.

But the thing is, I don't hate him. Not even a little. What I feel is so completely the opposite of hate, that I can't picture my life without him.

So it's time to get my shit together, figure out if I can trust him with my heart, and lay it on the line.

Chapter Twenty-Eight

Levi

I know she's home.

I saw light filtering through her curtains when I pulled into the parking lot, and it took every ounce of strength I had not to run across the hall and beg her to speak to me. Did she like my flowers? My note? Did I help repair even the slightest bit of damage I've caused? Probably not, but I'm determined to put in the time and the work necessary to prove to her that she can trust me again. The alternative is unthinkable.

After a quick shower, where I jack off again to more dirty images of my best friend, I head to the kitchen for dinner. It was another busy evening for the fire department and doesn't look to be slowing down anytime soon. My stomach growls, as it has a few times today, but I've been too worked up to eat. After delivering the homemade mac and cheese to Abby's fridge earlier this afternoon, the fire call came in for an out of control residential burn just on the edge of town. It might have only taken a short period of time to get it under control, but I ended up staying back at the station, working out and cleaning up some of the equipment.

It's not like I was super anxious to come home and stare at my fucking walls and surround myself in misery, ya know?

But now that I know she's home, I wonder what she's doing. Did she eat the dish I left her? What did she think about the flowers I spend an embarrassingly high amount of money on?

Do you know how much crow I had to eat when I called Payton for help? First off, she didn't even want to take my call. I believe her exact words where, "I hope you fall into a tub of honey, naked, and then step on a beehive."

Ouch.

But I was persistent, even though I kinda wanted to cower beneath the coffee table as she spewed big sister venom through the phone line at me, like missiles in an active warzone. (I'll totally deny that if you ever tell.) One thing's for certain, these sisters stick together. I feel sorry for the next sorry sucker that crosses one of them.

It took me basically confessing to her what I shared with Lexi early this morning for her to agree to help me. Fortunately, for me, but not so fortunate for my wallet, one of her distributers arrived this morning at the time of my call. That's how I was able to secure an obscenely crazy amount of red roses and one planted orchid. (Her favorite.) And being the stellar big sister Payton is, she didn't even charge me a delivery fee for running eighteen dozen red roses over to her sister's place.

That's because she charged me full retail price.

But I don't care. It's only money, and showing Abby that I'm serious when it comes to working towards her forgiveness is the ultimate goal.

That, and getting her back into my arms and my bed.

Fuck, my bed misses her.

My laptop sits on the coffee table, taunting me as it has for nearly twenty-four hours now. With the remote in my hand, I kick my feet up on the table, one of the *Lethal Weapon* movies on TV.

The movement, again, causes the computer to wake, lighting up my home screen. I should probably deactivate my account on that fucking dating site. I mean it's not like I plan to find someone to take on the perfect date. Nope. The only woman I want to date is across the hall sticking needles into her Levi-shaped voodoo doll.

With the computer in hand, I bring up the scene of the crime, my guitar profile picture filling the screen. My favorite instrument appears to be weeping in the picture, probably realizing he'll never be cradled against her sweet body while she gently strums its strings. I know my cock is weeping at the thought.

I'm just about to click on the settings to deactivate when a message notification pops up. I've ignored every request received since I set up the profile, so why would now be any different. I guess curiosity really did kill the cat.

My heart literally stops beating in my chest when I see the message. AngelEyes. Click. Click. Motherfuckin' click!

AngelEyes: *I don't know why you did what you did, but I want to know. No, I need to know. I don't believe you did it to hurt me, even though that's where my mind originally went. That's on me, and for that, I'm sorry.*

SimpleMan: *You have nothing to apologize for. Nothing. This is on me. I guess the only way to explain it is to start at the beginning. When I saw you signing up for this dating site, I guess I became jealous. No, that's not true. I was fucking crazy with jealousy. The thought of you dating someone made me mad with possessiveness. Why? Because you haven't been the only one fighting feelings for the other for a while. I wasn't kidding when I said I hadn't slept with anyone for a year. Every woman I saw was you. Everywhere I went, I saw your face. So I signed up for that site under the guise of keeping an eye on you. I should have come clean from the beginning, that first time we talked, but I didn't. I don't know why. I can only guess it was because I was enjoying talking to you more than I already was. So I kept it up. It was never to hurt you. Ever. Just knowing that I'm the asshole that put those tears in your eyes is crushing me. When you asked at the restaurant yesterday about it, my initial thought was to just deny. I knew you'd be pissed that I was SimpleMan and had been all along. I realized instantly that my lie was hurtful and wrong, so I had planned to confess last night when we got home. But then the fire call happened, and everything spiraled out of fucking control so fast from there. All I can say is I'm sorry. Hurting you was never my intention. I hope someday you can forgive me. I promise to work for your forgiveness every day for the rest of my life.*

I click send without rereading the message, feeling the slightest bit of relief that I finally told her a few of the things I've wanted to say. I just hope my apology isn't too late.

A few moments later, I see bubbles. Fuckin' bubbles!!

AngelEyes: *All lies are hurtful to some degree. That's why you're not supposed to tell them, especially to the person you consider your best friend.*

SimpleMan: *You're absolutely right. So fucking right, Abs. I wish I could go back and do everything over again. I wouldn't have lied. Hell, I probably wouldn't have signed up for the stupid site.*

AngelEyes: *Me too. I wish I knew where to go from here.*

SimpleMan: *Why don't we start over? Not the friendship, but everything else.*

AngelEyes: *Start over?*

SimpleMan: *Hey, AngelEyes. My name is Levi. I'm an EMT and fireman and a complete bonehead sometimes. My best friend would probably tell you I'm a bonehead most of the time, but that's OK. She's right. Yes, a girl. My best friend is the best fucking person I know. She's smart and sexy and sweet and forgiving. So fucking forgiving.*

AngelEyes: **blushing* A girl best friend, huh? Funny, I have a boy best friend.*

SimpleMan: *I bet he's the luckiest bastard in the world because you're in his life.*

AngelEyes: *Quite possibly. *winky face**

SimpleMan: *Tell me about your day.*

AngelEyes: *I'll be honest, it didn't start off so great, but it's starting to look up.*

SimpleMan: *Mine either. To be blunt, I messed up with my girl. I'm working on making it right.*

AngelEyes: *That's very noble of you. I'm sure she appreciates it.*

SimpleMan: *I hope so. And that's why I have to be honest with you now. I'm not looking to hook up or go on the perfect date with anyone but her. But I like you, Angel, and I'd love to be your friend.*

AngelEyes: *Since we're being honest, I kinda have a big thing for my best friend too. I've tried to fight it, but he's persistent and, well, he's pretty amazing. So I'm only looking for a friend too.*

I admit. This is the part where I fist pump victoriously in the air. My smile is so big it hurts, and my heart swells more than my chest cavity has room for.

293

SimpleMan: *Excellent. I think we'll make great friends, Angel.*

And then we spend the next three hours, until I had to go to work, chatting and talking as if we didn't know a single thing, yet knew everything at the same time. It was one of the best Friday nights of my life.

* * *

Saturday morning.

SimpleMan: *Just got off work. I'm going to sleep and then text my girl. I haven't talked to her since I was a dumbass on Thursday.*

AngelEyes: *You should definitely text her. I bet she misses you, even though you were a dumbass.*

* * *

Saturday night.

SimpleMan: *I texted my girl. It felt fucking amazing that she replied back right away.*

AngelEyes: *I bet she couldn't wait to hear from you. Even if she was angry and hurt, you can forgive those you care most for.*

* * *

Sunday morning.

SimpleMan: *I'm headed to the beach today to hang out with my friend Tucker. He's probably gonna want to know why I was such a douche to my girl. I'll tell him, of course, which will ensure that a year's worth of pussy-whipped comments will ensue. I can't wait.*

AngelEyes: *He sounds charming. Enjoy your teasing. #SorryNotSorry*

* * *

Sunday afternoon.

AngelEyes: *I spent the afternoon at my sister Jaime's house. While her boyfriend Ryan was away golfing, we searched the entire house for a hidden engagement ring that we're certain she's going to get soon. There may have been tequila involved.*

SimpleMan: **big cheesy grin* Tequila and sister shenanigans. What a great combination! Did you find it?*

AngelEyes: *Nope. But we did find the bottom of the bottle. I'm so sleepy. *yawning emoji**

SimpleMan: *Nap, Angel. I'll talk to you later.*

* * *

Sunday night.

SimpleMan: *How was the nap?*

AngelEyes: *Amazing until I rolled over and a thorn stuck in my hip.*

SimpleMan: *??? Explain. Where exactly were you napping? The jungle?*

AngelEyes: *My bed. But I have this embarrassingly amazing display of roses all over my room, and well, I kinda have been sleeping with some of them. They smell so good and remind me of my friend when he's not here.*

SimpleMan: *Lucky fucking flowers. I bet your friend wishes he was curled against you instead of thorny roses.*

AngelEyes: *That makes two of us, Simple.*

* * *

Monday night.

AngelEyes: *Work sucked. Since I took last Friday off, I was way behind. I had to put in extra hours to catch up.*

SimpleMan: *I'm sorry to hear that. I wish you'd let me help you. I know the proper uses for there, they're, their!*

AngelEyes: *That's one of the things I like most about you, Simple. Proper use of grammar.*

* * *

Tuesday night.

SimpleMan: *I'm off to work. Big plans tonight?*

AngelEyes: *I met my grandparents at the café for dinner. It was all fine and dandy until they started debating the benefits of anal beads and butt plugs. *insert grossed out emoji**

SimpleMan: **insert laughing emoji* I'm sorry I missed that. They sound like a hoot.*

AngelEyes: *They are the best. But don't tell them I said that. It would go to their heads and we'd never be able to live with them.*

* * *

Wednesday afternoon.

AngelEyes: *I just got a text. From my best friend. He wants me to come over for dinner tonight.*

SimpleMan: *And?*

AngelEyes: *I said yes. I'm really excited, but incredibly nervous too.*

SimpleMan: *Why are you nervous?*

AngelEyes: *I haven't seen him in a week.*

SimpleMan: *I bet he misses you. More than anything.*

AngelEyes: *I miss him. More than anything.*

SimpleMan: *Enjoy your dinner. Don't be nervous. Just be your charming, amazing self and you can't go wrong.*

AngelEyes: *Thanks for being my friend, Simple.*

SimpleMan: *The pleasure has been all mine, Angel. Go. Get ready. I have dinner to prepare for. My girl is coming over tonight and I can't fucking wait to see her.*

AngelEyes: *She's a lucky girl.*

SimpleMan: *I'm the lucky one.*

Chapter Twenty-Nine

Abby

My hand is shaking as I raise it to knock. Even though Levi, I mean SimpleMan, told me not to be nervous, admittedly, I'm terrified. Not of him, of course, but of the situation. We've talked daily since I messaged him through the dating app, including a few text messages, but he's been busy with work. Tonight will be our first time seeing each other in a week.

One. Very. Long. Week.

The door opens before my knuckles can rap on the wood, and there he is.

Gorgeous.

Smiling.

So damn sexy that I might have just gotten off standing here.

"Hi," I squeak out, my throat closed and my voice doing its best *Alvin and the Chipmunks* impression.

"Hey."

What do I do now? Am I supposed to give him a kiss? Shake his hand? Maybe do one of those one-handed, back slapping bro hugs?

"Come in," he says, taking a step back and opening the door widely. I start to cross the threshold when two arms wrap around my midsection and pull me against a firm, muscular body. Oh, this body. Being wrapped in his arms, my head tucked securely beneath his chin, is like heaven. "I'm not sure if this is appropriate or not, but I've missed you so much," he whispers against my hair.

"I've missed you too," I whisper, my lips caressing the stubbled skin of his throat. His scent surrounds me. He smells like the outdoors and musky soap, and just like that, my panties are wet.

Clearing his throat, he takes a step back, but doesn't release the hold he now has on my hand. His hazel eyes search me, as if cataloging every curve, every line, and every part of my body. "Dinner's about ready. I hope you're hungry. I went a little overboard," he says sheepishly, giving me that grin, the one with the hint of ornery, that I love.

"Starving," I tell him as he leads me into his place.

The table is already set for two, a bottle of white wine chilling in a bucket of ice in the middle. "I hope you're in the mood for steak," he says, pulling my chair out from the table. "I was at the butcher today and they looked amazing. So we're having prime rib, twice baked potatoes, with extra sour cream," he adds with a wink, "and fresh asparagus that I bought at the farmer's market."

"You did all of this today? After working all night?" I ask, watching as he brings dish after steaming dish to the table.

"Yeah, well, I caught a nap when I got home, but I was a little too anxious to sleep." Again, I get that sexy grin.

"It smells amazing," I confirm, my mouth watering as he places food on my plate. When he brings out the prime rib, I think I might actually orgasm on the spot. "Wow."

We dive in with gusto, neither of us really speaking much, but both of us stealing glances as we eat. We make it through almost the entire meal without many words spoken, but it's comfortable. It doesn't feel awkward or forced, but instead, it's the most natural feeling in the world. As if we've done this a million times, and I guess we have.

"Full?" he asks, starting to clean up the empty plates and bowls.

"Stuffed. Let me get that," I tell him, standing to take the stack of dishes in his hand. "You cooked; I can clean up."

"Not tonight, angel. These will keep until later."

I watch as he stacks the dishes by the sink, puts the perishable food in the fridge, and turns to face me. Suddenly, the sexual tension is so thick, I can almost feel it wrap around me like a warm blanket. Levi's eyes are dark, dilated, and are looking at me as if he wants to gobble me up as a midnight snack.

Before I realize it, I'm moving across the kitchen. Strong arms wrap around me as my body collides with his. When his lips meet mine, I swear I hear the angels singing from the heavens. My body erupts in happiness and need, my arms unable to hold him tight enough.

"God, I fucking missed you so much. I'm so damned sorry, angel," he mumbles against my lips before urging them open and plunging his tongue inside. This kiss is raw and full of need. It's as if we can't get enough of each other.

"I'm sorry too," I whisper as his mouth slides down the column of my neck.

"No. You don't apologize." His eyes find mine, muddled with lust and desire, as he says, "I can't take back what I did. As much as I wish I could have a redo, I can't. But I can vow to never lie to you again, angel. Never." His words are a plea for understanding and forgiveness.

"And I promise to never run away again, even if you're being a dummy."

"You can call me an asshole. I deserve something harsher than dummy." His smile turns wicked, predatory even. "My plan tonight was just to hold you in my arms, and maybe watch one of those cheesy rom-com movies you like so much."

"We can still do that. Naked. After you've made love to me." My words are bold, completely unlike me, but the way his face blazes with desire, I think they hit their mark. He just brings out this braver, more daring side of me.

With the quickness of a cheetah, he wraps me in his arms, picking me up easily as he walks towards his bedroom. My legs wrap around his waist, and there's no mistaking his level of excitement. Like some hussy, I grind myself against his erection, the balls of his piercing rubbing me in the most perfect, eye-crossing way.

"Stop doing that or you'll make me embarrass myself. It's been a really long week without you, sweetheart."

"You went a whole year without it before. Now, one week is gonna kill you?" I ask, my hands toying with the longer locks of his hair.

"That was before I had a taste of you." His words are the accelerant to the already raging fire between us.

Levi lays me on the bed, covering my body with his own. Our fingers are entwined, raised high above our heads as he devours my mouth in a bruising kiss. Shamelessly, I grind against his erection, wishing our clothes were gone. His hips thrust in sync with his tongue driving me wilder than ever before.

"Please. Hurry," I beg in a choppy out-of-breath way.

"On it," he says, jumping up to his knees. He makes quick work of shedding both of our clothes, even though he takes a moment to worship whatever part of me he's exposing.

He reaches for a condom, but I stop his movement with a hand to his forearm. "I trust you." And I do. So much it hurts. That's why I took it so hard when I figured out he was SimpleMan. But even now, after knowing what he did, I still trust him, because no one will ever compare to Levi. No one will ever hold my heart in the palm of his hand and treat it as if it were the most valuable treasure in the world. Sure, he hurt me, but that wasn't his intention.

I know that now.

"You do?" he chokes out, and if I'm not mistaken, his eyes cloudy with tears.

"Yes. There's no one I trust more than you."

He closes his eyes, his throat working hard to swallow, and when he opens them again, I see it. Love. No, he hasn't said the words, but I feel them. They radiate beauty and life from his eyes, his love shining brightly like a lighthouse on the coast. And that love is for me.

"Hold on, angel. This is gonna be a rough ride," he says with a sassy smirk before lining up his erection and slowly pushing forward. It's funny (not funny haha, but funny strange) how tight my body seems after merely a week without him.

Those magical balls slide easily against my inner walls, driving me closer and closer to orgasm. My breathing is erratic until he becomes fully seated within me. Then, he stops.

And stares.

He gazes down in awe at where we're joined together so intimately. He looks up to my eyes, a whirlpool of emotions shining brightly. Three little words are on the tip of my tongue, but then I can practically hear Payton shouting at me. *"You can't say I love you while having sex."*

So I bite my tongue and don't say the words I long to say.

Our bodies crash together, frantic and quick-paced. We're both strung too tightly to even attempt to fend off the sweet release that's barreling down on us. Sweat has broken out on his forehead as he drives into my body, each pump of his masterful hips bringing me closer and closer to euphoria.

Levi remains on his knees, but bends down enough to take my hips with his and my hands within his. I feel so much bliss with each thrust, my own muscles starting to tighten around him. And we all know that when that happens and I feel that piercing slide against me, it's pretty much over. My body can't recover from that kinda teasing.

Arching my back, I let him push me over the cliff, the bright white light of paradise drowning me and lifting me up all at the same time. Blood swooshes in my ears, but not enough that I can't hear the one name falling from my lips. "Levi." It's his name I call over and over again as he draws every ounce of pleasure he can from my orgasm.

And only then does he follow me over the edge, my name dripping from his incredible lips like a blessing and a curse. He shudders within me, grunting from the sheer force of his release, his sandy blond hair hanging down in his face.

His eyes meet mine, a mix of ecstasy and fatigue. Turning together, we remain joined, wrapped around each other as if the other was a lifeline. We're both sweaty, but that's okay. I mean, maybe we can move this party to the shower.

My hands are in his hair, my legs still wrapped around him, as our breathing finally starts to normalize. I tremble beneath his fingers as he softly grazes his fingers up my bare back and down to cup my butt cheeks.

"That was pretty...wow."

"Mmmhmmm," he mumbles, my cheek vibrating against his chest.

"We should do it again," I tell him, resulting in a hearty laugh.

"I'm still hard inside you from the first time and you're already asking for round two? What kinda monster have I created Miss Summer?" he asks, rolling me over and placing gentle kisses on my lips, cheeks, and chin.

Reaching forward, he moves a wild piece of hair behind my ear, caressing my cheek as he goes. "Thank you," he finally says.

"For what?"

"For giving me a second chance. For trusting me."

His lips are back on mine, a warm tingling sensation racing through my blood and landing straight between my legs. A mixture of his release and my own is running down my leg, but I ignore it. There's something I've wanted to do since the first time I saw him naked.

Licking my lips, I push him over so that he's flat on his back and crawl up beside him. He's already semi-erect, glistening with the wetness from our first go-around. My eyes devour him; the way the piercing makes his dick look even more appetizing and the way it hardens before me, without even touching him, makes my mouth water.

"What are you doing?" His words are gruff and his breathing labored.

"Something I've wanted to do since the first time you took off your pants."

He groans loudly, his erection jumping on his stomach. It looks angry now, the large pierced head turning a darker color. The smooth, velvety skin is stretched tautly over his length, a few veins popping out that beg to be traced with my tongue.

Just as I start to bend over, ready to lick him like a human popsicle, a shrill alarm sounds from within the room. I know instantly what it is; I've heard Levi's fire pager go off a million times. He's moving before I have the chance to taste him.

"Attention Jupiter Bay Fire. All units respond to a business structure fire at 614 Main Street, Jupiter Bay. Report of smoke coming from the building directly to the east. All units requested. Police and ambulance already in route."

"614?" I ask, as Levi jumps up and grabs a pair of jeans from his drawer.

"Yeah," he says, shoving his long legs into the denim.

"Isn't Payton's flower shop 612?" I ask, the words dying on my dry lips.

He turns and faces me. "Yeah."

I'm moving before he even answers the question. After the world's fastest trip to the bathroom to clean up, my legs slide into shorts and my shirt is pulled over my head. I don't even care that I don't have a bra on. "Come on, angel. You can call her on the way," he says as he laces up his thick work boots.

We're out the door, hand in hand, racing towards the scene of the fire. My heart is pounding and my legs are numb as we climb into the cab of his truck. The blue light flashes as he tears out of the parking lot, racing towards downtown Jupiter Bay.

My fingers shake and I almost misdial her number. Eventually, I get it right and it rings.

"Hello?" she asks, her sleepy greeting echoing through the truck.

"There's a fire."

"Where?" she asks, alert and trying not to panic.

"Next door to Blossoms and Blooms."

Her sharp intake of breath guts me, but not as much as the fear in her voice when she says, "I'm on my way."

Chapter Thirty

Levi

I pull up to the sidewalk, the police officer moving aside the barricade to grant me access to the scene. Abby's dancing nervously in her seat, her foot tapping a hole in the floorboard. Before I even have the truck in park, she jumps out.

"Abby, wait!" I holler, hopping down and making my way to the front of my truck where she's waiting. She's not looking at me, though; no, she's frantically looking down the block at the building that's engulfed in flames. The one right next to her sister's business.

The wail of the fire truck sirens fill the night, the blaze lighting up the sky better than any streetlight ever could. "Here," I say, as I hand her my keys and pull my wallet from my pocket. "Can you hang on to these for me?"

Her eyes are bright with fear. Fear for her sister, fear for me, I'm not sure. Knowing Abby, I'd say it's both.

"Come on, I'll show you where to stand so you're out of the way," I holler over the loud sirens. Taking her hand in my own, I lead her through the gathering crowd on the sidewalk. Everyone's pointing at the blaze as my brothers pull up in three trucks. They jump out, gear on, and ready to do battle with the fire.

Finding a spot over to the side where she can still see everything, I turn her to face me and plant my lips firmly on hers. "Stay over here. You'll be safe and out of the way. If anyone gives you any lip, tell them you're with me, okay?"

When she nods, I kiss her again, this time lingering a little longer on her lush, swollen lips than I should. "Be careful," she whispers, gripping onto my shirt as if to anchor herself to me.

"Always." With one more firm peck on the lips, I turn and head towards the truck.

"Abby!" I hear over my shoulder and turn just as Payton, Dean, and his five-year-old daughter, Brielle, run up to where she's standing.

I jog back as they embrace, Dean walking towards me with his daughter in his arms. "Keep them back," I tell him. Brielle's transfixed on the blaze, the fire dancing in her wide eyes.

"I will. She called them all."

"Don't let any of them get any closer. The blaze is too hot and spreading quickly. We'll do everything we can to keep it away from her place," I say, nodding towards Abby's oldest sister.

"Do what you can, but keep yourself safe," Dean tells me, putting a hard hand on my shoulder. "It's just a building."

"Levi!" Payton hollers before running at me. She wraps her arms around my neck and hugs me with everything she has. My shirt's wet from her tears, but I barely notice.

Looking down at her, I tell her, "Stay back. Don't come any closer, okay? I need to know you are all out of harm's way."

"We will. That business…" she starts, sniffling, "it means everything to me. But it's not worth anything if something happens to you. Please be careful," she whispers, pulling me into another hug.

"I will. I promise," I tell her, glancing over her shoulder to see tears in my girl's eyes.

"Hey," I holler, her emerald eyes locked on mine. "I'll be right back. Then we're going back to my place to finish what we started." The smirk I give her causes her face to flame. No, I can't see it, but if I know anything about Abby, it's that she embarrasses easily.

"Gross," Payton mumbles before pulling back out of my arms.

"I'll be back, angel," I tell her with a wink before turning and running towards the fire.

My gear is already there, thanks to Tucker, and I'm dressed and ready for battle only a few moments later.

"Ready to do this, Romeo?" Tucker hollers through his mask beside me.

"Only if you are, Juliet!" I yell back, blowing him a kiss.

Together, we grab our gear and set out to work. My main objective is to safely put out this blaze, and hopefully keep it from Payton's building. Then and only then will I allow myself to be distracted by Abby's intoxicating eyes and hypnotic thighs. After this is done, I'm heading home with my girl.

And to tell her how I feel.

Chapter Thirty-One

Abby

He's been gone a long time.

Every fireman looks the same, and there's no way of telling which one is Levi. That thought scares me. I watch, helplessly, as they run into the building that's on fire, and do everything they can to keep it from spreading to my sister's business.

My entire family is here.

Dean's mom arrived shortly after they got to the scene to take Brielle back to their house. Jaime and Ryan brought coffee from the gas station, and AJ and Meghan have both been doing everything they can to keep Payton calm. Dad, Grandpa, and Grandma showed up just in time to see the windows blow out of the building to the east, which used to be a shoe store. Used to be. Until it was engulfed by a raging inferno.

The only good thing about that is that the fire seems to be moving away from Payton's building. Now, three hours later, and after calling in mutual aid from two neighboring departments, they seem to have the blaze contained. We can see that Payton's place will have damage, smoke and water mostly, but that's better than the alternative.

"Do you see him?" Lexi asks, her hand wrapped firmly in mine.

"No."

"I've been trying to read the names on the backs of the coats, but they're too blurry," AJ says, standing on the other side of me.

"He went into the building about twenty minutes ago," Grandma says, causing us all to stop and look at her. "What? I have excellent eyesight. Not only could I read his name on the coat, but I'd know that ass from a mile away. He went into the shoe store with three other guys and a hose."

I glance from my grandma, not at all surprised that she'd notice Levi's ass (it is an amazing one), but more surprised that she didn't make a joke about hoses. Glancing back at the shoe store, I wait with baited breath for any sign of movement. Isn't it time for them to come back out? How long can they go on a tank of oxygen?

My mind races, my heart hammers in my chest, my worry escalates.

"Lexi, what do you think-" I start, but am cut off. She couldn't hear me anyway over the startling noise.

Shock races through my body as I gaze at the shoe store where the collapsing building rips off part of the façade. My world starts to crumble along with the building as, piece by piece, brick by brick, I watch it start to fall. My entire universe is in that store, the building caving in around him.

"Levi!" I scream before taking off towards the rubble.

Strong arms wrap around me, but I fight it, and fight hard. "Shhhhhh, Abby, you can't go in there. You have to stay here," Ryan says, pulling me while I kick and scream to get away.

More arms wrap around me, but I don't have a clue who they belong to. My eyes are glued to what's left of the front of that building. The one he went into. The one he hasn't come out of.

The one that's falling down.

Chapter Thirty-Two

Levi

I hear the floorboard groaning in protest beneath my weight. We've reached the point where it's unsafe to be in here; it could go at any time. Turning off the nozzle in my hand, I motion for my team to stop.

"Pull out, ground crew. That building isn't stable anymore," Captain chirps in my earpiece.

"10-4, Cap," Tuck says into his mic behind me.

Bill and Jonah are already moving towards the front, pulling on the hose, when the ground beneath our feet quakes. I glance up at Tuck and can see the realization in his eyes. We take off at a dead sprint. The ground underneath us opens up and the floor gives way, a small explosion ringing in my ear as I feel myself falling.

Just before the hole swallows me up, my mind drifts to Abby. Sweet, amazingly beautiful Abby. Her hair, her eyes, her smile. The one thing I should have said before I came running into the building.

The one thing I may never get to tell her.

Regret fills my body as the darkness surrounds me.

Eventually, black consumes me.

Chapter Thirty-Three

Abby

My eyes haven't left the building, or what's left of it. Two men came out. Two men haven't. The twisting pain in my gut tells me that Levi is one of the latter.

Dad has his arms wrapped around me, Ryan and Dean hover close, ready to jump if I try to make a break for it again. But I don't move. I watch.

Men rush into the building. Five, seven, ten. So many that I lose count.

Still, I watch. Wait.

I can see people moving in and out, trying with all my might to read the names on the backs of their coats. Glancing at Grandma, she must see my question reflecting in my eyes. The slightest shake she gives me sends my heart falling straight into my toes.

Turning my attention back to the building, I wait. I'm not sure I'm breathing, but I still wait and wonder and hope. My heart is flooded with so much hope, I'm afraid it might actually buckle under the pressure. My legs hold me up, but I'm not sure how. My family surrounds me, their touches offering both comfort and strength, but I don't really feel them. I feel nothing.

Numb.

This is what Meghan felt like, isn't it? This gut-wrenching pain and all-consuming numbness that devours you like a black cloud. This inexplicable emptiness that wraps around you and won't let you breathe, knowing that part of your soul has been ripped away from you.

It's the worst feeling in the world.

"No," I hear beside me. "Don't do that." My face is pulled and I'm staring into the fiery green eyes of Meghan. "Do you hear me? He's not gone. Don't you dare let yourself go there, you hear me? I feel it in my bones that he's alive, so you need to pull yourself from whatever darkness you were lost in and focus on getting him out." She holds so much conviction in her eyes that I can't help but grab hold with everything I have. I latch on to her hope and don't let go.

"That's it, Abby. Deep breaths. Don't let go," she whispers, pulling me forward and kissing my forehead. "He's okay. I feel it."

Even as my life spirals out of control around me, I reach for the calmness and don't let go. We breathe deeply, together, and let everything around us fade away. Meghan holds me, and jointly, we watch the wreckage of the building.

It takes about thirty minutes, thirty of the longest minutes of my life, before we hear yelling. EMTs and paramedics scramble through the hole in the structure, gurneys and stretchers waiting on the sidewalk. When they call for the backboards, I hold my breath and watch. And wait.

Firemen and EMTs clamber from the building in groups. It takes a few moments before I realize they're carrying the boards. With a fireman on each one. Both boards are loaded on a gurney, surrounded by those trying to help them, completely obstructed from view. I can't tell if the person they carry is moving or not.

Please, God, let him be moving.

"Let's go to the hospital," Dad suggests, gently gripping my shoulders and pulling me towards where their cars are parked.

Glancing back to the scene, I watch both gurneys being loaded into separate ambulances. I'm focused so intently on trying to figure out which one contains Levi, that I don't see the man running my way.

"Abby Summer?" he asks, breathing hard and searching our faces.

"That's me."

"Levi is asking for you. He'd like you to ride with him," he says with a smile. "Come on," he instructs, reaching out his hand.

Stepping forward, I glance over my shoulder. "Go. We'll meet you there," Dad says with a smile of relief.

My legs carry me towards the ambulance, and I hold my breath until I'm standing at the open doors. He's inside, talking to a paramedic as she hooks him up to something that looks like a car battery. I don't even realize the tears are falling until he blurs, but now that they've started, I can't seem to turn it off.

Blinking rapidly to clear my vision, my eyes finally land on the most gorgeous hazel ones I've ever seen. He's looking straight at me, concern written on his dirty, soot covered face.

"Come here," he says, his gruff voice ringing out through the night, his hand extended towards me. There's the slightest smile playing on the corner of his full lips, and even though they're a tad on the dirty side (Grandma would chuckle), I just want to feel them against my own lips.

"We need to go," the driver hollers back.

"Are you going?" the fireman says beside me, a warm smile on his face.

Without answering, I climb up into the ambulance and take a seat towards the back, out of the way.

"No way. Get up here with me. I need to hold you," Levi says as the paramedic continues her assessment of his condition.

"Are you sure?" I ask, looking at her for direction.

"Go ahead. He'd just whine and cry until he got his way anyway," she retorts with a smile.

"Zip it, Tori. I want my girl right beside me," Levi says, reaching his hand for me.

"Your blood pressure's high. Let's try not to elevate it any more, shall we?" Tori quips with a wide grin.

Gently, I make my way to where Levi's lying. I collapse onto the bench, tears silently falling to where our hands are now joined. He feels warm, alive, and I'm so damned grateful.

"Are you okay?" I whisper, resting my forehead on his bare shoulder.

"I am now," he exhales deeply into my hair.

"I was so scared," I confess, gazing up at him.

"I was too." My body shudders as he gently grabs a strand of my hair and moves it behind my ear, caressing my cheek and wiping my tears as he does.

"Listen to me," I sniffle. "I can't believe I'm thinking of myself right now. Of course you were scared. I can't imagine how frightened you must have been."

His eyes study me, his throat working hard to swallow his emotions. "Yeah, falling through the floor was a bit scary, but that's not what terrified me the most." He reaches for me again, stroking my wet cheek with his thumb.

"No?"

"I was afraid I'd never get to see you again. I was worried I missed my chance to tell you that I love you."

My entire body seizes up as his words permeate my brain. "Love?"

Levi smiles and nods his head. "Yeah, love. I'm glad you're here now because it gives me the opportunity to finally tell you that I love you. I've loved you most of my life; I was just too stupid to see it," he says with a smile, making me chuckle. "But I see it now, I feel it and know it, and I'm not letting you go. I love you, Abby."

"I love you, too," I whisper as tears of joy fall to where our hands are linked.

My lips meet his in a welcome kiss. His lips are warm and soft and taste like smoke, but I don't care. The fact that I can kiss him again at all is reason to celebrate.

A slow beep fills the ambulance, drawing my attention away from Levi. "What's that?" I ask, gazing down at his love-filled eyes.

"My pulse. It's soaring," he quips with a smirk.

Laughing, I try to pull away, but am stopped by strong arms. "Where do you think you're going?"

"I'm going to sit back and let them do their thing."

"What about my thing? I wouldn't mind you doing something to that," he sasses from the gurney.

"You're bad," I chastise, swatting at his shoulder.

"Maybe. But do you know what?" he asks, pulling me back down so that my head is lying on his shoulder.

"What?"

"I love you." I can't help but smile widely at his words and the meaning he puts behind them. "Get used to hearing it, angel, because I'm going to say it. A lot."

With a smile on my lips and my head against his chest, I close my eyes and drift off to the steady beat of his heart.

Chapter Thirty-Four

Levi

Labor Day Weekend

The lights are hot as I step up to the mic, my guitar hanging against my chest like an extension of my body. We've been playing at Lucky's tonight, our first gig since the fire. Considering I fell through the floor and landed in a concrete basement, I had no major injuries except a few lacerations and smoke inhalation.

Tuck hadn't quite been so lucky. When we fell, he landed hard on his right leg, busting it clean below the knee. Surgery was able to repair the damage, but my man is gonna be down for a while. Six to eight weeks until the cast can come off, but he's here tonight, sitting at a picnic table, nursing a beer.

"Everyone having a good time tonight?" I ask the crowd of locals gathered at one of our favorite joints. I offer them a smile, ignoring the group of screaming girls in the front, practically throwing their panties on stage.

Glancing around, it takes my eyes a few moments to adjust to the lights and find my girl. Abby is in back, drinking happily with her sisters. It's one of their crazy sister nights, and all six of them are in attendance tonight. Dean and Ryan are both parked at the bar, cans of pop in front of them, while they keep a close eye on the girls.

"You don't mind if I sing a song or two for you, do ya?" I ask, smiling at the response I get, but my eyes never leaving the emerald ones at the back of the bar.

I strum the opening chords of my new favorite song, the one that will forever be associated with my best friend. I belt out the words to "Angel Eyes," singing it for only one woman.

Abby sings along to the Jeff Healey song, and even though I can't hear her voice, I pretend that I can. I'm hypnotized, watching her beautiful mouth move along with mine. I sing the song for her, to her, only her.

When I sing the last note, I point, as I always do. She smiles back broadly, her body swaying a little on her feet. I'm not sure if she's had too much to drink or if she's been standing on those crazy high-heeled sandals for too long. They do amazing things for her legs, so I'm definitely not complaining, but I can't wait to get them off her later.

Along with the rest of her clothes.

"I'm givin' my man Gage a break and gonna sing one more song. That okay?" I'm assuming from the ear-splitting screams from the audience, they don't mind.

"Abby, can you come up here, angel?" I call into the mic. Paying no attention to the nasty faces the girls up front make, I watch my girl slowly make her way to the front of the room. "Up here," I tell her, reaching for her hand.

With her warmth within my hand, I guide her onto the stage and over to the chair Gage delivered. "Have a seat," I tell her. She looks at me sheepishly, her cheeks flushed with embarrassment.

"Hi, sweetheart," I whisper before kissing her lips.

"I've got a surprise for you all tonight. My girl, Miss Abigail Summer, is going to join me in a song," I tell the audience, her sisters hooting and hollering the loudest, all the way from the back.

"What?" she asks, her eyes filled with fear.

"Yes. You can do this," I tell her, reaching for my favorite guitar; the one I leave at home and never take to a show.

Strapping the guitar around her body, I give her a smile before taking the seat directly across from her. We're facing each other, not the audience. Gage positions the mics so that they're off to the side of where we sit, not directly in front of her face. I know that's one of the main causes for her freakouts.

"Just keep your eyes on me, angel. We got this."

"But…I don't even know what song we're playing."

"Yes, you do."

I start to strum the opening cords to Enrique Iglesias's "Hero." Her eyes light with recognition immediately, and I watch as her shaking hands take their positions on my guitar. Abby closes her eyes, the music washing over her, as she starts to play the song we've never played together, but both know the same.

Our eyes remain locked as I sing the opening lines to the song. I pause as we near the start of the refrain, and smile warmly when I see her mouth open. I'm transfixed on her as she starts to sing.

Her sweet voice washes over me, and I realize in this moment how damn lucky I am to have her in my life. I really could have fucked this whole thing up, and now I'll spend the rest of my life trying to ensure I never break her trust again.

When the song is done, you couldn't scrape the smile off her face with a putty knife. She's grinning ear to ear, her sisters cheering wildly from the front row where they now stand. Setting my guitar down, I reach for hers and remove it from her body. Then I take her in my arms.

"Thank you," she whispers.

"For what?"

"For making me do that. It was a rush."

"It was the song."

"It's a great song," she agrees.

"My kinda song," I say and claim her lips with my own. The lights, the stage, the crowd, the crazy half-drunk sisters screaming in the front row, all fade away until there's nothing–no one–but Abby and me.

That's the only way I want it.

Just us.

And the sweet music we make.

Epilogue

Abby

It's a Summer sister tradition that on the first Saturday of each month, the six of us get together. We take turns picking the location or activity, anything from margaritas and a movie to wine and painting classes at the small gallery uptown. One thing, though, is as certain as the sun rising over the Chesapeake Bay every morning; there will be alcohol involved.

Always.

Halloween decorations are everywhere, strewn from one end of the house to the other. There's a witch running amuck outside, but it's not our turn to watch her and keep her away from the candy bowl.

We're at Payton and Dean's place for an unusual sisters' night. The first weekend in October has brought a new kind of celebration, one where our entire family is together, instead of just the girls.

My sisters and I are all inside, whipping up another batch of margaritas. (This is our third.) The guys are outside around the bonfire, getting it burned down enough to make s'mores. According to Brielle, it's a necessity for tonight's celebration, and I, for one, agree wholeheartedly with her.

Yes, yes, there's a lot to celebrate.

First off, there's the fact that Payton's business is alive and thriving. It took three weeks to clean up the damage and make sure the building was a sound structure. Ryan took care of getting all the permits and inspections, and we're happy to announce that Blossoms and Blooms reopened this past Monday to a line of eager patrons and a fresh new look.

Of course, it wasn't easy to get it whipped back into shape. We had to replace the large picture window in the front and had to scrub everything, floor to ceiling. She has new tile flooring and a fresh coat of sunny yellow paint, and looks better than it did the first time she opened.

Payton also had to replace the electronics system in the building as it took on enough water damage to fry her computers, credit card system, and even one of the coolers. Thank God for insurance. It's the only thing that saved her from having to walk away from the one thing she built from the ground up. All in all, it was a learning and building experience for her and our family since we all devoted as much of our own time and energy to getting the business back up on its feet. And there was nothing better than seeing the smile on Payton's face when she flipped the open sign once again.

Thank God for small miracles. I like to think Mom had a little something to do with this.

Payton, with Dean by her side, started the adoption process for Brielle. No one really speaks of Brooke, Brielle's biological mom, but we know she didn't contest the adoption. In fact, she signed away her rights almost immediately. It's both a blessing and terribly sad. How someone can just walk away from their own daughter is beyond me, but then again, Payton will be an amazing mother to Brielle, and any future children they may be blessed with.

Their court date is in December to finalize the adoption. Grandma is already planning the party to celebrate the occasion. I'm also anticipating another big announcement from our oldest sister soon. I overheard Dean telling the guys that he was going to marry my sister as soon as possible. Of course, with everything that happened with the fire, I think his plan has been delayed slightly. But it won't be long…

And speaking of engagements, Jaime finally found the ring. It's on her finger.

Ryan knew she had been hunting for it after she accidentally found the receipt for his purchase. So one Sunday morning, she woke up and it was there. On her finger. I heard there were tears…and sex (hopefully not publicly).

"The fire's ready for s'mores," Brielle exclaims as she runs inside, in full witch garb. Apparently, she's practicing for Halloween at the end of the month.

"We'll bring everything out in a minute, sweetie," Payton says, pouring the frothy beverages into tall glasses.

"How many of these have I had?" I ask, taking a big drink of my peach margarita.

"Doesn't matter, Abs. Just drink up," Jaime says, holding the bottom of my glass and tipping it back a little more.

"Levi's gonna get lucky tonight," Lexi hoots from across the kitchen.

"He ain't the only one," Jaime smirks, taking a drink of her own glass.

"I miss buzzed up sex," Meghan says quietly.

"I'm sorry, Meggy, I shouldn't have -"

"No, don't be sorry. You're all still living your lives. You don't have to walk on eggshells because you're afraid of hurting me.

I *want* to hear all about your happiness, really I do. It makes me smile, knowing that you are all happy." Her words trail off as fresh tears threaten to spill from her eyes, but she's wearing a smile and it's genuine and full of hope.

"Hey, don't include me in that little happiness shhhhpiel." AJ stops and looks at me. "Is that right? Shhhhhpiel? Shhh-pee-uhl."

"Spiel. But you're close."

"I'm drunk. And I don't even have anyone to go have drunk sex with," AJ pouts, chugging half her glass.

I glance over at Lexi and see her staring off at nothing. She's still with Chris, but I wonder for how long. I know she mentioned the possibility of leaving him back a few months ago, but maybe she's just not ready. All I know is that she's miserable, and I hate seeing my twin like this.

"Payton, can I have drunk sex in your bathroom?" Jaime hollers, grabbing the pitcher and refilling her glass.

"No!" Payton exclaims at the exact same time Ryan walks in and yells, "Yes!"

Jaime smiles widely as soon as she sees him. "Awww, look. It's my fiancé. And he wants to have sex with me."

"Always, babe," he says, walking over and wrapping his big arms around her.

"Drunk sex is almost as good as drunk road-head," she whispers so loudly I think the neighbors heard.

"How do I sign up for the drunk road-head?" Levi whispers in my ear as his arms wrap around me. I shiver when his body aligns with mine, his warm breath caressing my ear.

"Are you asking me or Jaime? She was offering," I quip with a smile.

"You. Always you."

"This little lady is ready for s'mores," Grandpa says from the back door. "Why don't you all quit talking about road-head and sex in Payton's bathroom and get out here? The witch is ready," he adds with a smile.

"How did he know?" Lexi asks, each of us looking from one person to the other.

"I have excellent hearing," he reminds us from outside the door.

We all giggle (because we're drunk and giggling and booze go hand-in-hand) as we head outside and join the rest of the family. Dad and Dean are warming up the sticks that we'll use to roast the marshmallows, while Grandma and Bri get the graham crackers and chocolate bars ready.

"I love s'mores," I tell Levi, making our way over to the fire. There are not quite enough chairs, but I don't mind. I just take a seat on his leg and call it good.

"And I love you," he replies, a cheesy grin on his too-handsome face.

"Are we going back to your place tonight?" We hadn't decided anything when we set out for the night, but that's typical. We may never plan for which bed we'll fall into at the end of the evening, but we're usually together when it happens. Nights like these, we usually head back to his place. While those where he works late, I always find him in my bed when I wake in the morning.

"We are. Though, it doesn't matter to me. As long as you're naked and I'm naked, I don't care whose bed we're naked in."

"I love the way he says naked," Grandma says, interrupting our conversation. "It's all deep and dirty. Like he can't wait to strip you naked and take -"

"Why are you talking? You know he's talking about your granddaughter, right?" I exclaim, drawing attention from those around me.

"Oh, it doesn't matter who's having the sex, Abs, just as long as it's happening." She leans in closer and no amount of time could prepare me for what comes out of her mouth next. "It's the piercing, right? I heard all about it. Drives women wild with passion, Abs. I've been thinking of having your grandfather's love stick pierced," she says so matter-of-factly that I almost miss the gasps and choking noises coming from those around me.

My body starts to shake from Levi's laughter. "Please. Stop talking."

"Did it hurt, Levi? I heard they take a while to heal," she continues with a straight face.

"Uh, yeah, it didn't feel great, you know, when I had it done." Levi adjusts me on his lap to cover up his discomfort with talking about his dick piercing with my eighty-year-old grandmother. "And it took…a bit to heal."

"Like how long?" she goads.

"Ummm, six months?"

"Shame," she tsks. "There's no way I could go without riding Orvie's flesh rocket for that length of time." Standing up tall, she smiles down at me. "Here! S'mores!" she exclaims before flitting away as if she wasn't just discussing my man's junk.

"I swear I must have been having an out-of-body experience. No way did I just overhear our grandma asking Levi about his cock piercing," Lexi exclaims.

"Levi has his dick pierced?" Jaime practically jumps up off Ryan's lap and runs towards us. "Really? Can I see?"

"No!"

"Payton! Did you know Levi has jewelry…down below?" Jaime hollers across the fire, ensuring everyone and their brother hears her comment, and making hand gestures as if she's holding on to his balls.

"Really? Can I see?"

"No!" I exclaim once more.

"Why not? It's for scientific purposes," Jaime reasons.

"You're not a scientist!" I defend.

"No, but I could be!"

"You're just a nosey woman who wants to see Levi's junk piercing. Well, we all do. Whip it out, Levi," Lexi says.

"No way. You are not all getting a look at my man's junk. It's my piercing to ogle over, not yours!" I exclaim, completely forgetting that I could practically reach out and touch my dad.

"You always used to share your toys with me," Lexi pouts. "I just want to see it."

"Sorry, ladies, but the only woman getting a first-rate, birds-eye view of my piercing is the woman I love," Levi answers, curling me into his chest. My sisters all groan.

"I want to get my ears pierced but my friend Sasha says it hurts. You don't have earrings in. What kinda piercing do you have? Can I see it? Did it hurt? Boys don't have their ears pierced at my school. Did you get it done when you were in school?" My eyes widen dramatically as I glance over and see Brielle's sweet little face. Her innocence almost overshadows the fact that she's asking about a piercing she should know nothing about.

"Oh, um... Dean?" Levi hollers, fear actually written on his gorgeous face.

"Thanks, guys," Dean mumbles as he picks up his daughter. "We'll talk about piercing your ears later. How about another s'more?" he asks, earning him a chocolaty, toothless grin.

"Blame Payton," I tell him as he walks away.

"Me? Blame Jaime! She's the one who announced to everyone on the block that Levi has his cock pierced."

"Can we stop talking about it?" I plea.

"I know! Let's do presents," Grandma exclaims from her chair.

"Presents?" I ask, glancing around to all of my sisters.

"Last time we got a present it was the spawn of Satan," Ryan recalls, shivering as he thinks about their cat.

"Boots isn't the devil's cat! He's cute and loving and sweet and perfect," Jaime reminds him.

"You're cute and loving and sweet and perfect," he says, wrapping his arms around his fiancée and leading her towards a chair.

"So, I, like, really can't see it? I mean, I'm your twin. We're practically the same person," Lexi quietly says kneeling beside me.

"You have no shame," I tell her.

"None. And maybe if I were getting some at home it'd be different. But since I'm not, well, I think it's only fair that I get a peek."

"Not happening. Go away," I tell her with a laugh.

"Fine. Be that way, you stingy whore."

"What?!" I exclaim, unable to stop the full-belly laughter from erupting.

"Fine. You're not a whore. But you are stingy."

"I have lots of presents tonight," Grandma says, joining us in the backyard.

She hands a small bag of goodies to Brielle, who finds a witch's cauldron, green makeup, and striped socks, all to complement her Halloween costume. Then she hands a bag to Jaime and Ryan. They both look at it like there's a chance it could contain live explosives.

"I'm not opening that," Ryan says.

"It's an engagement present, Ryan Elson. You have to open it. It's a gift," Grandma chastises him.

Jaime carefully digs in, pulling a beautifully ornate glass vase from within. "Wow, this is beautiful."

"It is," Meghan agrees.

"It's the perfect size to hold lube, a cock ring, and those little bottles of warming gel that taste like fruit! All of that stuff is in the bottom of your bag," Grandma says proudly.

"Of course, it is," Jaime mumbles, carefully setting the vase inside the wrapping.

"Dean and Payton have one too. Theirs is in the bedroom waiting for them. I went ahead and assembled it," Grandma smirks with a sly grin.

"I can't wait," Payton groans.

"And one more gift," Grandma says, handing me a bag.

"Me?"

"Well, you and Levi. You're practically shacking up, having the sex every day, so I thought it was time."

My fingers shake and I can feel all eyes on me as I start to pull tissue paper from the bag. My sisters are each speculating on what's inside, each guess even more embarrassing than the last.

Pulling out the nondescript brown box, I'm surprised to find the word swing written across it. "You got us a swing? But we don't have a front porch." My mind is trying to figure where in the world I'm going to put a swing, and how exactly it fit inside the box. It must be one of those hammocks or something.

Levi digs into the box and pulls out the black contraption. That's when reality sets in. My grandma didn't give us a hammock. Oh, no. My grandparents gave us a sex swing! A freaking sex swing!

"Is this what I think it is?" Levi asks, glancing my way with mirth and surprise in his eyes.

"It is! Have you ever used one? They're so nice and really helps save the back of your partner, Abs. Grandpa and I love ours. Of course, Levi will have to figure out how to hang it from the ceiling. Or maybe Ryan could come over and help him build a stand? This way, you're not putting holes in your rental," Grandma reasons.

"There's no way I'm coming over to help with that project. Sorry, buddy, you're on your own with that," Ryan says, slapping Levi on the shoulder.

"You got us a sex swing?" I ask, dumbfounded.

"Oh, there's more! Keep going!"

I'm almost too afraid to look, but my face is already as red as a fire truck, so it's not like this humiliation could get any worse. Reaching into the bag, I find jewelry. No, not the kind of jewelry a normal grandkid would receive from her normal grandma. No, I get penis piercing jewelry.

"I don't even know what to say," I mumble, gazing down at several pieces of jewelry. There's a tiger's head, a fireman's helmet, a police hat, ruler, and an American flag.

"Do you know how many different heads they have for that jewelry, Levi? I found all of the best ones, perfect for role-playing. There's a tiger for when you're feeling extra ravenous, a fireman's hat, well for when you're the fireman putting out the flames in her loins. Then the police hat because everyone loves it when the cop arrests the naughty girl and has to show her the error of her ways in the back seat," she says, continuing as if the group, as a whole, isn't completely horrified by her fantasies.

"The ruler is for when you reverse it and she's the naughty teacher and you're the schoolboy, Levi."

"That's one of my favorite scenes," Grandpa says with a wide smile.

"And finally, the American flag because, well, it was buy four, get one free, and I was feeling patriotic."

"Now can we see it?" Lexi begs, her eyes wide and dancing with delight.

"Absolutely not."

"I kinda want to go home and try out the fire hat, angel. I'm feeling like dousing your flames," Levi whispers, kissing my neck. My entire body is suddenly alive and ready to see just how he intends to put out the fire.

"We should go home," I suggest, glancing over my shoulder at him.

"We should."

An hour later, we're finally making our way to Levi's truck. Dad was taking Meghan and AJ home, and Lexi caught a ride with Ryan and Jaime. So, it's just us as we head towards our building. The awkward gifts are on the floor between my legs, and if I were being honest with myself, I'm a little excited to see his new jewelry– in place.

"What are you thinkin' about?" he asks, reaching for my hand.

"The fireman hat," I say boldly, smiling across the cab at him.

"Me too," he agrees with a predatory smile.

"It's a little weird that my grandma bought you new jewelry for your piercing."

"A little? But I've learned to never underestimate the level of mortification that can come from such a small woman."

"You were embarrassed?"

"Not me. You. I was fine with it, but I hate that you were so uncomfortable."

"You know what will make me feel better?" I ask, unbuckling my seat belt. Levi eyes me questionably before returning his eyes to the road.

"What?" he asks, stopping at a stoplight.

"Road-head."

He doesn't know what to do as I reach over and unbuckle his pants, pulling them open and exposing his erection. "No underwear?" I gasp, gaping down, wide-eyed and mouth hanging open.

"I thought it might speed up the process tonight."

"I love the way you think," I tell him, moving over and kissing his lips.

"And I love you."

Another Epilogue

Lexi

The house is quiet as I enter.

Chris is either still out shmoozing some client, or already asleep. If I had to wager a bet, I'd say he's sleeping. He only does two things anymore: work and sleep. Sleep and work. He makes no time for me or anything else in his busy schedule.

I go to the stack of papers on the counter. They're all there, right where he left them. House plans, listings for property available around Jupiter Bay, kitchen layouts. There are even some financial statements for the investments he's made on our behalf recently. Everything's there, neatly stacked and perfectly organized.

Reaching down, I can't help but move the papers around, mixing up the financial statements with the house plans. There. Take that, Christopher.

Leaving the mess on the counter, I head over to the drawer where we keep pot holders. Down at the bottom, hidden beneath the contents is a sheet of paper, neatly folded in half. I pull that sheet from its hiding spot, carefully opening it up and revealing the secret I stumbled upon only earlier this morning.

My breath still catches, my heart still stops, my world still shatters.

How could he?

I read the report over and over again, wishing what I found weren't true.

But it is.

And it's time for me to go.

I can't stay, not anymore. Not when the man who vowed to love me, protect me, and give me everything I wanted in life was the biggest liar and fraud known to man.

Anger sweeps through me, just as it had the moment I found the paper poking out from under our bed. It had clearly been dropped, probably from his briefcase or something. It doesn't matter though; the damage is done.

My life's a mess, my dream in shambles.

But it won't be for long.

I'm taking back my life.

Starting now.

The End

Find out more about Lexi and Linkin's story in My Kinda Mess, coming soon.

Acknowledgements

As always, this entire process wouldn't be possible without the love and support of so many!

Nazarea and the InkSlinger PR team for their tireless promotion and work; Sara Eirew for the amazing covers; Dylan Horsch and Tiffany Marie; my amazing editor, Kara Hildebrand; Sandra Shipman for helping polish the story; Jo Thompson for proofreading and polishing expertise; Amanda Lanclos; Brenda Wright of Formatting Done Wright; Carey Decevito; Holly Collins; everyone in Lacey's Ladies; my husband and two kids' each and every one of the bloggers who helped promote and review; and to all of the readers.

THANK YOU for reading!

About the Author

Lacey Black is a Midwestern girl with a passion for reading, writing, and shopping. She carries her e-reader with her everywhere she goes so she never misses an opportunity to read a few pages. Always looking for a happily ever after, Lacey is passionate about contemporary romance novels and enjoys it further when you mix in a little suspense. She resides in a small town in Illinois with her husband, two children, and a chocolate lab. Lacey loves watching NASCAR races, shooting guns, and should only consume one mixed drink because she's a lightweight.

Email: laceyblackwrites@gmail.com
Facebook: https://www.facebook.com/authorlaceyblack
Twitter: https://twitter.com/AuthLaceyBlack
Blog: https://laceyblack.wordpress.com

Made in the USA
Lexington, KY
06 September 2017